Quantum Voodoo

To Yvonne,
Carl Peachey
Key West, 2012

Quantum Voodoo

By
Carl Peachey

E-BookTime, LLC
Montgomery, Alabama

Quantum Voodoo

Copyright © 2012 by Carl Peachey

Cover design by Kate Peachey

All rights reserved. No part of this book may be reproduced or transmitted in any form or by any means, electronic or mechanical, including photocopying, recording, or by any information storage and retrieval system, without permission in writing from the copyright owner.

This is a work of fiction. Names, characters, places and incidents either are the product of the author's imagination or are used fictitiously, and any resemblance to any actual persons, living or dead, events, or locales is entirely coincidental.

Library of Congress Control Number: 2012944829

ISBN: 978-1-60862-415-7

First Edition
Published August 2012
E-BookTime, LLC
6598 Pumpkin Road
Montgomery, AL 36108
www.e-booktime.com

Also by Carl Peachey...

Unnatural Selection

Immortal Logic

Acknowledgements

A hearty thank you to Bob Degrove, Bud Moore, Laura Black, Anita Pierce, Patrick McCarney, James Peachey, and Michael Shaw. My apologies for distorting the facts, but this is fiction. Special thanks to Tim Motes for editing.

Preface

*A*s an itinerant anthropologist, I have taken field notes over the years, and this tale is derived from some of those handwritten observations. Information that might have compromised others remained necessarily vague in my daily professional entries; however, reminders pertaining to matters of a personal nature were obscured within the text. I have kept these secrets for almost three decades, but it's time the truth was revealed.

For the sake of continuity, I have tried to intersperse events learned of after the fact into the timeline as it unfolds in the journals. I did not personally experience all the occurrences described on these pages, but after hearing other people's accounts, it is reasonable to believe that things happened this way. Forgive me if I am mistaken. If you have pertinent information, I'll be happy to listen.

Stephen Shaw, September 29, St. Augustine, Florida

Prologue

Lamanai, Central America, 350 BCE

Three weeks before the autumnal equinox, a thousand ecstatic devotees crowded the central plaza at the foot of a new temple. Dressed in their finest clothing, the members of the festive throng eagerly waited to receive the benediction that would ensure their individual safety during this dangerous time.

Wearing a smooth facemask hewn from a single block of pure jade, king *Balam Koh* (Jaguar Fang) presided from the temple steps, conducting the traditional ceremony that ushered in the *Wayeb'*, a period of five nameless days marking the end of the calendar year. During this annually observed unlucky week, boundaries separating the corporeal and spiritual worlds dissolved. Demons, spirits, and such were free to escape the underworld and cause havoc in the land of the living. A blood sacrifice entreated *Itzamna*, the god of creation, to keep the congregation safe. The reigning monarch advised the constituency to remain in their homes until the New Year was properly seated.

Taking his own advice to heart, the king settled in with close family, the sole members of society that knew the potentate to be mortal. The tribe's highest-ranking official would only appear in public while wearing the stone face. When the time came, his first-born son would don the mask and assume the role of leader, perpetuating the commoners' belief that King Jaguar Fang was an immortal demigod.

In the private royal quarters, the exquisitely carved jade rested upon a pedestal. On the third day of the *Wayeb'*, an evil spirit surreptitiously entered the well-protected private chambers, and the downfall of an empire began.

The fiend possessed the strength of many men, or so the legend tells. It would require a mighty warrior indeed to steal the face of a king. The details of the theft were later chronicled in stone. The jade mask was as heavy as a jaguar cub. Despite the burden of the object, the thief outran the guards and disappeared. Unafraid of the magic allegedly contained in the mask, the sacrilegious interloper intended to don the stone face in a distant land and thereby establish his own empire.

Although that particular new kingdom never came to exist, the artifact was revered by the subjects of subsequent dynasties, and borne throughout the ancient Mayan world. Images engraved on the icon were copied in stone carvings, and the tale was repeated in folklore throughout the region. Over the ensuing fourteen centuries the alluring facemask periodically surfaced, only to be stolen again.

Fleeing from pursuit, the most recent thief had carried the sacred relic deep into the densest jungle he could reach. Taking cues from hieroglyphs inscribed on the reverse surface of the object, he found a suitable hiding place.

The bandit did not live to return for the treasure. The ancient stone face of the king would languish untouched for a thousand years.

New Mexico/Arizona Border, 1985

A pair of quarter horses stood tethered to a scrub pine at the head of the trail. No hoof-prints were visible on the hard red shale. Mounts secured, the riders had continued on foot, climbing the steep side of the ridge, leaving no trace. At the crest of the imposing mesa, the smell of a campfire lingered faintly in an arid breeze. Softly padding on feet clad in traditional leather moccasins, the duo maintained an almost complete silence.

Cloaked in a shroud of moonbeams, a young woman waited expectantly. In the dim light, she appeared a wild goddess. The men were mesmerized. The long curls of hair were like nothing they had ever seen. Her skin was surely pale as the moon itself! After exchanging a sidelong glance, the strangers approached. The exotic maiden spoke in a hushed voice.

"Did you bring it?"

"Of course," came the subdued reply. The man gestured toward a large flat boulder, and the three furtive attendees sat down, cross-legged. The ceremony began; ancient ritual incantations were solemnly whispered in voices quivering with enchantment.

The young woman accepted the peace pipe, and a light from a white-tipped strike-anywhere match. Not exactly a traditional source of flame, but for this particular secret rite it would have to suffice. She savored the sweet smoke, holding the vapor in her lungs until she felt they would burst. There was no way of knowing that the drug being ingested was not what had been promised.

In subtly accented English, the man spoke again, saying something about flying, but the edges of the world were becoming fuzzy. The woman reached for the pipe again and tasted the metallic succulence. Reality melted away.

Pennsylvania, Modern Era

"Denied funding?" The words seemed to echo embarrassingly throughout the building. Petersen slammed the door and paced the empty room. Two winters in this snowbound hellhole, a major breakthrough, and now his grant money was to be cancelled? Back to the drawing board, the endless written proposals, the jerk-offs with the purse strings expecting him to brown-nose?

It wasn't going to happen. There were people who were happy to pay, thrilled to possess the latest technology. Petersen happened to know just such a person.

Despite his anger and disappointment, Donald Petersen wasn't planning to sell vital secrets to a foreign state. Carlton Jains was a successful American businessman. The technology was secure. When the government changed its mind, the patents could be purchased. Fairly run-of-the-mill instruments had been used for the quantum mechanics experiments. Relocation was merely a huge pain in the ass.

Creating a weapon had not been the original motivation for starting the project; it was just the easiest means of acquiring financial support. Donald Petersen didn't give a damn about the source of the money, but believed that his findings should remain classified. At least the armed forces could keep a secret.

Inventions developed for the military are frequently adapted for commercial purposes by civilian entrepreneurs. Jet aircraft, the Internet, microwave communications, cyanoacrylate adhesives...hell, Petersen knew his discoveries would spawn myriad technologies. How could the Department of Defense be stupid enough to cut the program? The research was critical!

Fuming, the physicist began packing up his office.

Part One

Miami, Today, March One

After passing through airport security, I went to check the status of my flight on the schedule board. A familiar figure stood facing the screen. Despite a considerable lapse of time since our last meeting, I immediately recognized my old friend from behind and couldn't resist a reference to an inside joke, commenting, "You're a long way from the beach, Sandpiper."

The woman turned immediately, gasping my name aloud. "Stephen Shaw!"

The exclamation simultaneously conveyed recognition, astonishment, joy, and question. We hugged, her head snuggled against my chest. Gossamer hair snagged in the stubble of my day-old beard, obstinate as a cobweb. It felt exactly as I remembered. Our laughter echoed in Miami International's departure mezzanine.

"Airports are always full of beautiful women."

She accepted the compliment with a blush, chuckling, "Is that what you're doing here?"

"Not this time." I checked the clock on the flight schedule screen. This was going to be a very brief reunion. She followed my gaze and I said, "Guatemala City. You?"

In reply, she took a newspaper clipping from the side pocket of her purse, saying, "I called you, but your number has been disconnected."

"I moved to Europe."

"Yes, I heard."

A tall man, fit but gray, approached. Ignoring the encroachment, I began unfolding the worn sheet. The date at the top of the page was September of the previous year. The stranger joined us, saying, "Come on, Piper. They're boarding."

I smiled at the woman. "I guess the nickname stuck." She flushed again, and introduced me to her friend.

"Jon, this is Stephen Shaw. Stephen, Jonathan Ashe."

I don't think Jonathan Ashe was impressed, although my name was apparently familiar. He sized me up and dryly intoned, "Oh. Of course. Nice to meet you."

After exchanging an indifferent handshake, I opened the news clipping fully. It was a special feature article from a Sunday edition of the Arizona Republic. A color photo below the fold showed what appeared to be a group of Native Americans on horseback. In striking contrast to the other members of the group, one of the riders possessed a flowing mane of bright red hair.

I looked up at Piper's worried expression, wondering aloud, "You're going back again?"

"I have to."

Jonathan Ashe said, "Piper..."

I refolded the paper and scribbled my new phone number at the top. Jonathan Ashe snatched up the clipping, grabbed Piper's arm and hustled her toward the gate. My own flight was boarding momentarily, and I too rushed through the concourse. We did not even exchange a goodbye.

As Taca flight 321 became airborne, I noticed a single fine hair clinging to the shoulder of the denim shirt I was wearing as a jacket. The sandy blond had long since turned gray, but even from the back there had been no mistaking Elizabeth Locke. Those long legs, tiny body, and her tendency to sprint rather than walk had inspired me to bestow the moniker "Sandpiper" upon her, what, twenty-five years ago? Was it possible that so much time had passed? Although we lived less than one hundred miles apart, I had not seen Piper for probably close to fifteen years.

The seatbelt light went out. I reclined in 12A and closed my eyes.

It was my first postdoctoral research appointment after earning a degree in anthropology. The southwestern United States was not my preferred choice for exploration, but my research partner, Pauline Denzer, thinking the project a brilliant place to start, pulled some strings to get me funded. The expedition's principal investigator, an Austrian archeologist named Hermann Eicher, had been earning quite a reputation by making forays to sites entailing hardship under extreme environmental conditions. Professor Eicher had been one of my instructors, so it seemed natural for me to join the group.

This particular trip would not be as dangerous as some of his previous ventures, but did require tackling rough terrain in a remote area. Eicher had a map showing the location of known petroglyphs in a mountainous area called the Mogollon Rim, but he also wanted to search the surrounding region in case there were other stone carvings awaiting discovery. Piper and another degree candidate, along with three seniors seeking credit before graduation, were to join Herr Dr. Eicher and me.

Our little troupe gathered in the Arizona desert during the first week of June, and prepared for the arduous trek into the mountains. Two members of the party, both of them men, had become ill and failed to show, leaving the graduate students, Elizabeth "Piper" Locke and Sharon Reynolds, along with a much younger undergrad named Scarlett Taylor.

Eicher was ready to turn back and regroup, but the three women cried foul, insisting that they were qualified and able. The few weeks that would be lost during reorganization would push the exploration into the heat of summer, increasing the difficulty of the climb. We voted. The verdict was unanimous; the expedition would continue as planned.

If only we could have guessed that five of us would ascend the mountain, and just four would return.

The flight attendant served me a soft drink. I was happy for a distraction. Extraordinary events had brought me to today's juncture, and I hardly needed to relive odd occurrences now almost three decades in the past.

The passage of a few recent months had seen my world unseated. I had lost my job, stacked most of my possessions in my friend Charley's garage, and moved to Austria.

A developing romance with an anthropologist named Ingrid Luft had led to an attempt at a permanent relationship, but a previous dalliance with an alluring young Croatian woman called Magda had resulted in an unexpected pregnancy. The process of conception is not exactly a mystery, and I had been foolish to presume that precautions had been taken. Although I had fallen for her seduction under dubious circumstances, I felt strangely paternal, and at least somewhat responsible. I intended to lend a little financial support. This attitude did not go over well with Ingrid, my new paramour.

It came as no surprise that Magda decided to return home to Bosnia to deliver the baby. I knew that her parents were no longer living, but there were probably other relatives. In the closed society of the Republic of Austria, a foreign national was a second-class outsider. Now that there was peace on the peninsula, going home to the Balkans made sense.

Against my new girlfriend's wishes, I had accepted an invitation to join a potentially lucrative expedition in Central America, intending to use the profit to set up a trust fund for the unforeseen child. I had been idle over the winter, and had few things to wrap up in Europe. A new mission gave me a much-needed kick. After leaving Austria, I had returned to Florida, picked up some old field notes from storage, and prepared for a trip to a different climatic zone.

I assumed that lugging a computer and phone around the rainforest would more likely be a liability than an asset, and left mine at Charley's house. Fishing under the seat, I extracted a weathered leather-bound journal from my backpack and pondered the drawings that I had made years before. On that expedition, I had been concerned with Neolithic era petroglyphs, and mostly recorded detailed replications of the particular pictographs that seemed relevant to my research. Mayan glyphs were a sideline, but I had copied some for fun. All these years later, I had awoken from a nightmare, suddenly realizing the possible importance of what I had seen. Strange what the subconscious chooses to regurgitate during rapid eye movement.

Settling in for the duration of the flight, I scoured the disorganized pages of freehand sketches and pencil-lead rubbings for clues.

March Two

The meeting I had come so far to attend took place in a lavish home overlooking Lake Peten Itza. A car and driver had been provided at the airport in Guatemala City, and the two-hour ride allowed me time to acclimate.

My host, Hector Ramirez, was a wealthy international executive, but his heart belonged to his old mother in Guatemala. From childhood, she had regaled him with ancient tales of valor and treasure, stories that had fueled the young man's desire to excel. Now that Nana was in her eighties, Señor Ramirez was determined to bestow expensive gifts upon her.

Nana protested that material wealth would not be of value on the next part of her journey. It was far more important that the world was better for her having passed through it. A civil war had raged since her childhood, pitting the diverse ethnic roots of her family in opposition. If the Señor wished to bring treasure, let him return that which had been looted from her homeland, restore to its proper place a glorious symbol of an archaic civilization once as powerful and educated as that of ancient Egypt. Nana could die in peace, knowing she had played a role.

When his initial searches produced no results, Ramirez spoke to the directors of several museums and universities, and my name was repeatedly suggested. Along with a degree in anthropology, my credentials include references from my frequent expeditions related to a variety of fields. My speculations concerning the basis of certain myths, rituals, mores and traditions have led to surprising discoveries. Ramirez believed that would prove true in this case as well.

The Guatemalan offered to pay for all my flights and operating expenses. I had nothing pressing, apart from a great need of the bounty that was being offered for the recovery of a certain artifact. Depending on where the ancient treasure was found, Señor Ramirez would cover the cost of extradition and repatriation, as well as paying me a huge cash reward. All I was being asked to do was locate and secure the object, and make a telephone call.

Hector Ramirez was a handsome, cordial man, impeccably dressed and coiffed. After proudly leading the way through the elaborate house, he opened a door into a torch-lit courtyard and gestured for me to have a seat at a glass table. Pulling up a chair, he amiably began speaking in surprisingly eloquent English.

"You are undoubtedly aware of the Mayan creation myth?"

"I have a limited acquaintance with the English translation of the Popol Vuh."

"Yes, of course. The commonly accepted version of a three thousand year-old legend as redacted four centuries ago by a Franciscan monk. Still, I suppose it will suffice as a frame of reference. The story I plan to tell you is not included in that account. This tale was handed down to me by my mother."

Apparently the citronella torches were intended to keep the rampant invasion of flying insects to a minimum. The smoke wafting around us was thick, the citrus scent sweet. Ramirez poured two small glasses of Anejo, and we toasted. Draped on the wispy aromatic mist that drifted through the flagstone paved patio, his soft, slightly accented words evoked an aura of mystery.

"My mother is what you would term a Mayan, of the Mixtec tribe. My father is Hispanic, but that is a different story." He swallowed the rum and set the glass down before continuing, "The deserted ruins of ancient Mayan cities exude such a powerful presence that there is a tendency to believe that when the sites were abandoned, the culture also vanished. This is not so. The modern Maya have been forced from their tribal lands, much in the same way as your Native North Americans."

I nodded my head, swallowed the ounce of well-aged liquor, and sat back to listen.

"As you probably know, in all of Central America, only Guatemala possesses jadeite deposits. Early native inhabitants prized the stone, and traveled from all over the isthmus to obtain it. Not all the miners paid obeisance to the ruling emperors. Carrying large chunks of jade as a sort of currency, many defectors fled to other areas and established new kingdoms.

"In what is now called Belize, a primitive cultural center existed. One of these precious stones became an icon in the center of power. Carved as a mask, a huge piece of purest quality jade was the face of the king. As the ancient city at Lamanai began to take shape, the mask was the sole image the people recognized as their ruler. The artifact was passed from father to son. Only appearing before the public as a were-jaguar with a face of stone, the king was believed a demigod, perhaps even an immortal."

Ramirez had apparently become absorbed by the story, and absentmindedly poured more rum while gathering his thoughts.

"During this period, a great temple was erected, rising above the jungle. The base of this enormous pyramid was decorated with statues.

"A symbol representing a detail adorning the holy structure was carved into the back of the already ancient mask. The hardened stone was difficult to work, and there was great fear of the magic contained within the artifact. The glyph was little more than a tracing."

Matching his subdued tone, I inquired, "A jaguar?"

Ramirez looked up and slowly focused on my face, as if I had only just entered at that moment. We tossed back the little glasses of liquor, which seemed to clear his thoughts and throat.

"Yes, a jaguar, or were-cat is the assumption. From there, the huge piece of precious stone vanished. Periodically, references to this legend have resurfaced in the lore of subsequent tribes."

Some of this I already knew. A thousand questions came to mind, but I was not about to disturb the recitation. Ramirez seemed happy to have a drinking companion. The tiny shot glasses were brushed aside, and the next round of precious aged rum was served neat in eight-ounce tumblers. With the issue of libations settled, Ramirez continued.

"A fable has been passed down through hundreds of generations. The language has changed, but always the story remains the same.

"In the ancient kingdom, a spirit from the underworld captured the face of the king and escaped. Without the were-cat's magic, the emperor lost both supernatural power and royal status. The dynasty began to lose its vitality. Only one worthy of becoming godlike – half human, half jaguar – could retrieve the mask, and return the empire to glory. Any impure man who attempted to wear the face would suffer a horrible death at the hands of the gods."

Señor Ramirez paused for effect before continuing, "These old fables may seem fanciful, but they were important enough to be passed down orally during a period when Mayan hieroglyphs were being systematically destroyed by the Spanish invaders. Only in the last few years is the calligraphy of this ancient language beginning to be taught again, reconnecting the aboriginal population to its rich history.

"The sites of the ancient cities have been looted for centuries, stripped of their treasure. The return of this virtually priceless artifact would symbolize the birthright of the Guatemalan Maya, as well as draw deserved attention to the value of the original Meso-American culture. The object I seek is the one of which the legends tell, the jade mask of the jaguar king."

In the fickle flickering of tiki torch flames, the courtyard flora seemed to dance. We finished the rum in silence. Ramirez wished for me to locate an artifact that had gone missing over two thousand years ago. The task seemed impossible, surely made to order for a fool such as I.

Señor Ramirez provided me with a written rendition of the tale, including an English translation. The driver took me to my hotel. Despite the effects of the rum, I immediately began to plan. The extraordinary story provided some descriptions, but did not include any reference to the place where I intended to begin the search. I hoped my memory was correct.

As a graduate student, I had traveled to Central America to study petroglyphs, some of them as much as seventeen thousand years old. Pyramids and stelae at the accessible Mayan sites belong to a culture much more recent than the hunter-gatherers of the Archaic Period that I had been investigating at the time.

Along with the rudimentary paintings ascribed to the earliest inhabitants, elaborately carved stone "totems" from later cultures can be found throughout the isthmus, in areas occupied continuously since at least eighteen hundred years BCE. Most of ★ these monuments display glyphic writing in addition to intricate artwork. Some of the oldest script still defies translation, although many scholarly interpretations have been proven to be accurate. On my previous visits to the area, the notes I made concerning the Mayan architecture and stonework were more in the line of casual intrigue than investigative science. My sketches were of random images that caught my eye.

All Meso-American jade does indeed originate from one single source along the Motagua Fault Line in what is now Guatemala. Several weeks previously, following Hector Ramirez' initial phone call, I had reviewed my journeyman's knowledge of the Mayan empire, including the prevalence of jaguar symbolism. With hieroglyphics on my mind, I had woken from a vivid dream in which I visited the ruins and perceived certain carved symbols as conveying a different meaning than that of generally accepted interpretation, a slant subconsciously picked up elsewhere. If I could match the tale preserved in ancient sculpture to similar stories recorded at other locations, I might be able to follow the chronological trail of the legend, find the final chapter, and thereby locate the relevant artifact.

★ BCE - Before Common Era - a non-religious alternative to use of BC. in designating the first period of the Gregorian Calendar

March Three

Señor Ramirez' home rests almost at the geographic center of the ancient Mayan world, providing convenient access to numerous archeological sites. At nearby Tikal, the pyramids angle upward at a steeper gradient than do the ones at other notable Mayan city ruins, lending the structures a peculiar quaintness. I meandered along the causeway into the heart of the ancient city. In the windless morning air, the temples, monuments, and ball courts neighboring the central plaza seemed solemn and austere. Surrounding these ancient structures, the aura of human presence is intense; in my imagination, thousands of voices reflected from the walls, phantom echoes of the tumult emitted by primeval hordes.

Exploring in the fleeting silhouette of shade cast by the main temple, I examined a basalt pillar displaying engravings that depicted a series of figures. The first image I noticed was what I construed to be a man struggling to support a head too large for his body, followed by a warrior brandishing a spear. Another carving portrays a man bearing a staff across his shoulders; at one end of the yoke hangs the exaggerated face from the previous rune, at the other, the head of a jaguar cub. Other symbols in the stone depict a figure running from pursuit.

My slant on interpretation came from sketching a similar carving as an undergraduate visiting the newly sovereign nation of Belize in the early nineteen-eighties. To me, the stelae at the site were extraneous to the illusive stone-age inscriptions I had traveled so far to study, but I had examined the distinctive etchings with fascination, trying to glean possible relevance to Mayan daily life from the depicted myths.

Similarly, I now imagined this pictograph showing a pole with a figure at each end as representing a balance; the royal head was as heavy as, or equal in importance to a wild cat, the culture's most powerful totem. The next series of pictures seemed to support this outlandish theory. Despite the cumbersome burden, the fleeing man appeared to outrun a pack of soldiers.

Figures chiseled into freestanding boulders recount mythology and history, tales perhaps well known to the ancient populace, but variously interpreted by modern scholars. Here at Tikal, glyphs imprinted on stones resting out in the open have eroded or been vandalized. Some ruins have been looted to supply museums and art collectors. I could easily presume that these missing panels of hieroglyphs may have imparted details of Ramirez' tale, or other fables yet undiscovered. It had taken a dream state for my brain to connect these distantly related images one to another, and now I was planning to trace ancient mythological inscriptions through Meso-America based on fleeting impressions formed in an uneasy sleep.

I took photographs of the stela, and wandered among the neighboring pillars checking to see that no others bore relevant carvings. Back at the hotel, I compared the digital camera images with rough pencil drawings I had made years before at various sites. In the quiet surroundings, the pages triggered other memories, and my habitual real-time reminiscence took over without my noticing.

Eicher's proposal was based on combining two teams of specialists on an expedition to Arizona. Undated primitive artwork is scattered throughout the region. The idea was for archeologists to catalogue the stone-surface inscriptions, separating pure pre-Colombian Amerindian imagery from that displaying Spanish influence or other Old World symbolism. Cultural anthropologists would try to relate this material to a cross section of the modern local populace and determine whether the inhabitants had become completely homogenized in blood and belief, or if some indigenous ethnic strains and their lore survived intact.

From the outset, our little group formed cliques corresponding to our respective disciplines. Stolid, busty Sharon immediately teamed with Dr. Eicher, leaving the brilliant birdlike Elizabeth and spacey Scarlett with me in the cultural anthropology crew. Even during the hike, we grouped this way, Eicher and Sharon leading, Elizabeth and me talking shop, and little redheaded Scarlett following dreamily behind.

The trail was steep and difficult. At times we were forced to doff our heavy external-frame backpacks, mount large boulders, and hand our baggage up. We took frequent rests, thankful that we had not waited until the summer temperature climbed into three digits.

It was during one of these breaks that Elizabeth scurried off into the scrub brush to retrieve what turned out to be a desiccated cow-horn, prompting my original "sandpiper" comment. She immediately became "Piper." It seemed fitting that such a unique woman would go by an uncommon name.

The memory dissolved as mysteriously as it had developed. I set aside the old journal and went to bed with the images from the stelae fresh in mind. Perhaps another dream would reveal more secrets.

Carlton Jains III spent his formative years in Northwest Washington D.C., an area where affluent enclaves abut average middle class neighborhoods. The residents are a constantly revolving mixture of government workers, foreign dignitaries, executives, lobbyists, media professionals, support crews and blue-collar workers, but the children are just kids. At the local playground, the swing-set or seesaw might easily be host to an African diplomat's child, a Swede, a Thai, and a midwestern farmer's daughter.

Carlton's massive family estate overlooks Spring Valley, a rolling old-growth forest sprinkled with sprawling mansions of brick and stone. Less than half a mile from this spectacular collection of homes, modest wood-frame houses originally intended for families of military members serving in the nation's capital form a neighborhood along what was once called

"Aqueduct Road," paralleling the water main that serves the city. The area has become desirable and well known, but back when Carlton Jains visited the home of his childhood best friend Donald Petersen, Potomac Palisades was an unnoticed and sleepy riverside suburb.

Despite a marked difference in social station, the boys formed a bond that would last a lifetime. Carlton was heir apparent in an established capitalistic clan, well tutored concerning the management of money. The boy's destiny was clear; there was no question that he would follow the family tradition and carry on the business of financial investment. Even his semi-arranged marriage to a suitable debutante seemed predestined. Throughout life, Jains merely went through the expected motions, accustomed from birth to the perquisites due an eminent entrepreneur.

Young Petersen's future, however, was a continuously morphing sequence of inventions. Seeking a lifetime vocation, the child experimented endlessly.

Carlton Jains was constantly amazed; where he saw only a mud-puddle, Donnie Petersen described a primordial lake teeming with exotic creatures. Jains watched his restless buddy create elaborate structures made of drinking straws and coax colonies of ants to traverse the labyrinths. The precocious child bred guinea pigs, made popguns from vinegar mixed with baking soda, caught and dissected small animals and insects. Eventually banned from experimenting in his mother's house or environs, Donnie established a secret hideout in a vine-tangled slope overlooking the Potomac River, a perfect sanctuary in which to fabricate stink bombs and culture maggots without interference.

Jains was not surprised that his childhood pal had become a brilliant scientist; it was Petersen's nature. The tycoon was still fascinated by the now grown-up experiments, despite their being largely unintelligible. Although his old friend tried to explain the need for financial assistance using scientific terms, it was a simple description of what could be done with the resulting technology that eventually persuaded Carlton Jains III to lend financial support.

March Four

The quiet colonial island city of Flores provided a welcome respite from the stress and cold weather I had endured in Austria during the winter months. Selfishly, I savored the summery indolence induced by the equatorial heat. Rather than forging ahead with searching the ruins, I holed up in the hotel, got caught up in my journal, and wrote a letter to my girlfriend relating the details of Ramirez' quest.

After spending years as a bachelor following my divorce, I had finally met Ingrid Luft; a woman with whom I believed a long-term relationship was possible. Was it my fault that I had a past? That there had been other lovers? Was it wrong to assume partial responsibility for a night of passion?

From my point of view, a wish to assist a woman that accidentally carried my biological child was not a viable reason for my new partner to become jealous. I wasn't abandoning our relationship; helping out with some cash was simply my way of dealing with guilt. The heart, however, follows its own logic. Interaction with Ingrid had become strained. I tried to be sensitive and imagine how it would feel if the tables were turned.

I took strength from a healthy dose of fine Guatemalan rum, and tried to channel the restorative power of a warm evening breeze blowing from the lake.

Following a high-society wedding, Carlton Jains' wife, Margaret, had moved into the house in which her husband had come of age. She respected the established boundaries, and seldom entered his half of the ground floor. The semi-arranged marriage had been rather practical and emotionless, their two girls raised by nannies while the parents socialized with their country club clique. Now, with the children off in college, Margaret was free to exploit the benefits of wealth, and spent most of her time traveling with friends. The relationship worked for both Carlton and "Maggie," maintaining the expectations of their families and social set without interfering with each other's personal agenda.

Jains no longer wore a suit, or went to an office. Brokers handled his investments, and he called the shots from home. A private trainer helped keep extra pounds in check, and trips to a tanning salon ensured that his gold jewelry showed to advantage against an off-season suntan that suggested affluent leisure. Despite the foppishness of his affectations, Carlton Jains was a tough bargainer that had rebuilt a deteriorating family fortune.

Donald Petersen met with Carlton at the old family mansion in the hills overlooking Spring Valley. Mrs. Jains familiarly greeted her husband's old friend, and left the two men alone.

Jains was thrilled to join Petersen in a business venture, although had Donald asked for a personal loan it would have been refused. Wealth was something to which Jains was accustomed, and it conveyed no particular thrill. Power was a different thing entirely. A certain amount could be bought, but omnipotent dominance was priceless.

For as long as he could remember, Carlton Jains had been bedazzled by Donald Petersen's scientific dexterity. If Petersen said he was going to make something happen, there was little doubt. Jains had every intention of being in control of the incredible force; still, it was a lot of money for an unproven technology.

Petersen tried to explain the reason for so much expense.

"To be able to do this, CJ, I'll need a klystron, a linear particle accelerator, photo-optic relays…"

Jains looked up from his smart phone. "Hold up, Don. You know I don't understand all that shit."

The physicist made to continue, "Computers…"

Jains held up his hand, and Petersen became silent. Both men understood perfectly. The tone of their relationship had been predestined on the day they met.

After school let out for summer, Carlton Jains was enjoying the few rare days of freedom between the end of the semester and the start of summer camp. The pudgy eleven-year old flung downhill on his ten-speed, exhilarated by the rush of air, momentarily forgetting how hard it would be to pedal on the return trip.

Carlton parked the bike near the deserted railroad track and made for a trestle over the canal. Older kids sometimes jumped from the bridge into the shallow water, or climbed out on the precarious perches of the structure to paint graffiti on the metal sections of the span, but Carlton was content to peer down at the thirty-foot drop through the gaps between the ties.

On the far side of the bridge the boy continued along the tracks, playing tightrope walker on the rails. Trails wound through the woods, leading from the railroad berm down to the river. He ran to the bank and skipped flat pebbles across the water.

When hunger set in, Carlton realized that the afternoon had disappeared and set out for home. To his dismay, older boys from the neighborhood had taken over the railroad bridge. There was a distinct possibility that they would bully a younger child out alone, but the next crossover was miles down the towpath. Knowing the danger, he pressed on, hoping for deliverance.

They ambushed him at the center of the span. Three ruffians wrestled him over the steel I-beam plate girder that supported the tracks. With nothing between him and a life-threatening fall, Carlton stopped resisting. The bullies forced him out to the end of a T-bar suspended high above the muddy water. Whether the others really intended to push him off, the height was dizzying, and his bladder let loose. As the stain spread down his shorts, the bullies taunted and jeered, but Carlton didn't cry; something inside of him snapped, and he would never be the innocent child again. He turned toward the older boys in a rage.

For a moment, Jains thought that his anger had miraculously brought the wrath of God upon his tormentors. Pops and hisses filled the air, followed by smoke and a thick stench. One of the older boys was screaming after being hit by a flying incendiary, and missiles were exploding all around. The bullies ran scrambling over the ties to the far end of the bridge. The barrage continued until they had fled into the woods.

Carlton was so dumbfounded that he forgot to be scared, and climbed back over the rail to the relative safety of the bridge. From the bank he had been trying to reach, a figure appeared in the bushes, a boy about his age, beckoning. Carlton hustled toward his rescuer; the older kids would be back, armed with rocks. Approaching the end of the trestle, he heard laughter, and then came an admonition to hurry.

Petersen introduced himself when they a gotten a little distance from the bridge. He showed off his weapons, a homemade slingshot with a launch guide like a crossbow, and munitions consisting of little plastic balls made from gumball containers. "Ammonium sulfide," said the newcomer, but Carlton didn't understand the words. Soon they were both laughing about the incident as they continued along the railroad tracks.

Carlton's bike tires had been slashed by vandals. Petersen came to the rescue again, leading the way to a modest wood-frame house. Carton used the garden hose to clean up, while the other boy persuaded his mother to give the newfound friend a ride home. The Petersens were duly impressed by the Jains' mansion.

It was the start of a symbiotic relationship; Donald Petersen had the scientific ways, Carlton Jains the financial means. Their friendship was cemented during the teenage years; eventually becoming scorned as nerds, the pair had frequent need for revenge, and took great pleasure in the creation of devices and schemes of retribution. Never again would Jains silently suffer as a victim; every trespass was cruelly avenged.

"Bottom line, Don," the wealthy man continued. "Just give me the bottom line. What's it going to cost?"

March Five

Carlton Jains' grandfather had fallen under the same spell as Theodore Roosevelt and Ernest Hemingway; he loved to hunt. In an era when large game was still plentiful and the safari was considered a noble endeavor, wealthy men played at the sport. Among other locations, the senior Jains sought trophies in the wild terrain of the southwestern United States. Stalking mountain lion and black bear, he ran up against an obstruction when a rancher refused to grant access to a large tract of land in the foothills of the White Mountains of Arizona. The macho mogul simply bought the ranch for more than it was worth, sent the homesteader packing, and continued to pursue elusive beasts. Of no further concern after the old man's death, the property remained in the family portfolio, merely an unremarkable real estate holding that steadily increased in value, a safe investment that had slowly turned three hundred thousand into one-point-five million.

When Petersen described the isolation and open space required for the experiment, Carlton Jains immediately thought of the remote preserve. The open acreage seemed perfect, and significantly lowered the cost of investment.

After formulating a plan, Jains handled the leasing of a recreational vehicle. Petersen excitedly placed orders for the required equipment to be delivered to the site. The laboratory supply salesman had dealt with the physicist for years, and didn't question the purchase of sensitive chemicals and machinery. He concentrated instead on figuring his commission as the list grew.

In the relative coolness of dawn, I returned to the stelae at the ruins of Tikal. For several hours, I perused and studied the intricate stone-carvings, hoping relevant glyphs would be evident somewhere. After a short break during the hottest hours of the afternoon, I continued to roam among the pillars unrewarded. Exiting the site, ready to call it a day, I noticed a deteriorating pockmarked relic situated away from the organized row of intricately inscribed boulders that faced out from the temple. The solitary monolith had been angled in a different compass orientation than any other object at the site.

Stepping back from the carved stone, I realized that lines created by the placement of smaller etchings had once surreptitiously described a single rune. From fifty feet away, a giant rendering of the elusive symbol that had become embedded in my subconscious appeared, a clue the size of the entire boulder. It was surprising that the idea of a symbol on a large scale had not occurred to me sooner. Many Central American sites display enormous statues and masks.

The huge ideogram fit both my dream and the tale told to me by Hector Ramirez. The symbol appeared to be identical to the one I had copied so many years ago at the Temple of the Jaguar in Lamanai, but the details had long since worn away. It had taken hours to go through the photographs I amassed in preparation for this wild goose chase. So far, this was the only match. Perhaps a stone located elsewhere contained clues.

The rulers of Tikal also built the city of Copan, beyond the current border in Honduras. The site has suffered from erosion, but it was possible that an inscription related to the tale remained intact. Now that I had reinforced the notion that the hieroglyph might have traveled widely throughout the ancient kingdoms, the sister city seemed worth a try. I caught the last flight of the evening into Guatemala City.

Margaret Jains' springtime schedule had become an annual pilgrimage. By the time her daughters returned to school after the semester break near the beginning of March, winter would become unbearable. Maggie and two of her girlfriends would fly to the French Riviera and soak up some sun. For the remainder of

Lent, they would make a pilgrimage to Lourdes and purge at a neighboring spa until Easter. After shopping in Paris or Milan through the end of April, Maggie would return to Washington in early May and enjoy the city in the blush of spring until the heat of early summer forced her to retreat to the seashore.

    Carlton despised the very thought of this pious regimen, and used Maggie's yearly absence as an opportunity to run with his old school crowd. Following the incident on the bridge, Jains had learned to use his social stature to dominate and bully, and surrounded himself with others that would do his bidding. Over the years, the men had graduated from cocaine and marijuana to single-malts and Havana cigars. This year, Carlton skipped the reunion to join his oldest friend in a more productive adventure. With the exuberance of teenagers on a lark, the middle-aged duo set out for Arizona.

March Six

On the advice of the hotel concierge, I hired a car and driver from a tour company to take me to Honduras. Apparently it would have required an entire day to reach the ruins by bus. It took almost that long by car.

After checking in to a hotel in Copan Ruinas, I went looking for local knowledge at the nearest watering hole. I'm a bit taller than the average Honduran, and felt a little conspicuous as I gazed over a cluster of red-brown faces.

I fully expected distrust; Europeans decimated the prosperous indigenous population that originally defined civilization in the Americas. Empires that had flourished for hundreds of years before the birth of Christ fell prey to the lust, greed, and diseases of the self-proclaimed conquerors from the old world. Modern regimes have deviated little from this vile legacy. The Honduran Ladinos had every right to regard me, a foreigner, with wariness.

Eventually, civilized men drinking together sense their similarity and form a bond; in the end we are merely specimens of the animal named "human," brought to a common denominator by the very nature of meager mortal existence. I paid for a few rounds, as was probably expected. After a mass exodus to the rear of the building for group urination against the wall, a marijuana cigarette was circulated. I don't care much for the stuff, but my refusal would have engendered distrust. I took in as much air and as little smoke as I could get away with convincingly. As the joint burned away, my humanizing initiation was complete.

These men had no compelling reason to volunteer assistance to a stranger, but after I made clear my scholarly intent, they seemed to respect my courage or stupidity. I'm not sure which.

The conversation became an animated exchange of anecdotes, punctuated with laughter and gestures intended to overcome my limited Spanish vocabulary. They clamored to tell me the most likely places to search.

After one last jovial visit to the straw pit out back, I found my way to the hotel unmolested. My room had been searched, but not ransacked. It was neither a surprise, nor a major concern. Everything of value in my possession on this trip was carried in a knapsack that remained on my person constantly, my companion for all the years I had spent in the field. Australians use the term "Waltzing Matilda" to describe the habit of carrying a "tucker bag." The backpack was safe next to me on the bed. I was accustomed to my "Matilda's" presence and didn't count "jumbucks." Sleep was instantaneous, and regrettably, dreamless.

The motorhome made good time on the smooth pavement of Interstate 81. As the east coast megalopolis fell behind, the traffic thinned. The forty-foot RV rolled along as if on autopilot. Whiling away the miles, Petersen talked about the experiment.

"Before you can understand what I am about to accomplish, there are several concepts that need to be grasped, or at least accepted. Speaking scientifically, do you know what the term 'emergence' means?"

Jains propped his feet on the dashboard, resting his eyes behind dark glasses. "Not a clue."

"Well, take for example an insect, say…a bee. The individual animal has little capacity in the way of cognitive processing. It simply reacts to chemical stimuli by performing functions that have been 'programmed' into its nature. Some bees make wax forms; others fill the holes with honey. Each bee only performs one specific job; there are bees with different 'instructions' that provide other necessities. Yet as the hexagonal wax cells are built, a pattern emerges – the honeycomb – a structure that is quite beyond the conceptual capabilities of the individual members of the hive. Other types of emergence include patterns shaped by a variety of influences, wind on sand, for example, or the formation of sugar crystals and what have you."

Jains nodded, and said resignedly, "I can accept that it occurs, as long as we don't go into who or what 'programmed' these traits."

Familiar with his companion's fair-weather Catholicism, Petersen smiled, saying, "Believe me; I had no intention. Now picture similar assemblages occurring in a bio-molecular setting. Configurations of elemental particles form atomic structures. Groups of these atoms comprise molecules that combine as amino acid compounds, the building blocks for proteins. Following a sort of blueprint, the proteins help build specific cells. The cells come together and comprise a single entity, a bodily organ for example. How do the cells know when to stop reproducing?"

"What keeps your nose from growing forever?"

"Exactly. Somewhere in all that 'programming' are instructions that tell cells what to become, and how to communicate to each other that the job is finished."

Jains was suddenly skeptical of his friend's creativity. "I hope there's more to it than that, Don."

Petersen was unperturbed. "I'm just trying to make clear my approach. Change anything at the subatomic level and these instructions become modified. A malfunction takes place, and there is a different emergence. Cancer for example. The mutated cells spread and grow unabated, displace the normal growth, and eventually destroy the very organism from which they derive life-support."

Removing the designer shades, Jains blandly glanced at the scenery. "Killing off your host doesn't seem like a particularly brilliant evolutionary tactic. Why are they still here?"

"Mutation is crucial to the process of life. Without it, nothing could adapt to environmental changes: no new traits would ever develop. However, that's totally not the point."

"I'm sure." Jains faced his friend. "So, what? You found a way to spread cancer?"

Petersen's eyes remained on the road. "Hardly. In fact, perhaps a cure. However, an individual emergence event is not the larger focus of my work, although controlling one would certainly prove the viability of my concept."

"So wait a minute. You're saying that a cure for a disease that has meant a horrible death for millions of humans throughout history is a minor sideline, compared to what you are working on?"

The question elicited a half-smile. "Oh my, yes. The results of these new experiments will revolutionize humanity's conception of existence. We will enter an astounding phase of comprehension and development, and it is vital that this technology remains under rational control."

"Or?"

Petersen's grave reply seemed to suck all the oxygen from the vehicle's cab.

"Or the continued existence of the entire planet is forfeit."

March Seven

I woke in a cold sweat and lay awake in the grey of predawn wishing I could snooze a little longer. A sudden recollection prevented my return to slumber. My chance meeting with Piper had brought back long dormant memories.

Sharon was a big girl, loud, brassy, and sharp as the sting of a whip. Eicher fell under her spell. By the end of the second day, it was obvious that a love affair would ensue. I don't think that the two of them were even remotely aware of the "vibe," but sex-charged pheromones permeated the air. Eicher had enough sense to pitch his tent away from the safety of the central fire. To me, dividing the group hadn't seemed such a good plan at first, but I was grateful for his foresight when muted grunts and moans of pleasure escaped on the wind.

In the morning, Sharon was defiant, apparently expecting reproach. I doubt if it came from any member of our party; there was certainly none from me. The team explored the stone formations; the artifacts that had brought us here were scattered, and locating primitive drawings that had escaped erasure by time and weather required considerable effort. The group continued to be divided; Eicher and Sharon catalogued every find; the rest of us attempted to decipher meaning, and assign significance.

Evidently, Sharon was pushing a personal agenda of which I was unaware, at least until our third night camping.

The memory melted under a hot shower. I wanted to get an early start. The latent effect of the previous evening's cocktails was enticing me to sleep in.

Petersen seemed content to drive, hours at a stretch. The next segment of the journey would follow I-40 west for over fifteen hundred uneventful miles. From behind the wheel, the physicist continued to cajole his new backer with descriptions of the experiment.

Carlton Jains was beginning to savor the prospects of power that his scientific friend was suggesting. Putting aside the trepidations that were a natural reaction to the implications, he was impatient to explore the weapon's potential.

"Wait a minute, Don. You're telling me that you are inventing something that is capable of destroying the Earth?"

"That's certainly not my intention, but like that old song says, 'If I don't do it...'"

"Somebody else will?"

"That's the tune, but seriously; the one that gets there first will be able to detect and control any other attempts. I intend to be that person."

Jains stared across empty fields as the vehicle rolled along. "So what is it, a black hole?"

Petersen chuckled. "That would probably provide pertinent data, but no, nothing like that. My current line of reasoning came about for mostly philanthropic reasons. I know you think I experiment just for the sake of experiment itself, and certainly that was true of me as a child. I have come to realize that my youthful inquisitiveness was merely a period of training. There had to be a higher purpose."

"A higher purpose?" Jains was intrigued by the term. "So now you intend to become a god?"

"Nothing could be further from the truth. What I meant was, I trust my clear scientific mind to use reason, not only to unlock secrets of the physical world, but also to disseminate sensitive information wisely. I simply cannot trust that other researchers capable of discovering this technology necessarily possess similar scruples."

Jains employed a theatrically insipid tone of voice, saying, "Dorky Petersen, master of the universe." Both men cracked up at this. Throughout childhood, Donald Petersen had been a self-described "unrepentant nerd," and took his revenge on scornful peers through trickery such as feeding laxatives to the neighbor's cat, or putting an egg in the school bully's gasoline tank. Recounting these antics could even now reduce the pair of old friends to juvenile hysterics.

Petersen recovered his composure. "I think you're going to like this."

"I don't know if I can stand it. Go on."

Petersen's voice was deathly serious. "How much do you know about quantum entanglement?"

Stelae carved as portraits are a prominent feature of the ruins at Copan. Amazingly detailed stone pillars depict dozens of ancient monarchs, and describe the circumstances of their dominions. The city was occupied continuously for over two thousand years. Artifacts at the site were created during dynasties spanning the Mayan reign. A thorough examination of every inscription would have taken days, but between the information from the previous evening's encounter at the bar and the assistance of the local tour guides, all the likely carvings were systematically ruled out.

By evening I was reasonably convinced that no stone pictograph featuring the jaguar king I was seeking was to be found in Copan. Other Mayan ruins are situated throughout the area, but I had no evidence that particularly suggested extending the search in this direction. The legend had come west from Belize, but apparently had not traveled south from Tikal.

Historically, jade was often carried north into what is now Mexico. In a civilization predating the Mayan, the Olmecs were famous for intricate works in the ornamental gemstone. I wondered if the object I was seeking had followed along the same timeworn path. I decided that after one more night in Copan, I would return to Guatemala and head for Piedras Negras, the source of the jade. Starting at the original quarries, I would follow the ancient migrations of the semiprecious stones.

Alone at the end of the day, with nothing but my dog-eared journals for entertainment, my past kept me company.

In many ways, the setting had been exactly how, in the naivety of youth, I had imagined an archeological dig. Stone-age inscriptions and artwork inspired fireside conjecture espoused by energetic and youthful scholars. The central bonfire became our think tank. The flames were not intended to warm the group; the fire was built to keep critters at bay, but it provided a convenient forum. Caught up in discussion, I don't think that any of us paid particular mind that the youngest member of our troupe was not participating. I assumed that she was taking note, and the silence was due to studious observation.

I had brought a flask, and under the influence of rum, our speculations assumed an aura of educated brilliance. Piper and I began to establish a close rapport. There were undercurrents at work that did not become apparent until much later.

The highway seemed endless. Jains absorbed as much science as he could take in at a sitting. After a beer and a nap, he would be ready for more. Petersen drove on relentlessly, deep in thought except when answering questions.

Eventually Jains took a turn at driving, and talked to stay awake.

"So let me get this straight, Petersen. What you're telling me is that quantum teleportation entails the creation of entangled particles, and it makes no difference how far apart they are?"

"Right. As long as both particles are necessarily described by a third entity with which they are linked, their behavior is associated, and the state of one will dictate the nature of the other. They remain connected in time, despite being separated in space."

"So your 'teleportation' doesn't physically disassemble something in one place and reassemble it in another?"

"Not in this scenario."

Jains gave a disbelieving look. "So it's not like…"

"Not like on TV, no." Petersen realized his own nap would have to wait. "Do you remember what I told you about emergence?"

Jains was trying to put it together. "About the patterns? So your teleporter is going to transmit its state to distant particles that will then form new configurations…where is this leading?"

"You are still missing a few pieces, but if the particles are entangled, and an influence on one affects both, and if the particles are part of a larger entity…"

"Then changing the corresponding particles' behavior would affect that entity…Petersen, that's diabolical!" Jains drummed a martial rhythm on the steering wheel. "But I still don't get the part about the patterns."

"Imagine a cancer, forming cells and spreading throughout an organ. Transmit information that influences the behavior of targeted particles to alter the atomic structure of the abnormal molecules, and the cancerous cells begin to behave as the originals did. Stimulate intracellular communication, and healthy tissue forms in emergence."

"I thought you weren't working on a cure."

Petersen yawned, and snuggled against the seat-back. "That's true, at least not directly, but as an added benefit, why not? The number of ways to use this technique is as endless as the number of waves in the ocean. Quantum teleportation is already being applied in radiology. It will revolutionize communication, and computing."

"What about the all powerful weapon you described?"

"Picture this; I create a duplicate of a specifically targeted molecule. Through electromagnetic waves, particles from my model become entangled with corresponding entities in the target. I know when that happens because of the reaction of my particles. Now I influence the motion of my particles…"

"…And it affects the target."

"Well, let's say information is transmitted to the target, regardless of the distance. Then, using radiation, I initiate the genesis of an emergence event based on the new information. Obviously this is a gross simplification of an extremely complicated process, but now you see why it's so important."

"Regardless of distance, even if something blocks the path?"

A shadow of death once again seemed to chill Petersen's voice. "There will be no hiding place."

Despite his sudden thrill, Jains involuntarily shuddered at his old friend's grim tone. The development did not sound like good news for the school bully.

March Eight

There was no way of knowing if I would ever have reason or opportunity to visit Copan again. To more fully experience the ruins considering my limited time, I took a guided tour without the distraction of searching for clues.

By mid-afternoon, the driver arrived for the return trip. On the ride back to Guatemala City, I stared out the window, thinking again of the memories I had visited the night before.

Hermann Eicher had discovered the erotic stimuli that would cause Sharon Reynolds to vocalize, and did not hesitate to perform them. I don't know that this precipitated things, but hearing moans of ecstasy was certainly not a deterrent to physical desire. As I lay awake, the zipper on my pup tent was quietly manipulated from the outside.

Piper was wearing a man's white shirt, and I immediately realized that there was nothing underneath. I started to ask, "Are you...?"

She shushed me, whispering words that at the time meant far more to me than any term of endearment.

"I'm on the pill."

Kneeling in the doorway, she unbuttoned the shirt and reached to pull off my shorts. She stretched out on top of me, downy softness tantalizing against skin parched by desert aridity. The confines of the little Dacron shelter provided an inconvenient milieu for this type of encounter, but we successfully conducted our slippery business despite the clumsiness of unfamiliarity. That may seem almost crude, but what stands out instead is our complete freedom and release, the joy of youthful discovery, the peaceful bliss of a post coital embrace.

We savored our satisfaction. I am happy that I can remember these moments separately from the ones that followed.

The RV rolled on through the night, and arrived at the deserted acreage of the long-forsaken hunting preserve just after dawn. After deciding on a site for their camp, Petersen and Jains waited at the turnoff for two semitrailers loaded with equipment to be delivered.

The encampment was clustered at the foot of a ridge that rose abruptly at the western edge of the desert, providing shade from the soon to be blistering afternoon sun. Propped up on wooden blocks, the steel shipping containers provided a perfect workspace.

After the teamsters left, Petersen and Jains began unwrapping the equipment and setting up the laboratory. The financier griped about doing physical labor, but to help maintain secrecy he had agreed to assist personally rather than hire workers. As each component was integrated, its function was discussed.

A fifty-kilowatt diesel-powered generator located a hundred feet from the trailers provided electricity. Four liquid crystal screens were the monitors for a bank of computers. The klystron and accelerator were bulky but mobile, mounted on wheeled carts. In a practical long-distance application, a target would have to be at a sufficient distance from the point of transmission to allow a beam of radiation to be deflected by the subject and detected by a remote sensor, ultimately as distant as an orbiting satellite.

Jains began to open a box marked with the international symbol for poison and warnings in three languages. Petersen intervened.

"Better let me take care of that one, CJ."

Jains stepped back to read the label. Petersen continued, "The gas doesn't smell bad, but it is extremely volatile and toxic."

The moneyman was perfectly happy to leave it be.

March Nine

Mayan-style culture in Guatemala goes back well over three thousand years, although Neolithic era predecessors haunted the area for centuries prior. Before this trip, I had never visited the country. Cold war era fear of communist insurgency in Latin America led to U. S. support for the Guatemalan military. Following a CIA backed coup d'etat, the arms and training detoured on an insidious path. In a civil war that lasted almost fifty years, subsequent factions of the government committed genocide against an estimated two hundred thousand Mayans. Traveling to the region hadn't seemed a good idea at the time of my previous visits to Central America.

As I was already in the capital city, searching the sources of jade along the Motagua River struck me as a logical pursuit. Entering the rain forest is an enchantment after the bustle of densely populated urban areas. The jungle engages the senses as if a single giant living organism. The raucous calling of birds infuses the sullen humidity with relentless cacophony. Prolific plant growth is unbridled and omnipresent. Dense and moisture-laden, the air itself seems to have an organic presence. My breath came hard after the long sweltering hike from the highway.

Jaguar themes permeate Mayan mythology, reflected by recurrent motifs in the extraordinary stone carvings. I didn't find the oversize representational architecture that adorns the temple at Lamanai, but there were other sculptural interpretations of transmogrifying wildcats and men, further expanding upon the folklore. If I was willing to entertain the idea that the artwork changed stylistically over time while continuing to represent the original legends, the thread of the tale might be discernible in cultural centers that were occupied more recently.

After a professionally gratifying but fruitless visit to the eroded ruins, I began to believe that if archaic commerce in jade might reveal the trail of the piece I was seeking, museums would be a more productive place to look. Virtually no semiprecious stones are still to be found *in situ*; the remains of ancient cities are works created from common basalt. If I had found symbols or architecture similar to that of the jaguar glyph, there might have been something to go on.

The Epi-Olmec culture flourished in the Yucatan Peninsula at around the same time that the temples in Tikal, Copan, and Lamanai were being constructed. Although their stonework is stylistically different from that found in the Peten Basin, they too fashioned many portraits of their rulers. The ruins of their cities lay to the North. My next stop would be Veracruz, Mexico. I headed for the hotel.

While arranging the final positioning of the equipment, Petersen continued to elaborate to an astonished Carlton Jains.

"It's easy to presume that humans represent the pinnacle of evolution, the sole practitioners of higher cognitive processes, wardens of the planet. That opinion is a bit presumptuous and arrogant; something like ninety-seven percent of our genome is the same as that of a mouse."

"Why are you telling me that?"

"Because as far as eventually creating a weapon goes, the genome is where the unique molecules that I intend to model are found."

"I'm not sure I follow."

Petersen lifted a heavy water-bottle onto a dispenser, and paused to stretch the kinks out of his back. "Let's say I want to target you specifically. I have to use something that is unique to you, for example, your DNA. The particles I wish to manipulate are already positioned and functioning in the subatomic configuration that comprises the amino acids that make up your genetic code. I create identical models-clones, if you will-that correspond exactly to those particular molecules. Using gamma rays, a channel of communication is opened between the originals and the models, and some of the subatomic particles become entangled. Then I begin to influence the activity of the molecules, and therefore also the particles, in my clones. This triggers a corresponding alteration in the targeted molecules.

"The radiation stimulates your cells, provoking reproductive activity similar to an immune system reaction. Following the new quantum instructions in your DNA, your cells mutate to match my altered prototypes. Once the process is underway, intracellular communication takes over the replication process. No further interference is required."

"What are you doing to my DNA?"

Petersen drew a flask of water from the jug. "I might remove or repair a gene that causes a deleterious effect. Alternatively, I could take advantage of our animal commonality, and cause your human sections of code to become like those of, oh, say, a pig?"

"You're joking!"

"Quite serious, and can you imagine the effect this might have, the knowledge that you can be identified by your unique molecular signature, anywhere on this planet or beyond, and the very essence of your corporeal being altered, without the position of your precise location having any bearing?"

"Let me get this straight. You don't know where I am, but my molecules react the same way as your model."

"Particles."

"Right. Particles. On a subatomic level. I get that; but how can you possibly make a model of the atomic state of me?"

"Quantum state? A physical corollary to a mathematical description? That is unnecessary for the process. Copying DNA is simple. Once there is material to work with, I merely alter the code, link it to the target, and transmit the information."

Petersen poured the water into a reservoir atop one of the machines. Jains shook his head. It made no difference whether he understood, as long as it worked.

Back at the hotel room, my vanity disrupted a burglary. Almost feverish after exploring the ruins in the heat, I turned up the air-conditioner and went to take a shower. Stripping my clothes off, I caught the reflection in the wall length bathroom mirror and paused. I sucked in my gut and stood up straight. My stomach still protruded. Too many hours sitting at a desk, too many Austrian cappuccinos, beers, schnitzels and strudels. There was nothing I could do about the flecks of gray in the stubble on my chin, but a diet and some exercise definitely loomed in my future. I heard a bump, and felt a rush of warm air.

A man had climbed onto the balcony and opened the sliding glass door. I yelled, "Hey!" The startled intruder vaulted the rail back down into the garden. I ran to the door, but there was no way I was going to leap after him and give chase *au naturel*. I wrapped a towel around my waist, and called the front desk.

Petty theft hardly comes as a surprise in a country where seven million people subsist below the poverty level. I was sympathetic; there was little the hotel could do. It did seem peculiar that the break-in occurred precisely upon my entering the bathroom, considering that the hotel room had been vacant all day. I looked around at my possessions. Was it possible that upon not finding anything on a previous search the perpetrator now wished to get a look into my knapsack? Had Señor Ramirez sent someone to ensure that I was not stealing the artifact I had been sent to find?

Although the incident was a bit unnerving, I did not feel seriously threatened. However, I took the backpack with me and latched the bathroom door while in the shower.

A little wound up after the incident, I found sleep elusive. Lying in bed, I tried to review the few clues I was working with in the search for the ancient mask. Thinking back to the jaguar symbol recorded in my journal, I became sidetracked.

Sharon had been the instigator all along, regaling the other female members of the team with boasts of sexual prowess and credos of women's liberation. Piper was apparently determined to prove she was a modern woman, not a prude. I can testify on her behalf; the new nickname fit in more ways than one.

Now that their liaison was no longer a secret, Eicher and Sharon became quite unabashed, at least judging by the noise coming from the tent. Piper and I had our own little party going, and fueled with rum, our erotic liaison continued long after the rest of the camp had finally become quiet for the night.

After a grand finale of sorts, like most typical males, I fell asleep. Piper woke me before dawn, and in a confusion of exhaustion and alcohol, I thought she wanted more sex. The importance of what she was saying did not immediately register when she told me that Scarlett was gone.

March Ten

The early morning flight to Mexico made several stops along the way, but the view from the air was spectacular. The size and density of the jungle impressed upon me the tremendous resolve it must have taken to create a major civilization in such an inhospitable environment.

Upon arriving at the hotel in Veracruz, I called my girlfriend in Austria. I had hoped that this phone call would be focused on my current adventure, but Ingrid delivered the news that Magda had given birth to a girl. This led to a discussion concerning my personal motivation for the trip to Central America. We had been through it all before. Ingrid repeated something she had said at least a dozen times in previous conversations.

"I don't understand why the woman is so eager to go through all the complications of raising a child for whom she cannot reasonably expect to provide proper care."

"Magda is a Bosnian Catholic Croat. For her there was no option but to deliver the baby."

"No option? This is going to set her life course! She's just a child herself!"

"Maybe taking responsibility for an infant will force her to mature emotionally."

"That's another thing; she's part of a satanic cult. How can she suddenly espouse the Christian faith?"

"It's the same thing, isn't it? Belief in Christ presupposes the acknowledgment Satan."

"How can you be so callous?"

"You're the one suggesting that I abandon an innocent child! A child that is wanted by its mother, I might add."

"You're defending her!"

"I'm saying that I'm partially responsible for the child, at least genetically. I'm not suggesting that I marry the woman; I just want to provide some assistance for the baby."

"Stephen, it's not your responsibility! Her seduction of you was extortion! Now instead of information, she wants to guilt you into giving up some cash. Don't you see? While you are expending all your energy on this idiotic bounty hunt, she's going to be knitting booties and eating bonbons! Picking out cute pajamas!"

That was a heart-wrenching comment. I had assumed that it was too late in life to consider child rearing, but Ingrid was younger. What with all the confusion surrounding the early phases of our relationship, the topic of a family had never been fully explored. Did Ingrid really want children? Was this just a manifestation of her fear that I would leave? Even marriage had never been discussed; I had moved to Austria to explore the possibility of forming a long-term partnership, but Ingrid and I had agreed to move slowly. Moreover, both of us had lived single lives for so long that the thought of relinquishing personal freedom was excruciating. Although we slept together most of the time, we maintained separate apartments.

Now that things had changed, my actual motivation was no less murky. Like a cowbird's hatchling, my offspring would receive nurture in a surrogate nest. While I was unwilling and unable to assume the role of primary caregiver, I hated to think of my accidental descendant facing a childhood of total deprivation. Contributing financially was my way of absolving guilt. I had arranged for a test to prove paternity, but it was hardly worth the cost. Admittedly, I had been a willing participant. There was little doubt the child was mine.

Ingrid's voice came quiet from the phone. "I know that you're not going to change your mind."

"Ingrid, you know I love you, but if I can't be free to do what I feel is right, I will be useless."

Ingrid remained silent for a few moments before breaking my heart.

"I miss you."

"I miss you too."

The exchange was bittersweet, encompassing the rift between us.

Jains was itching to hear more about the weapon's capabilities. Petersen continued to explain the system while his partner tried to glean practical applications from the information.

"If there is a physical specimen from which to create the model, communication can be limited to interaction between only the designated particles. Operating in an open environment, however, no computer could possibly crunch the numbers to analyze or recognize, much less target and influence individual quantum entanglements from amongst all the other matter in the universe. Furthermore, completely separate particles that are naturally linked would be affected, even if they belong to entities other than the target."

"Meaning that you could inadvertently transform a bunch of molecules that you didn't intend to alter, and you wouldn't know it?"

"Right, not a good thing. So if I don't have a DNA sample, how do I isolate the target? First, I have to reduce the number of variables to an amount acceptable for the computer to process. I established a hierarchical regimen of other sciences, to locate particular molecules systematically. Starting with a specific geographic area, a series of thermal images reveals mammals in the target range."

"I thought the location was irrelevant."

"To the teleportation, it is. As a byproduct of isolating the desired cells, the general area of the intended subject becomes apparent. Once the subatomic array has been established, the 'template' so to speak, the position of the target makes no difference. If I possess a specific group of molecules to start with, the target is accessible, and entanglement is possible, this part of the process would be unnecessary."

"So you will know the exact location of the subject."

"In order to isolate the DNA from a distance, and protect other entangled particles from being affected, the broadcast will be pinpointed. So, yes. An exact location could be noted during this stage."

Jains had intended to take notes, but played with the pen instead of writing. "So first you use temperature to narrow the choices."

"Right. Then I match the resulting statistical projection with a previously established prototype, in this case, the heat signature of a human body. Assume that there are now multiple targets in that range. A continuous barrage of upper frequency hard gamma radiation is concentrated toward specific molecules of each individual, and a subatomic 'image' derived from the resulting pair production is relayed to me by way of a modified free space optic link. This 'blueprint' is matched to what we already know about the target we are seeking."

"Where does that information come from?"

"Data input of a genomic configuration derived from a physical description, height, weight, race, hair color, eye color and so forth."

Jains perked up. This sounded like a perfect targeting method. "Incredible! You have a machine that is capable of doing that?"

"The same technology that is making the teleportation possible is spawning computers that will render even the largest and fastest processors of today as obsolete as abaci. I will soon have access to a trapped ion quantum computer that is being built by geeks. Most people believe these machines are years from being developed."

"Geeks?"

"For lack of a better term. Physics engineers working clandestinely. There is a general belief that if government became involved, pure science would take a backseat to politics."

"But you were working on this for the government."

"I couldn't tell them about my access to the quantum computer, and without that kind of technology, the project appeared as a pipe dream of the distant future. That's why the fools cut my funding."

Jains gave up on the notes. "So now quantum computing is a reality?"

"It's in its early stages. I suppose it's just as well that I finish the project in secret. I don't know if society is prepared to handle a weapon of this magnitude, although the medical aspect will hopefully be viable within a few years."

"What's the medical aspect?"

"A noninvasive remedy for pretty much anything that ails you."

Mexico seemed to be welcoming me with open arms. Ordinarily, winter is the busy season and I expected crowds, but tourism had been suffering a slump. The locals seemed pleased to see a foreigner. Following the incident at the hotel in Guatemala, however, I was taking no chances. I kept my wallet and passport in the front pockets of my jeans.

After the rain forest, even the provincial towns of rural Veracruz State seemed like a return to civilization. This produced mixed feelings. The previous few months had been full of intense interpersonal dynamics. Disappearing on an adventure by myself had turned my focus outward, freeing feelings that had been suppressed. I was not ready to give up the tranquil solitude; there were still matters that remained heavy on my mind. Besides my current problems, memories of the expedition to Arizona continued to haunt the silent moments.

Scarlett had taken her backpack and bedroll, so apparently she had not simply gone for a pee. She had been asleep in her tent when Piper left to visit mine. There was no sign of her at the petroglyphs. Fearing the worst, Eicher, Sharon, Piper and I fanned out within sight of each other, and began searching. After four hours it was clear that Scarlett was not in the immediate area. I could not imagine that she would have undertaken the difficult return hike solo with no food or tent.

Eicher became extremely upset; the coed had either met with some misfortune while the expedition leader was engaged in sexual relations with another student, or had gone to complain about the activity. Disclosure of indiscretions between faculty members and students would result in a scandal that could ruin all of us. Eventually we decided; Eicher and Sharon would go for help; Piper and I would remain at the camp in case Scarlett returned. The sex would remain a secret unless Scarlett tattled.

After the pair of archeologists departed, Piper and I continued to search, returning to the camp at regular intervals in case Scarlett showed up. Mid-afternoon, we heard a woman's voice calling our names. Rushing toward the sound, we realized it was Sharon, and she was desperate.

Two hours down the trail, Eicher had been trapped in a rockslide. A falling boulder had pinned his leg to the ground, and there were injuries to his head and torso. After ensuring that his vital signs were stable, Sharon had frantically raced back to the camp. We immediately packed our supplies. Descending the mountain carrying an injured man would take an entire day and there was no telling what provisions we might need. I preached calm. Keeping our wits was essential to Eicher's survival.

Having anticipated a destructive type of device, Jains was surprised that the medical outcome of the experiment would be so imminent.

"A remedy for everything?"

Petersen continued, "Damn near. I can't bring you back if there's nothing to work with. You would have to remain alive long enough for corrected cells to reproduce and create new tissue. But picture, oh, clogged arteries. Change the composition of LDL cholesterol to match the beneficial HDL. Sclerosis? Remember the emergence? Reprogram the bad cells and you've got a new liver. Target and alter a virus, bacterium, cancerous growth, or genetic defect, all at a sub-molecular level, and all through an electromagnetic wave."

"I thought we were talking about developing a weapon."

"I wasn't originally intending to create an implement of destruction, but I couldn't find anyone interested in financing speculative advanced research for a non-pharmaceutical medical application. Without the enticement of a lucrative drug patent, my proposals were ignored. The military, on the other hand, seemed eager to provide funding for a quantum-based weapons system. It was the easiest way to get money for developing the technology. Manipulation of genetic material is just one possible application.

Whether therapeutic or detrimental, the process is the same. Once the idea gets around, other uses will be plainly apparent to our enemies. Another reason to keep the new computers a secret; we need to stop allowing our technological advances to be hijacked and turned against us."

March Eleven

Mayan cities were laid out geographically to reflect the astrological tenets upon which the ancient mythology was based. Careful attention was paid to celestial alignment. Most Central American pyramids face precisely fifteen degrees east of north, the direction of the rising sun on the longest day of the year. However, I found that several sites in Veracruz, and some in Tabasco, are oriented eight degrees west of north. Excited, I turned back to the page in my journal dated March five. Sure enough, that was the precise direction that the isolated stela in Guatemala was facing!

A primary belief in a specific deity and the orientation of monuments toward a corresponding constellation could denote a connection between sectarian factions that survived the rise and fall of the predominant cultures. Perhaps religious dissenters had stolen the mask. The ancient icon may have accompanied the splinter group as its beliefs and architecture spread. At any rate, since I first noticed the weathered old monument in Tikal, this was the only thing that even vaguely resembled a clue.

Archeologists are constantly faced with the task of deciphering hieroglyphs containing ancient knowledge and philosophy. I was looking for a practical application, not mythology. While a startling revelation would be welcome, I was merely hoping to uncover a folk tale, not a religious doctrine. Man has always made attempts to immortalize his achievements. The Mayans inscribed the legends and mythology of their gods and royalty into stone. I was hoping that accounts of notable mortal endeavors had also been recorded.

At the ruins in Mexico, on a famous stela at La Mojarra, I unexpectedly found a partially eroded glyph that almost matched the one at Tikal. This confirmed that the stylized image derived from the jaguar structures had migrated into the Yucatan! A glyph that had been modeled after the sculpture adorning a pyramid in Belize had traveled for hundreds of years, appeared in Tikal near the start of the first millennium, and again in Epi-Olmec ruins dating to around 250 CE. It was possible that the vehicle for the symbol's journey had been an etching on the inside of a carved jadeite mask.

For this preliminary experiment in the desert, Petersen had placed a solar-powered optical collector on a stand, three miles from the control station. A tightly focused gamma frequency beam would be fired at the subject and the resulting emissions picked up by a monocular lens. The electromagnetic wave would be relayed back to another receiver mounted on the trailer. The refractive pattern would be reverse-engineered to recreate the most often repeated molecular configuration; that of the target's nuclear DNA.

The current subject was a laboratory rabbit. Along with the resonance and refraction data, Petersen had the advantage of being able to work from a sample of the animal's actual DNA. This segment of genetic material could be used to calibrate the gamma rays, and check the accuracy of the engineered cells.

Petersen's present experiments were focused on developing the ability to acquire all the information that would be needed when the advanced technology was in place. While rudimentary entanglement and teleportation could already be accomplished, meaningful manipulation of extensive groups of interactive particles would have to wait for the new generation of computers. Petersen's buddies assured that eighty linked quantum bits, or qubits, would provide one hundred fifty-trillion gigabytes of processing power. That kind of capacity would be required to analyze, model, alter, and link the millions of nucleotides comprising a strand of DNA.

Two thermal imagers would triangulate the position of the laboratory animal, caged approximately halfway to the receiver.

Quantum Voodoo

When the heat sensors were locked onto the position, the klystron would fire bursts of finely tuned electromagnetic radiation through the linear accelerator to the target.

March Twelve

The most prominent jaguar image that adorns the temple at Lamanai is constructed of stone lintels stacked so that the edges facing out form a pattern. Vertical spacers between long stones form depressions that describe the eyes, nostrils, mouth, and ears of a cat. Paint and plaster surface details that once filled out the figure have eroded.

The glyph in question had been drawn to represent the large stone edifice, shown as two long horizontal lines resting on four short verticals defining the eyes, two pairs of horizontals resembling whiskers beneath that, and a divided square at the center of the figure to illustrate the nose.

At the site in Veracruz, the symbol carved on the stone had been slightly modified. The erosion was severe, but the graphic representation was clearly identical to the glyph derived from the statue adorning the pyramid in Belize, the third and chronologically most recent bit of evidence I had found.

At the Xalapa Anthropology Museum, I was allowed to make a photographic print of the glyph. Although the staffers were eager to help, they knew of no corresponding image carved in jade. The rune was definitely not a recognized alphabetic symbol. Even though I had found the example locally on an artifact of known age, that only implied that the mask or someone with knowledge of the pictograph had traveled in this region of Central America during the heyday of a civilization that died out a thousand years before Columbus sailed to the new world. I decided to search at sites belonging to the most recent cultures first. The latest appearance would have to be the closest geographically to the eventual resting place of the artifact.

Ramirez had said that his mother was Mixtec, the predominant indigenous culture in the area at the time of the Spanish arrival, an ethnic group that is still viable today. In Pre-Colombian times, the Mixtec civilization was centered in the western part of the modern state of Oaxaca, in Mexico. Traces of the fable could still remain.

I took a crowded bus across the country to an area less often frequented by average tourists. A new factor was introduced at these more recent ruins. By the time of the Mixtec's ascension, writing had advanced from etchings on stone to the use of "foldbooks" made of deerskin. In their quest to spread Christianity, the Spanish invaders burned as many "heathen" manuscripts as they could. Few of these remarkable works survive today. The only complete examples of these codices are currently in the possession of museums in Germany, Spain, and France. I would not be able to examine them personally. I had no idea if I would be taken seriously enough to have the texts searched for signs of my symbol, secret marks that could easily have been concealed within the elaborate illustrations.

Another remarkable trait of the Mixtec sites is that new edifices were built near or on top of the monuments of preceding civilizations. Ruins intermingled at a single location can belong to cultures that flourished hundreds of years apart. I began with the most recently constructed buildings.

After pondering sophisticated sculptures that surround the central plaza of a Classic-era site, I wandered down a path that led to an overgrown rock garden attributed to a previous Zapotec occupation. An enormous oblong stone had recently fallen, crushing a scrub cedar. It was a sudden reminder of what we had to deal with on the trail in Arizona, more than a quarter century before.

When we reached the scene, Sharon's panic became completely understandable. We were faced with an extremely nasty situation. Eicher was awake, but in a state of shock and intense pain. The first aid kit did not contain morphine; the reliable old opiate had recently been replaced by a relatively new wonder drug. I asked the women to collect some flat rocks, and gave Eicher several Tylenols.

Darkness was falling as we drove wedges under the boulder, lifting the enormous stone enough for Sharon to help Eicher pull the trapped leg free. Now the question was, should we send a runner for help, or try to carry Hermann Eicher down? Considering the disappearance of our young colleague, I was opposed to splitting up the group, or leaving one person alone to protect the wounded man. Taking him with us would get him medical attention sooner, and we needed help with searching for Scarlett.

Using aluminum tubing from the tents, we fashioned a travois, and strapped the Dacron tent cloth over it. With the pressure off of the leg and the drugs beginning to take effect, Eicher's shock symptoms began to abate. I immobilized the crushed limb with a crude splint, and we moved the wounded man to the improvised stretcher. We padded with our bedrolls as best as we could, but it was going to be a damn painful ride.

My backpack became a harness. With a folded blanket protecting my lower back, the pointed V of the travois rested against the bottom of the external frame, distributing the weight to my shoulders, torso, and hips. Traveling downhill, Eicher was nearly parallel with the ground, in a half-seated position. Piper carried a Coleman lamp ahead. Sharon followed, tending to Eicher's discomfort and easing the rear feet of the stretcher over the rough spots. Energized by adrenaline, we hastened down the trail despite the coming of night.

Even though an evening breeze blew from the Acula River, the back of my shirt was soaked with sweat. With my rucksack dangling from a shoulder, I walked back toward the plaza, wondering what Piper could possibly find in Arizona after all these years. I knew that she had periodically returned to the scene of Scarlett's disappearance, but I assumed the incident had slowly taken on less importance. Over a week had passed since our chance meeting at the airport. Maybe it was time to reestablish contact with the rest of the world.

Damn! A sudden violent blow knocked the wind out of me. I hadn't heard a thing. The second hit knocked my knees from under me, and something smashed into the back of my neck. Dizzy and woozy, I fell forward. By the time I shook it off and stood, the assailants had already run a hundred yards away, at least two figures that I could see. I foolishly clutched at my valuables. The experienced traveler knows better; that reaction gives away the location of the money, but the reflex is immediate and all but unstoppable. My wallet and passport were safe, but my knapsack was gone.

Jains helped get the klystron ready to be moved for the next day's experiment.
"So wait. You use this machine to fire a gamma ray beam through the target...how does that show you one particular molecule?"
Petersen wheeled the machine nearer to the door. "Standoff sensing. For now, the computer creates a sort of virtual diagram of the photoelectric effect. Eventually, the Compton scattering will provide a better 'picture'..."
"Don't get too technical on me, Don."
"Sorry. The frequency of the beam is calculated to resonate with a molecular entity of a particular size. As gamma rays pass through an object, the photons strike other particles. Photons and electrons burst out from the point of impact, providing a sort of...negative blueprint, if you will.
"At this point, the quantum states of the particles comprising the entity become associated with those in the electromagnetic waves of my beam. To make it simple to understand, picture a loop. I transmit a signal and after the ray exchanges particles with the object's matter, the resulting energy hits the receiver and is relayed back to me. Using the characteristics described in the electromagnetic waves, a corresponding atomic state is created, which becomes the basis for the next transmission. The process repeats an infinite number of times at the speed of light, linking the target with the model."
"And the subject doesn't feel anything?"
"Unless he has gas."

Envisioning an unsavory explosion, Jains was almost afraid to ask. "Then what happens?"

Petersen let out a loud fart, laughing so hard that his breath came in gasps.

Jains too was crippled with mirth, realizing that he had been had, just like when they were kids. "Why, you rotten son of a..."

Petersen continued to guffaw. "When electromagnetic radiation passes through, you don't feel a thing."

The constabulary in a town the size of Mitla is invariably aware of the delinquents operating within its jurisdiction. As often as not, miscreants are blood relatives of the officials, and the resolution of petty crimes depends upon cutting a deal that satisfies the question of familial loyalty, as well as that of a small profit to be turned somewhere along the way. The police were apologetic. I tried to make my position clear without offending. The contents of the backpack, notebook and camera, were of little value to anyone other than me. Its return was worth a small reward.

No information was forthcoming. I believe that the police were honestly unable to locate the stolen goods, and the implication of ineptitude disgruntled them. It also meant there was no graft to be had. Before leaving town, I made a cash donation at the local Catholic Church. This seemed to please the policeman, and I hoped it would encourage him to continue searching for my belongings.

March Thirteen

I relocated in Oaxaca de Juarez, a larger town sixty kilometers to the northwest of Mitla. At the country store, I found a black wide-lined composition notebook like the ones used by elementary school students. In a motel room furnished in decorative early eighties PCV lawn, (stylish as well as durable), I tried to reconstruct my technical notes. I jotted down a quick account of my recent exploits, starting with my original flight to Guatemala, and ending with several renditions of the jaguar glyph.

While any traveler might fall victim to petty larceny, this was the third incident in a week. I had to believe that the theft of my shoulder bag was related to my current quest. As far as I knew, only one person was privy to the details concerning my visit to Central America, but it seemed inconceivable that Hector Ramirez would be behind such an asinine assault. Thinking he should probably be warned, I started a list of people to contact. Realizing I possessed no way to get in touch with Piper, I remembered what was on my mind just before those bastards mugged me.

Piper had run ahead to get the jeep, and backed as far up the trail as possible. With Eicher lying in back, we headed for the Ranger Station in Duncan. They radioed for an ambulance; the nearest hospital was in Safford, thirty miles away. After calling Greenlee County Airport to request a helicopter search, Ranger Johnston arranged for horses to be delivered to the foot of the trail at dawn. Piper and I would join the posse, and lead them to the campsite; Sharon would accompany Eicher to the hospital.

I called Pauline Denzer at the University. Ever my protector, she agreed to contact Scarlett's parents with the bad news. My body ached from the exertion of towing the sledge. Exhausted, Piper and I checked into separate rooms at a local dude ranch, and slept in beds for the first time in six days.

March Fourteen

Archeological sites in this rural area of central Mexico are not marked or segregated as such. Remarkable stone artifacts can be found simply scattered about in fields and forests. Local directions will get you close, but locating and assessing what is there is up to you. While the weathered relics were fascinating, there seemed little chance of stumbling onto any meaningful clues.

I showed copies of the symbol to the locals that offered to be my guide, with no success. I would have to go to a museum to check the glyphic script inscribed in the deerskin books.

The klystron and accelerator were positioned outside the trailer. The caged rabbit waited alone, a mile out in the desert. Inside the makeshift control room, Petersen and Jains stood before a screen alive with a pattern of letters and numerals scrolling too rapidly to be individually registered by the human eye.

Petersen explained, "I'm only displaying this to demonstrate the immensity of the numbers we are talking about. This is a statistical representation of the lab animal's genome. We isolate a single molecule of DNA, and derive an atomic model. Manipulation of the entangled particles is based on an acceptance of the probabilities, as we cannot know the precise location of the actual components."

Jains was startled by the vagary. "Probabilities?"

"Right. We know the elements that comprise the organic compounds. Within those atoms exist probable relationships that are essentially immeasurable. Nevertheless, their influence is felt in the physical world. To work with them, I am forced assume that the system is operating according to my expectations. The only proof is in the results."

"How do you mean?"

"It is possible to know that a phenomenon occurs, without being able to explain exactly why. It would be idiotic to believe that the only extant entanglements are those of human creation; interaction at the quantum level takes place universally. The only way to prove that my experiment is effective is to have acceptance in the functionality of the unknown, put it in motion and observe the results."

Jains shook his head in confusion. Petersen moved to another terminal and began manipulating a figure on the screen. "This is the gamma ray control station. I ran the thermal imagers already, and locked on to the target. The photon beam is tuned to a frequency that will resonate exclusively with specific molecules of DNA. When we have a match with the configuration that is loading," he gestured at the screen with the scrolling data, "our communication channel can be established."

As the stream of symbols came to a halt, the cursor sat flashing, waiting for data entry. Petersen activated the gamma ray generator. A different window came to life, and began displaying a numerical process, similar to the one describing the rabbit's genome.

"This time it won't take as long; as the sections pair up, only the mismatches will be highlighted. The strands are identical, so the process is incredibly fast."

Confident that there would not be any glitches, Petersen moved to another machine to prepare for the next phase of the experiment. An annoying beep that indicated an anomaly startled him. On the screen, numerous sequences highlighted in red splotched the otherwise black stream of figures.

The scientist was furious, and slowed the progression of numbers and letters. After several minutes of silent reading, he shouted, "Fuck! It's contaminated! This is human DNA!"

I needed a break from searching for signs of the legend, and decided to write to several friends whose addresses I knew by heart. Sending postcards seemed nostalgic in this age of instant global communication.

As I browsed a card-rack in the hotel lobby, an image suddenly leapt out at me. One old card showed a mountain peak that bore a striking resemblance to a pyramid, as they appear when reclaimed by the jungle. Was this a yet undiscovered temple, or possibly a natural formation that may have been imitated by the ancients?

The caption read, "Sierra Madre Occidental." I asked around the reception area, receiving nothing but shrugs in reply. No one knew the location; the mysterious peak was somewhere in the rugged mountain range, an area of two hundred thousand square miles. The picture went into my little black notebook, tucked between my sketches.

I sat in a little café, really more of a mom and pop convenience store with a couple of picnic tables out front. Over several spicy Micheladas, impressive local interpretations of the famous Mexican beer cocktail, I penned what were hopefully witty greetings from a lazy and forgotten little corner of the world. After word got around the neighborhood that a stranger was in town, about a dozen small children gathered nearby, smiling and trying to catch my eye. I rewarded their patience with a handful of pesos before leaving.

I was totally flabbergasted upon returning to the hotel. The desk clerk informed me that the police had telephoned. My backpack had been found. I immediately called the station in Mitla. They told me that my bag had mysteriously turned up at the precinct house. Yes, the notebooks were in it, also my camera. It was hard to believe that there had been no complicity by the local officials, but I was happy to pay the reward for the return of my possessions. I immediately set out for the little township.

The alguacil was extremely proud to give me back my things, despite maintaining that the knapsack had simply appeared on the front stoop. A quick check showed that nothing was missing. After handing over the cash reward, I showed him the postcard, hoping that he had traveled more widely in the region than most of the other residents. He informed me that reddish boulders like the ones in the foreground of the photograph were found mainly in the northern portions of the extensive mountain range.

Petersen checked the thermal imager, and confirmed the presence of a human in the test zone.

"Ordinarily, I would have reconfirmed the position of the subject before initiating the gamma ray, to make sure the field was clear. With the target confined to a cage in the middle of the desert, I was not expecting an intrusion. I see now that as part of the routine I will have to double-check the subject immediately before firing the photon beam."

"So the experiment is a failure?"

"No, merely incomplete. We can come back to it after dealing with the intruder, but something far more important has happened. Considering the radiation exposure, I hadn't planned to move the process into human subjects until running many more tests. At this point, however, I possess a statistical molecular image of this person's DNA!"

"Meaning?"

"Meaning that with a sample of their physical DNA, I can make a comparison with the virtual model captured by the computer. We need to find this person, and obtain some cells. I would have done this eventually, but it seems we have a volunteer."

March Fifteen

Back in Oaxaca, I took advantage of the hotel's modern communication facilities and checked the voicemail on my phone service. My astonishment at hearing the excited voice of Jonathan Ashe immediately turned to dismay. Somewhere in the rugged mountain terrain where Scarlett Taylor had disappeared, Piper too had gone missing.

Part Two

Mayan Lowlands, 1016 CE

The marauders were tall fierce hunters staging forays out of the North. Descending from the heights of the Sierra Madre Mountain range, they discovered cultivated valleys providing continuous sustenance to clans that remained in one place long enough to warrant the construction of elaborate cities. The warlike nomads recognized the value of maintaining a permanent domicile, and began to infiltrate the civilizations. Along with greater height and strength, the northerners' violent rites slowly blended with the religious rituals of the original inhabitants. Their offspring became a powerful people, spreading into the Yucatan peninsula for centuries, waging war with neighboring tribes until the arrival of Spanish conquistadores led by Hernán Cortes predicated the eventual demise of the burgeoning Aztec empire.

Three hundred years before the arrival of the Europeans, a lone warrior carried the ancient mask across the lowlands, spiriting the treasure away from a city suffering defeat at the hands of the nascent Aztecs. A party of invaders with no knowledge of the artifact gave chase. After eluding the pursuers for three days, the soldier hid the jade face, and stood to fight. By sheer numbers of foe, he was overcome.

Capture of a mighty warrior was a feat superior to that of slaying a great beast. Although the lone man was prepared to fight to the death, he was bound and taken to the conquered temple. The prisoner was confined with the slaves, and forced to dislodge and transport huge boulders as the monuments were sacked and the tombs pillaged. Gradually weakening from food and water deprivation, the warrior came to understand that he would never escape. Working a large stone, he chiseled a symbol that would not be noticed by the guards, a message to members of his own tribe.

Along with hundreds of other slaves, the captive was marched north to an Aztec shrine. The Vernal equinox was occasion for an enormous celebration. On this day, sunlight animated an optical illusion on the walls of the Aztec temple. The priests demanded blood to placate the gods.

The prisoners were drugged, painted, and escorted to the altar. The executioner split the sternums of the human sacrifices with a single ax blow, and deftly removed the still beating hearts. One at a time, the vital organs were placed on the flat surface of a ceremonial altar, doused in oil and lit afire, even as they vainly convulsed to pump the blood that now instead ran in a gory stream down the slope of the pyramid.

Arizona/New Mexico Border, 1985

Scarlett Taylor had sacrificed useful space in the backpack to make room for a couple of extras. The paperback book was worn to the brink of disintegration. The hashish pipe and a half-ounce of kief wrapped in foil were essential tools. The coed was on the way to discover "nonordinary reality."

Scarlett attended college because that was what was expected of the daughter of a pompous, well-to-do social climber. School turned out to be a great way to connect with the wildest partiers, and the newly legal-age socialite began to run with a crowd of whom her parents were sure to disapprove. It was her way of getting back at Mom and Dad for perceived slights.

Southwest Florida had been a perfect choice. A vacation atmosphere permeated the surrounding beach communities. The curricula were designed to attract students of Scarlett's social stratum and ilk. The most likely culmination of four years of higher education would be either a suitable marriage, or a career in the entertainment industry. The unlikely cause of her suddenly altered life course was cow-pies.

Psilocybin flourishes in dung. Heat and humidity encourage the growth of fungi; Florida provided the perfect natural environment for transplanting sacred spores from the West. The hallucinogen was soon plentiful in the southeastern states, and relatively unknown at the time. A rosy alcohol buzz and a little peer pressure emboldened Scarlett to ingest a magic mushroom. The mind-expanding experience triggered a transformation.

Scarlett discovered philosophy, as seen through the kaleidoscopic perspectives of the nineteen-sixties' counterculture. She became immersed in the music and writing of that decade. This new pursuit came with an added bonus; it pissed off Mom and Dad extremely.

At the end of her junior year, Scarlett found a way to turn her penchant into a subject major. A friend turned her on to a book by an anthropologist named Carlos Castaneda. The tales of psychotropic adventure were infatuating. The first three volumes describing Don Juan Matus became her gospel. She signed up for courses in the human sciences.

In her fourth year, Scarlett suddenly began scoring well. In support of anything that improved his daughter's grade point average, Daddy wished to reward his little girl for the newfound academic interest. She turned down a new convertible, and a trip to Paris in favor of an archeological dig in the desert. Her parents were impressed by the sacrifice, and put their financial support behind the project. The University was thrilled by the large donation. The senior would be welcome to join the expedition in Arizona.

Smoke inhaled from the pipe had produced euphoric hallucinations. Twirling and dancing, the young woman followed the pair of men along the mesa. Under the influence of the drug, descending from the ridge became a form of flying, little leaps distorted by altered perception into visions of airborne acrobatics. With pupils dilated to the periphery of the iris, her eyes saw night as day. Tiny phantasmagoric creatures scurried away from the trail. Enchanted insects glowed with phosphorescence. The breeze was magical, swirling beneath her, seemingly visible. Sparkles shimmered from every surface. Two noble equines stood patiently waiting, sleek and muscular, mythical in proportion.

From astride the horse, Scarlett felt as if the earth had dropped away. Strong arms steadied her from behind. With heightened awareness, she could feel the man's hard body against her back; smell the sweetness of his sweat. The air rushed past, coolly rifling her long red tresses into a super-hero's cape. Clouds rolled in fast-forward across a purple sky pulsating with paisley patterns.

Energy from the powerful beast welled upward with every stride, coursing through her veins, pulsing with her heart. Every bone and tissue vibrated, every sense became stimulated in a joyous feeling of oneness with the world, with life, with God, with this horse and its riders. The hallucinations became physical; with her skin tingling, the intensity built to a crescendo. Scarlett's young body convulsed with multiple orgasms.

Today, March Fifteen

Jonathan Ashe was bellicose when I returned his call, demanding to know the details of what had happened on the expedition all those years ago. It was not open for discussion.

"Look, Jon. If Piper wishes for you to be privy to her past, she will tell you about it. I'm not going to betray her trust to someone I hardly know."

"Damn it, Shaw! Piper has disappeared and you have clues. I demand to know what the hell is going on!"

"Don't be ridiculous. Piper told you everything that is pertinent, or you wouldn't have accompanied her. Maybe you should tell me what has happened. Believe me, I will help if at all possible."

After a huff of breath came a pause. I hoped Jonathan was regaining a little composure. His voice was lower as he continued.

"All right. I have some familiarity with the area, and arranged to meet with some para-psychological professionals."

"What, a clairvoyant?"

"Among others."

"Piper went along with this?"

I could sense Jonathan's hackles rising.

"Listen here, Shaw. I know that you and Piper call yourselves 'serious' scientists, and pooh-pooh certain fields of inquiry, but there are paranormal phenomena that you and your high and mighty theories cannot explain!"

"That may be, but I'm still surprised that she would have gone along."

The exasperation was apparent in Ashe's next reply.

"Piper thought it possible that someone involved in the 'counterculture of Generation X,' as she put it, might have seen or heard something that was withheld from the authorities at the time."

"And you found nothing."

"She didn't give it a fair chance..."

"You got into an argument, and Piper stalked off."

Piper Locke had a low threshold for crap, as well as little patience for fruitless confrontation. I was guessing that she simply moved on to a more pragmatic approach.

"Look here, Shaw, I don't know what kind of relationship you..."

"Jonathan. Jon," I interrupted. "May I call you Jack?"

"That's not funny."

"Let's try to keep it real, Jon. I knew Piper years ago; it has nothing to do with you. All right? Let's stick to the facts."

The connection was silent for a moment.

"That's the problem. She walked off yesterday, and I don't know where she went. This area is full of unpredictable cosmic energy. Anything could have happened."

I wasn't about to get into that. "Well, you must have a better idea than I. Didn't she tell you where she planned to start?"

"She said something about a Park Ranger, Officer John something..."

"Ranger Johnston. He'd have to be in his seventies or eighties by now. Why don't you start with him, and call me back?"

"That's the best you can do?"

"I'm in the middle of rural Mexico, Jonathan. Stop imagining things and get serious."

Jonathan took down the phone number of the motel. I told the desk-clerk where to find me if an urgent call came.

Local knowledge and horses cut travel time to the ridge to three hours. The route was more circuitous than the path our original expedition had taken, but required no "portages." Ranger Johnston and the two deputies were experienced horsemen. Piper could ride, but I was a novice. They ascended the butte at a brisk trot. In keeping pace, I developed a condition on my rump that surely threatened to prevent my return to a desk chair in this lifetime.

As we approached the petroglyphs, a helicopter could be seen traversing the mountain range. Starting at the expedition's original campsite on top of the ridge, we used the remaining hours of daylight to check the area. I did my part on foot, thankful to give my backside a reprieve. My long-suffering mount was no doubt equally relieved.

After spending the better part of the afternoon searching, we had not turned up a single clue. Officer Johnston received a radio message from the helicopter crew. They too were empty handed. The Park Ranger requested that they continue to widen the search, but it was obvious that the horseback attempt was futile. The posse turned downhill in the waning sunlight.

I harbored guilt about Scarlett Taylor, but never to the degree that it tormented Hermann Eicher. The way I see it, had we simply been asleep the girl could have vanished just the same. I suppose that as leader of the expedition Eicher felt ultimately responsible.

Piper's sudden disappearance reminded me of other aspects of the earlier situation, the helplessness, frustration, and growing fear that Scarlett was no longer alive. I immediately checked into travel options. Arizona was at least two days away.

I spent the rest of the day writing, reluctant to leave the hotel and become incommunicado. I was just getting ready to go find some dinner when the switchboard operator rang my room. To my surprise, it was Piper calling to let me know she was safe, and to apologize for Jonathan's disturbing me. I was eager to hear the details.

"Oh, Stephen. It was the strangest thing. No one seems to know anything about the picture in the newspaper. We've been here for two weeks, and all we have done is visit gurus, clairvoyants, card readers and shamans. I know Jonathan means well, but I finally got fed up and went off on my own. You know I have revisited the petroglyphs from time to time over the years."

"I knew you went back a few times."

"Well, in the past I have started at the top of the ridge, and tried to figure out which way Scarlett could have gone. This time I thought I would circle the base of the mountain instead. I parked at the southern end of the escarpment and started hiking. After a while I saw a little shed of some sort, off in the middle of nowhere. I went over to investigate. It was a rabbit hutch with one single white bunny in a battery cage."

"A rabbit?"

"Yes, a cute little thing, all alone out in the desert. He was perfectly tame; I couldn't resist petting him. The temperature drops rapidly out there at night. I decided that if I couldn't find the owner, I would come back and take him with me."

"You got busted for rabbit rustling?"

"Don't be ridiculous, Stephen! I kept going north, and after ten or fifteen minutes, a small truck came barreling out of nowhere. There were two men with guns and they were extremely agitated, demanding to know who I was and what I was doing on private property."

"Good thing you didn't abscond with Br'er Rabbit."

"Very funny. Anyway, these men accused me of some kind of industrial espionage! They drove me to their camp, which consisted of a couple of shipping containers and a mobile home. They refused to let me leave until they had time to check out my credentials and prove I was not a spy. They took away my phone, and locked me in the camper overnight."

"Jeez!"

"Can you believe it? In the morning, they apologized, and told me that they were working on something for the Department of Defense, tres hush-hush. My identity had been confirmed, but apparently my DNA had contaminated the experiment. They asked for a cheek swab so they could rule out my genes!"

"Seriously? You gave it to them?"

"I just wanted to get out of there. After they took the saliva sample, one of them drove me to my car."

"Did you report them to the sheriff?"

"Not yet. I don't know if it's worth the bother. The scientist, Donald Petersen, showed me his Department of Defense identification card and said the less publicity the better. I believe they were telling the truth. What I'm wondering is, could this have anything to do with Scarlett's disappearance?"

"Was someone working out there twenty-five years ago?"

"My question exactly. It makes me think of all that hoopla about Roswell that was going on at the time. That was top secret. The entire area is full of alleged spiritual vortices and mysterious phenomena, not to mention open-pit mines for the extraction of radioactive ore. Maybe Scarlett saw something sensitive and they silenced her."

"Wouldn't Ranger Johnston know whether anyone was working out there back then?"

"He passed away last year."

"Well, I still think you should report them to someone. There should have been signs posted or something."

"I hopped over an old fence that had some signs on it, but it was so rickety I didn't think it was current. It makes me wonder if Scarlett inadvertently trespassed. These men seemed like the types that would not think twice if you happened to get in their way. I'm going to try to find out more through the Defense Department before getting involved in some kind of confrontation with a couple of armed nut cases."

We promised to stay in touch. It was possible that Piper had finally stumbled on a clue to a mystery that had befuddled us for almost three decades.

Petersen proudly demonstrated that the samples derived from the gamma ray transmission perfectly matched those on the swab they had taken from the intruder. Jains was becoming bored with all the technical details, and wished for some action.

"So now we are going to manipulate her DNA?"

"Take it easy, Carlton. Like I told you, we will need the new quantum computers before that becomes viable. In any event, I have no intention of destroying an innocent person."

"Don't be so squeamish, Donnie; you're the one that's creating this whole mess."

"With noble purpose."

"You said you are going to move the experiment into humans. This is a perfect opportunity!"

"Let's stick to lab animals for the time being."

"So what happens next?"

"Apparently, you don't realize the incredible breakthrough that this represents. Under normal academic conditions, I would submit a paper that would astound the scientific community. Remote electromagnetic imaging of molecular DNA!"

"Under normal academic conditions."

"Okay, I concede the point. Now that we have proven the viability of our system of collecting genetic information, what happens next is that we try to produce a measurable effect in specific cells of our little furry friend."

"Didn't you just say you couldn't do that yet?"

"I'm glad to see you've been paying attention, Carlton. I meant not in humans, or on a large scale, but it is possible to influence a simple compound. Even though we don't have a quantum computer, I intend to entangle identical groups of particles and manipulate them from a distance. The effect should be an emergence event on specific cells of the rabbit."

"Incredible! See why I say you shouldn't be so squeamish?"

"Don't worry. We're going to reverse the effects in the end, and it won't affect the meat."

Jains looked to see if his friend was serious.

March Sixteen

Hector Ramirez had come of age in a time of political upheaval and shaky regimes. Despite the complications, the savvy young entrepreneur established a thriving import/export concern. Sensing a niche market as organic produce and "natural" products became desirable in the United States, he began trading with rural economies that created items that fit this profile out of necessity. No insecticides or other chemicals were used on the crops, mostly because none were available. Food and textiles were produced as they had been for centuries, and labor was relatively inexpensive. Between the high quality products and weather conducive to year-round growing seasons, Ramirez' exports became staples in the American marketplace. When fierce competition began coming from a new source, it was imperative to assess the threat.

Inexpensive goods from the Orient began to flood the world markets. Opportunities abounded as these products became integrated with the local economy. Chinese imports began to come under scrutiny when they were found to contain various toxins. The list runs the gamut; carcinogenic preservatives in meat and fish, melanin in baby formula, banned insecticides in fruit and vegetables, caustic chemicals in everything from shoes and furniture to drywall and cement. The United States has a federal agency capable of discovering and protecting against dangerous products. Not necessarily so everywhere else. When the US Government blocked the importation of items already in transit, there was a quick profit to be made by the expedient unloading of these second rate and frequently dangerous sundries. Developing nations became easy prey.

Hector Ramirez considered it his duty to expose the profiteers and their deadly game, not only to protect his business interests, but the health of his countrymen as well. His interference stymied an imminent influx, making him extremely unpopular with the middlemen left holding the bag. In a part of the world where assassination is common, Ramirez had become a walking target.

Now that I had my journal and phone numbers back, I called the people on my list before going back into the field. Señor Ramirez was apologetic when I told him of the break-in and mugging.

"*Mis disculpas*, Señor Shaw, my apologies. A man cannot wear shoes such as mine without stepping on some toes. I do have enemies. I have stated publicly that I wish to recover this artifact. It is entirely possible that someone is trying to interfere. I sincerely regret if this has placed you in a dangerous situation."

"Well, despite having found traces of the legend, there is nothing significant to report. I confess that I'm a little unsure how to continue." I explained about my plan to follow the jade. "I assume that the next stop is Mexico City."

Ramirez assured his continuing support, and recommended several museums that house extensive collections. I promised to keep him informed.

It looked as if I had more investigating to do elsewhere in Mexico, but I was a little distracted, wondering if Scarlett Taylor's disappearance really had anything to do with a rabbit out in the desert.

Scarlett's father arrived by way of corporate jet, and a limousine the size of a school bus. It was a little like being introduced to a lizard that was attired in a three-piece suit. Brent Taylor was immediately prepared to place blame on everyone within earshot. I actually expected a physical assault. The impression he made was less like one of concern for his daughter than that of outrage over the disruption of tee times at the country club.

After demanding the girl be found and vehemently suggesting a heinous termination of the careers of everyone involved, Taylor posted a reward, got in the limo, and disappeared in a huff.

The national media picked up the story and ran with it-a missing debutante and a sizable reward made for exciting copy-but nothing tangible came along. In the absence of a single clue, there was naturally talk of extraterrestrials and portals into other dimensions. The search expanded into the vast National Forest.

Carlton Jains had tied on a good buzz, and was sleeping it off in the RV. An occasional snore echoed down the hall of the metal trailer, keeping Petersen awake. Scientific ideas began to evolve in his continuously restless mind. Eventually the physicist gave up on sleep, and slipped quietly out the door.

Jains had made a good point; the woman's interference provided a brilliant opportunity for experimentation. Without the quantum computers, the ultimate outcome was not achievable; Petersen had been telling the truth about that, but perhaps in the meantime the entanglement could be tested on a simpler scale. Something noninvasive and benign, something easily verifiable without causing harm to the subject.

To make a comparison with the data collected through the gamma ray transmission, Petersen had already reproduced a workable amount of Piper Locke's DNA. As he relished in the providence of possessing bona fide samples, a simple approach occurred to him, an innocent experiment that fulfilled all the requirements. Besides, Dr. Locke wouldn't even mind the effects. No, she wouldn't mind this at all.

Arizona/New Mexico border, 1985

Scarlett's eyes opened to an intense pinprick of red, the naked sun in a cloudless sky. Achy all over, her body was dehydrated from both physical activity and psychoactive smoke. The men were seated on the ground near the horses, and came to her immediately when they saw her wake. One of them kneeled, was he somehow familiar? The water from the canteen he offered tasted like the elixir of gods.

Saying, "This will help," the man held out a foil pouch containing an effervescent pellet of concentrated vitamin C.

Scarlett gratefully accepted the orange lozenge, and let it dissolve in her mouth with more water. The man spoke again, "Keep drinking. We'll talk when you feel better."

Scarlett looked around at the sandy hillocks and scrub brush. The ridge that the University expedition had camped on was nowhere in sight. This hadn't been part of the deal, but she had to learn about the ceremony and experience the altered state or the trip to the desert would be a waste. Getting to her knees, she realized that the effects of the drug had not completely dissipated. Her throat was raspy, her words faint.

"Why are we here?"

"You wanted to fly, to ride the horses."

The intense erotic experience came back like a dream, and she flushed with embarrassment.

The voice was kind, continuing, "My name is Carmine. This is Josef. We were your guides last night. This is where the inner journey led us."

"When will it lead us back?"

"When it is time, you will know it. The old Doctor says you seek knowledge. Before he will consult with you, he wishes for us to show you some things. If you still wish to understand, that is."

In reality, the "medicine man" with whom Scarlett had made the deal had been perfectly happy to take the money, and forget about it. Carmine and Josef had accepted a small payment to make delivery of the drug. The kidnapping had been Carmine's idea. If the student could afford two thousand dollars for peyote, the parents could afford considerably more in ransom. PCP would work better than Mescaline. The minute the young man saw the girl, everything changed. Carmine was smitten immediately, and after witnessing the sexual climaxes on horseback, positively enflamed.

Josef believed the whole scheme was a seriously bad idea, and the men argued. Finally, it was decided; the girl would make a choice, and they would stick to it. If the answer was no, they would return her to the camp. If Scarlett wished to continue, Josef would drive the horse trailer home alone. Carmine would have to take the girl into hiding, and make it on his own.

Scarlett tried to shake off the grogginess. "What do I need to do before meeting the medicine man?"

"Then you wish to continue?" Carmine looked to be sure that his partner was listening.

"Of course."

Carmine smiled warmly. "Then we will go to the sacred mountain, a very spiritual place."

Josef turned away, rolling his eyes. *Spiritual place my ass. I see where this is going.*

"Josef will return to the reservation and report to the old Doctor. They will meet us when you are ready." Carmine rolled up the thin blanket Scarlett had slept upon, and repacked the saddlebags. He handed the redhead a ruby colored cactus fruit. The flesh was sweet, and quenched her persisting thirst like nothing she had ever experienced.

"I'm sure you are sore and hungry," he continued. "Would you like to walk a little while, to loosen up?"

His smile was perfect and bright. Scarlett joined his side as he led the horse. Josef disappeared in the distance leaving an ephemeral trail of dust dissipating on the wind.

Today, March Seventeen

Mexico City is a vast bustling metropolis of approximately nine million souls. I had stopped there briefly during my travels elsewhere, and always vowed to return. It was a thrill to have an excuse for a visit. It was also a bit overwhelming.

Ramirez had paved the way with an introduction to an assistant curator named Marta Villa-Rosa at Mexico's spectacular Museo Nacional de Antropología. Ms. Villa-Rosa was familiar with the fable, and related her belief that the mask had not been seen since around the year 1,000.

My head was swimming after examining the museum's impressive collections, including the famous Mayan sunstone, and other extraordinary artifacts from all eras of Meso-American history. No complete Mayan codices are on exhibit, but along with some other original fragments, the museum's files contain an extensive series of photographs of the fig-bark paper editions that are kept in Germany, France, and Spain. I painstakingly examined a copy of the Dresden Codex, and was finally rewarded with a tiny clue. There it was; the graphic jaguar glyph appeared on the margin of a treatise that had been written sometime around the twelfth century! I copied the surrounding text, and went to consult a modern translation.

Petersen was cuddling the laboratory rabbit, and gently stroked its long silky ears. Unaware of his cohort's late night experiment, Jains nursed a hangover while observing the proceedings.

"Remember, I cannot know the state of the particles. I must trust that an influence on one set will affect the other."

Jains massaged his temples, grumbling, "I still don't really get that."

"Subatomic particles are constantly moving. Their location is strictly a probability. If I attempt to measure them, they become influenced and are no longer valid."

"So you've said. I have the feeling that I'm going to wind up taking your word for it."

"Picture a race car speeding around a track. When it is moving, you cannot pinpoint its precise position in space. If you freeze it long enough to fix its location, its progress in time becomes immeasurable. If you accept that it is impossible to simultaneously measure speed and location to an exact degree, the car will probably continue to circle the track and pass your position at relatively predictable intervals, information you can use."

"OK, I guess that makes sense."

"So the particles' spin or flavor doesn't really matter; the characteristics of the atoms will change without my ever knowing their exact composition."

Tucking the critter in the crook of his elbow, Petersen took the lid from a small contraption, revealing a glass test tube full of liquid. He gestured at the hapless hare, saying, "These are cells cloned directly from the subject's tissue."

Turning toward a machine that resembled an enlarged torture device from a dentist's office, he swung a pneumatic arm toward the table. "The material in the test tube is identical to, and in the same state as specific cells of our bunny rabbit. Finely tuned gamma rays go through the linear accelerator," he pointed across the room at the complex apparatus, "and hit a nonlinear crystal. The photon stream is scattered, and some of the resulting particles become entangled. Half of the now associated photons are directed at the subject, the corresponding photons are transmitted to the cloned cells."

"Any chance this method going to cure the hangover someday?"

This question received an unsympathetic chuckle. "I'll see what I can do."

Petersen aligned the swing-arm over the box, carefully centering it above the sample cells before replacing the lid. He crossed the room and put the rabbit back into the wire cage.

"Rabbits are very social creatures, you know."

Jains just shook his head. "Is that it?"

Petersen responded by patting the mechanical arm poised over the tube of liquid.

"Next comes an influence on the state of the particles that will be linked to the subatomic structure of our gentle subject. After that, we'll send the new configuration long distance."

While the altered cells incubated, the two men drove the rabbit back to the shelter isolated in the desert.

My little breakthrough with the codex didn't bust the case wide open. The glyphic text apparently had nothing to do with Ramirez' fairy tale. I listed my clues, or rather, all references to the mask and appearances of the symbol I had come across. My investigation followed a timeline consistent with the sporadic development of various cultural centers. It was a little too neat, which probably meant that I searched for what I suspected had happened, and neglected the possibility that had I looked in the other directions-farther south instead of turning north, back in time instead of forward-there might have been corroborating evidence that conflicted with my current view.

The real problem was that there was no logical next move. The jaguar glyph was apparently still being used in the thirteenth century, but in a context that could have referred to an actual feline as easily as a living person or mythological being. I could not tie the probable location of the jade mask to any specific time and place.

March Eighteen

After the gamma ray transmission, the test rabbit had been returned to the laboratory. While waiting for cell development, Petersen was working on other techniques to be implemented when the quantum computer became available. He tried to interest Carlton in watching a demonstration of gene-splicing. Jains observed the microscopic images for a while, but by the time the experiment had been completed, he had become bored. The powerful instruments sitting idle presented an irresistible attraction. He began fiddling with the machinery. Petersen was not amused.

"Don't play with that, CJ."

"I'm just checking it out."

"Unbound electrons accelerate through a potential of two hundred thirty volts, producing thirty-eight million electron volts in the klystron. You'll blow your brains out."

"This knob sets the frequency?"

"I'm warning you, Jains. Don't mess around with that thing."

"I'm not going to turn it on, Don. I just want to see how it works."

"That knob changes the intensity of the beam. The black graduations are for short distance applications, but if you set the pointer in the red range, the radiation will burn holes in your eyes. Satisfied?"

"At what distance?"

"What are you planning?"

"I just think the thing is cool. It's not every day that you get to fire a ray gun."

"There's a reason for that, Carlton. It's not a toy."

"Can't I at least fry a saguaro or something?"

"Just forget about it, OK?"

"All right, all right. No need to get upset. I'm a little bored, that's all."

"Well, go find a saloon or a bawdy house or something. It's difficult enough to concentrate without worrying about what you are up to."

Arizona, 1985

A spring-fed stream flowed out of the foothills. Scarlett and Carmine camped and watered the horse. After the drugged ordeal the night before and the long hike through the desert, they were exhausted. Dusk was barely falling as they went to sleep. In the morning, they continued toward the mountains, following the clear ice-cold stream uphill.

Carmine recounted native fables, trying to imply spirituality, making it up as he went along. The unfamiliar tales sounded exotic, even if somewhat idiomatic. Scarlett's new companion seemed gentle and honorable. With no reason for doubt, she let her belief in mysticism cloud her judgment. The drugs that the establishment fought so hard to suppress surely were the key to enlightenment! The book she would write would guarantee her degree, and a pedestal in the academic world. The movie rights would be worth a fortune!

In the evening time of sharing, Scarlett brought out the kief that had been smuggled all the way from Amsterdam. The yellowish *Cannabis* pollen was as potent as hashish. Giddy with intoxication, the stoned couple splashed in the creek. Returning to the campfire, they hung their clothes to dry, sat naked on the blanket and shared the pipe. The attraction was undeniable. This time, riding a man, not a horse, induced Scarlett's sexual ecstasy.

The kief proved a remedy for the hangover from the psychedelics. It became a daily routine; in the morning they shared a calming smoke and hiked beside the horse until finding a tranquil place to camp; as the sun went down, they took peyote and had sex. Bodies satiated, their minds were free to roam.

Periods of lucidity became briefer. Time turned into a blur, a useless aspect of a forgotten plane of reference.

After about a week, supplies were running low. Carmine announced that Scarlett was ready. It was time to consult with the medicine man. Doubled up on the horse, the intoxicated couple made their way along the crest of the mountain.

Today, March Nineteen

I don't know why it took so long for the thought to dawn. What if the glyph really was a reference to the sighting of an actual jaguar? Despite their size, the beasts are extremely elusive, preferring dense rain forest habitat that is conducive to their style of hunting. Unlike their close feline relatives that are stalkers, jaguars prefer to hide and attack by surprise. In the modern era they avoid confrontations with man by traveling along terrain that is unsuitable for human occupation. Wouldn't the same be true of ancient times?

At a downtown library, I found a map showing the habitat of the ferocious cats. While they have been wiped out in a large portion of a range that once encompassed the entire landmass stretching from the southwestern United States all the way to Argentina, jaguars still have a stronghold bisecting Central America that coincides dramatically with the location of the Mayan civilizations. To ensure the protection of these endangered animals, human traffic is restricted in many sensitive eco-zones. Perhaps the modern jaguars were unwittingly guarding the mask of a king that had plied their ancestors with blood sacrifices.

March Twenty

Thanks to Ramirez' influence, the curator allowed me access to the museum's computer room. Looking into the plight of the wild felines, I discovered that their modern-day range includes the mountains of the Sierra Madre Occidental, extending into southeastern Arizona.

Naturalists warn that the Federal Government's effort to seal the Mexican border could place the already fragile jaguar population at further risk in North America. Confirmed sightings in Arizona are extremely rare, and without access to the gene pool to the South, it is likely that the great cats will vanish completely from the southwestern United States. There are efforts underway to protect the jaguar's access without stymieing smuggling interdiction programs.

As I studied the layout of the Sierra Madre, I noticed that pre-contact Uto-Aztecan languages – the native tongues spoken throughout the North American west – had spread along this range of the American Cordillera. I printed the map, and referred to a graphic showing the habitat of the southwestern wildcats. The areas indicated on both charts were nearly identical. The strangest coincidence was that both regions included the rugged Arizona Mountains where Scarlett Taylor had disappeared, and Piper had run up against the peculiar scientists.

I admit that frustration was getting the better of me in the search for the mask, and that what was going on in Arizona seemed more enticing at the moment. However, if the jade followed the same trails as the jaguars, and there were clues to be found in Uto-Aztecan lore…well it certainly seemed like a good excuse to go north, investigate Piper's predicament, and work my way south along the wildlife migration corridor. I remembered the old postcard and the reddish rock formations of the northern Mexican Mountains, and decided to go.

Feeling ridiculous in a surgical mask and gloves, Jains followed Petersen around the lab, asking questions. The scientist secured the laboratory animal with the restraining harness. After taking a DNA sample from the rabbit and preparing it for replication, he began examining one of the creature's beady red eyes with a magnifying glass.

"So two days is all it takes?" Jains was pleased that some activity was finally taking place.

"The cells of the eye reproduce extremely rapidly, and the new growth can be observed without complicated surgery or biopsy. Look at this; there's your answer."

The scientist moved aside so that his friend could peer through the eyepiece.

"I'm not sure what I'm supposed to be looking at."

"Around the rim. Do you see the cloudy area? Those are the beginnings of artificial cataracts, induced by the entanglement."

"That's incredible!"

"The entangled biophotons provided a pattern for the cells to follow. The radiation excited new growth." Petersen began extricating the rabbit. "After we have documented the physical analysis, reversing the process should return the critter to normal."

"For a guy who is inventing such a monstrosity, you seem awfully attached to that rabbit."

"This little fellow is very important to me; he is going down in the record books!"

March Twenty-one

In Phoenix, I bought a go-phone, rented a car and drove northeast toward the Sitgreaves-Apache National Forest. This time around, I was not going to climb the mountain without means of communication.

I didn't think there was anything to find in the remote town of Duncan but it seemed sensible to visit the Ranger Station and let the park staff know I would be out in the wilderness. I was hoping they would know the location of the camp that Piper had stumbled onto, despite its being on a large tract of private land. In any event, the law enforcement headquarters seemed the best place to start.

The U.S. Park Rangers were sympathetic, but had no memory of the disappearance of Scarlett Taylor. Piper had apparently not contacted the Forest Service on her most recent visit. Questions about scientists working on private land were answered with shrugs. To follow the trail, I would have to start at the south end of the ridge and continue on foot as Piper had done.

Cacti and scrub brush receding from the two-lane highway accented the dusty terrain; southeastern Arizona seemed just as desolate and untamed as I remembered. I drove into the foothills and parked at the end of the mountain ridge, where the packed dirt road gave way to loose sand.

In contrast with the predominant aridity of the region, dark purple cumulus clouds clung to the horizon, threatening rain. I rolled up a plastic slicker and stuffed it in my knapsack. If the clouds continued to linger where they were gathering in the western sky, the temperature would remain perfect for hiking. I still carried my expired university ID card, and was prepared to talk archeology should the men that had held Piper hostage accost me.

    The ridge rose steadily from the desert floor toward the tree line of the mountains, a massive wedge of stone slicing abrasively through a threadbare carpet of evergreen. After hiking for half an hour, I approached a western style fence marked with faded cardboard signs that read "No Trespassing." The apparent choices were either scramble up the ridge, or hop the split rails and continue along the base of the escarpment. This appeared to be the point where Piper must have entered onto private property. I swung over the weathered crossbar.

    Continuing along the base of the mountain, I searched the horizon. The rain remained mercifully at bay. I widened my distance from the ridge, and continued to parallel it. A small structure became visible, resting on top of a distant hillock. It almost had to be the rabbit hutch.

    The open-sided shed was empty, except for a makeshift plywood table that presumably had once held the wire cage. From the top of the hillock, it was possible to see a fair way into the distance; nothing unusual was visible on the scrubby hills that rose intermittently above the desert floor. From here, Piper had ridden in the abductor's truck. Tire ruts continuing north soon disappeared in the windblown sand. Following my compass, I settled into a steady pace, prepared for a long walk.

    After another half-hour or so, I began closing in on a promising topographical feature. Perpendicular to the stony ridge, a line of trees encroached on the desert turf. At the edge of the copse stood two large shipping containers and a mobile home, as Piper had described. Upon hearing the hum of a generator as I drew nearer, I turned left and began ascending the mesa, hoping to approach the encampment unseen amongst the trees.

    As I entered the woods, shots rang out and whoops came muted on the wind. I took cover, and the sound of another volley echoed along the ridge. After a few moments, I became confident that the gunfire was not being directed toward me; someone was shooting at a target for sport. Nonetheless, I tried to keep behind scrub brush and boulders as I made my way through the strip of forest abutting the camp.

Two figures were moving in the clearing at the foot of the hill. A man was aiming a shotgun at something I could not see. A second man approached, bare on top with an unkempt fringe of brown and gray haloing his head. It was obviously the pair that Piper had described. Their raised voices echoed clearly across the open space, and I crept to the edge of the woods to listen. The bald man seemed upset.

"Damn it, Carlton! When are you going to grow up?"

"Fuck you, Donald. Guns are part of my heritage."

"So? We don't need to draw attention to ourselves."

"Yeah, yeah. It's okay for you to fire a fucking gamma ray and rearrange somebody's molecules, but you get all pissy if I take out a couple of stupid squirrels."

"You're drunk."

"So what? Shoot your quantum gizmo at me."

"Can't you just take your toy gun and go somewhere else to terrify wildlife? It's impossible for me to concentrate."

"Oh, don't be so sore, Petersen. I was just blowing off a little steam."

The shooter began to break down the weapon. The other man shook his head and walked away. Had it not been for Piper's encounter with the strangers, I doubt if I would have paid any attention to what had been said. Taking note of the weird conversation, I retreated through the trees and climbed the ridge, hoping for a strong enough telephone signal at the top.

Microbiologist Charley Pulaski is my old drinking buddy, and most reliable friend. In contrast with his genius IQ and scientific savvy, he is a beatnik born in the wrong era. Charley "digs" jazz, and embraces the colorful language and mannerisms used by the beat poets of the nineteen-fifties. He mixes this in with the "hip" vernacular of nearly every contemporary culture and adds the technical jargon of advanced science. The result can be linguistically stupefying. If anyone could make sense of what I was dealing with, it was Charley.

At a clearing partway up the mountain, the bars on my phone indicated reception of a signal. My friend answered with his usual dry nonchalance.

"Pulaski."

"Hey Charley, it's me."

"Yo, my brother. Home to roost?"

"I'm in Arizona."

"Ballin' the jack?"

"Not exactly." I hadn't the faintest idea what that meant, but I was pretty darn sure I wasn't doing it. "Do you remember my friend Piper?"

"Dame with the gams? Keeper of the flame?"

"That's the one. She ran into something weird out here. I want to get your take."

"Lay it on me, slim."

I told him about the rabbit, Piper's abduction, and the DNA sample she had given. After relating the circumstances of my current position, I asked, "Have you ever heard of a scientist named Donald Petersen?"

"Negativo, compadre."

"Any ideas about a gamma ray or a quantum gizmo to rearrange someone's molecules?"

"Sounds like gibberish to me, Stevie, and that's one thing I do know; gibberish."

I didn't tell him that it was one reason I thought he could help. "Can you check on this 'Petersen'?"

"Man, what's your thing? Every time you drop a dime, some screwy shit be on the line."

"It might have something to do with the disappearance of Scarlett Taylor."

"Whew! That old thing still buggin' you, huh?"

"Please, Charley? Through scientific channels?"

"Got it, dude. Petersen, Donald. I'll drift it past some cats."

I made my way south along the side of the ridge for half a mile before descending to the less demanding terrain of the desert floor. The temperature was likely to drop by forty degrees when the sun went down. I intended to be back at the car before that happened.

March Twenty-two

After two weeks of tamales, an American breakfast was definitely in order. I found a suitably greasy establishment and ordered the three egg special. I was lingering over coffee when Charley called. At first I thought the ring tone belonged to someone else's phone; it had been so long since I carried one. Inside the aluminum diner, the reception was poor; I went out to the parking lot to talk to my friend.

Charley started with his usual offbeat lingo.

"You ready now, professor?"

"You found something on the scientist?"

"Got the goods on Petersen, D. Graduate degree at MIT. Micro RNA, PhD. Bustin' his hump for the Dee-oh-Dee."

"Did you practice that?"

"It just be that way."

"Translation, please?"

"Your boy's a genius. Did some noteworthy investigation into intercellular communication, you know, the mechanism that cells use to turn gene expression on or off. Went to work on something top secret for the military. Apparently they pulled the plug, and he disappeared. Typically, when you do top-secret contract work for the government, they make you sign a nondisclosure, noncompete agreement."

"You mean he's not allowed to continue to develop whatever he was working on?"

"Usually for a couple of years."

"Is that all?"

"Sources suggest that he was recently working on quantum teleportation."

"You think he is beaming rabbits around in the desert?"

"Not likely. It doesn't work that way."

"So what is he up to?"

"Hard to say. Given his background and what you told me, maybe the effects of radiation on cellular mutation."

I thought of the weird conversation. "A ray gun?"

"There's a dated concept. I don't know, Steve. I'll keep looking into it, but I'd stay out of the line of fire if I were you. The guy's no slouch."

I had the feeling I was going to need more help from Charley. When he switches to plain language, it means serious business.

March Twenty-three

I hoped to find out who owned the land where the improvised laboratory had been built. There was a plat at Greenlee County Assessor's office in nearby Clifton. The property in question had last changed hands in 1930. The taxes were current, paid automatically by a corporation whose constituents were not individually listed. A sportsmen's organization leased hunting rights to the acreage, and sent the rental fee to a bank. The hunters maintained the fences and signs. As the property was vacant, desolate, and abutted wild parkland, the locals paid little attention. Although I intended to continue to look into the current ownership, I had no resources for instigating that kind of search.

The town of Duncan lies along a road that borders the National Forest. I revisited the Park Service's Station there, hoping that with a more accurate description of the location, the Forest Rangers might have further information for me. While waiting for officers to return from the field, a casual conversation pointed out that the last confirmed itinerant male jaguar in Arizona had recently been euthanized under apparently dubious circumstances.

That fact seemed somehow relevant to my search for the mask. The northernmost jaguar of modern times had roamed the mountainous area near Nogales, on the Mexican border. I noted the area on my map, wondering about the color of the soil.

It was a little late by the time I called Ingrid Luft; Arizona is seven hours behind Austria. Ingrid seemed perky, considering the hour. I had warned her that on a trip such as this one, my travel plans could change instantly, but my presence in the States seemed to be a puzzling surprise. The conversation ended up being reassuring; despite plenty of differences concerning our personal relationship, at least Ingrid and I could still argue about science without rancor. She had been studying a discovery recently reported from Siberia.

"Think of it, Stephen, an entirely distinct species of humanoid, a branch that separated from the ancestral tree before the arrival of Neanderthal man and modern humans!"

"The more we learn, the less we know."

"I would expect more from you than a tired cliché."

"Well, I have been a little out of touch. From what you tell me, the scientists responsible for this revelation may be reacting more cautiously than their predecessors, but there is still a tendency to attempt to paint a complete picture of the past from necessarily limited information."

"That sounds like something you would study, the human need to explain the world even while recognizing the limitations of the arguments."

"I have observed that in groups there is frequently a member that points things out to the others, objects that are plainly evident to all. Probably a habit held over from describing the world to inquisitive children. Yet the group respects this individual's need to be the explainer. 'Look! A pond! See the ducks?' The members of the troupe say, 'Oh,' and nod their heads."

Ingrid was starting to laugh. "That's hardly an indictment..."

"How about this? Picture a nineteenth century paleontologist, smoking his pipe in a wood-paneled drawing room. When asked about the bones found on the latest expedition, he is hardly going to admit to being clueless. 'Dinosaurs were huge, vicious, green lizard-like creatures!' Of course they were! Then the protective spikes are proven to be feather follicles. The fearsome raptors are believed to be the predecessors of modern birds. Other saurians gave live birth and coddled their young. Few lay-persons over the age of ten can tell you the latest theories."

"That hardly applies to science as it is practiced today."

"Of course it does. If you excavate prehistoric remains and don't establish their archeological significance, they are just old bones. Citing limited evidence, you offer creditable conjecture, and you may even be correct, but all you can really prove is that conditions at the site were conducive to the preservation of skeletal tissue, not that creatures necessarily congregated there, or that evolutionary changes occurred based on what is known about the modern environment at that location. I know I'm guilty of doing the same thing myself, but it's informed speculation, not scientific method."

Ingrid snickered. "So you doubt the conclusions drawn by experts that are smart enough to create and evaluate modern data?"

"As the data becomes refined, new conclusions can be drawn with ever more accuracy. I don't doubt the relevance, but information is not static. Evolution did not occur in a vacuum, overnight, or in a neat orderly sequence. It's better to learn of possibilities than to build a theory based on facts not in evidence that later prove to be inaccurate."

"I see your point, but without a rudimentary picture or common ground for discussion, how can opposing views be debated?"

I conceded that a platform is needed for discussion, but until there is enough information to support a comprehensive theory, the attributes of early humanoids, as well as denizens of the Mesozoic, remain necessarily vague in my mind's eye. I didn't answer immediately, and in the moment of silence, Ingrid continued, "Hermann Eicher thinks the implications are so dynamic that he has created a special credit for students that do research on the subject."

I hadn't forgotten that Hermann Eicher was my girlfriend's boss, but it certainly had not been foremost in my mind during this phone call. I briefly flashed on my connection with the Herr Direktor.

Eicher remained in the hospital for over a week. Sharon, Piper, and I stayed in Arizona until the expedition leader was stable enough to fly home in an air ambulance. During the first part of his long recuperation in Austria, the other three of us returned to the University in Florida, and tried to salvage what we could of the project.

I wondered how much Eicher had told his underling.

"Has Eicher ever talked to you about our expeditions?"

"Only that he holds you in the highest esteem. He has cautioned me never to underestimate you."

I thought about that comment for a while after we ended the call. I hoped the archeologist had meant it in a good way.

March Twenty-four

Resuming my investigation of Piper's abduction, I hiked north as before, hopped the fence and crept through the woods to the encampment. The trailers were quiet; there was no sign of activity. Other than one small truck and the RV, no vehicles were parked in the area. I found a lichen-encrusted boulder to lean against, with a good view of the camp, and began writing in my journal.

The sound of a twig snapping behind me sent a chill up my spine. I turned to see a man armed with a shotgun, approaching through the trees. I recognized the target shooter from my previous visit. His voice was reedy and cynical.

"Well, well, well. What do we have here?"

I rose, and wished him good afternoon.

Through an evil grin he hissed, "And what, may I ask, are you doing on private property?"

"Just out hiking. I'm studying the petroglyphs in the area. I saw the camp, and wondered if there were other archeologists working out here. Since no one seemed to be around, I decided to wait up here, so as not to startle anybody."

The grin became a sneer. "Yeah, right. Like I'm falling for that." The shotgun loomed more menacingly in my direction. From my perspective, the barrel looked enormous.

"Honestly. Here, I've got an ID card." I moved very slowly, retrieving my expired University identification from my pocket. As Piper had said, the creep seemed like the trigger-happy type. Keeping the weapon between us, he snatched the laminated plastic and ignored it while continuing to appraise me skeptically.

"There are no petroglyphs around here. Make things easy on yourself and tell me what the fuck you are doing on my land."

"Looking for Indian artifacts. See there? You just made my day easier. No artifacts nearby. Give me back my card, and I'll clear out."

"I don't think so. I think we should take a little walk down there to the trailers, and you can tell me who you are working for."

"The University of Southwest Florida! Look at the card!"

"I'm not buying that bullshit." He waved the blunderbuss at my chest. Suddenly the muzzle seemed the size of a cannon barrel. An engine turned over in the distance and settled into a monotonous drone. I nervously put on my knapsack and turned down the slope, with a gun at my back.

One of the shipping containers had a door at the center of the long side, with wooden pallets laid as steps leading up. At the top of the platform I hesitated, and the man with the shotgun growled, "Go on." I opened the door to a room full of computers and machinery. The balding man that I had observed on my previous visit turned toward us from the table where he was working. This would be the scientist, Donald Petersen. He seemed startled by my presence.

"What the hell is going on?"

The man with the gun responded immediately, "I caught this asshole spying from up on the hill."

I began to interject, "I told you, I..."

"Shut up." He kept an eye on me while continuing to speak to the other man. "I'm not letting this one off so easy. He's up to something."

"Just stay cool, all right?" The scientist turned toward me. "What brings you into this neck of the woods, mister...?"

"Shaw. Stephen Shaw. As I tried to tell your friend here, I'm an anthropologist..."

"He's lying, Donald. Said he was an archeologist before."

"No, I didn't. I said..."

"And I said shut up!" He circled around to my left, brandishing the shotgun. The scientist became visibly nervous.

"Be careful, Carlton!"

Carlton cocked the weapon and pointed it in my direction. I could see his finger on the trigger. His face had become red, and sweat beaded on his forehead.

"Tell me what the fuck you are doing up here, or so help me..."

Petersen moved toward the enraged man saying, "Calm down." Carlton gestured with the barrel in a dismissive motion as the scientist reached out a hand. Events happened so rapidly at that point that I'm a little unsure what actually occurred.

The shotgun went off, the sound exponentially amplified in the confines of the metal container. A large machine mounted on a stand exploded in a shower of sparks. The men seemed to be struggling for control of the gun. An enormous electrical cable burst loose and writhed across the floor, knocking into a shelf full of beakers. Something that smelled like denatured alcohol spilled to the ground. The liquid ignited and a sheet of fire flashed across the room.

I bolted through the door as a larger blast shook the trailer, and a ball of flame burst from the doorway behind me. I sprinted as fast as I could toward the cover of the trees. Nothing followed except the crackling hiss of a blistering conflagration.

I should have returned to see if the men needed help, but the memory of the madman with the gun and sound of the explosions gave my feet wings. I turned across the slope and ran south, blood pounding in my ringing ears.

Part Three

Arizona, March Twenty-four

When I had covered enough distance to make me feel safe from pursuit, I caught my breath and called the Ranger Station. Record snowfall and a wet spring allayed fears of a wildfire, but the officer on duty immediately notified the fire department and sheriff's office.

After descending to the desert floor, I jogged the rest of the way to my car. By the time I drove to the state road, a steady flow of emergency vehicles were headed to and from the property.

Inside the blackened trailer was a smoldering mass of molten plastic mixed with metallic remnants. There was no sign of life. Thankfully, no sign of death either. The Fire Marshall estimated that the forensic investigation would take weeks.

March Twenty-five

The sensible thing would have been to get out of Arizona immediately. I don't know why I didn't simply head back to Mexico; I guess my curiosity outweighed the potential danger. As long as I was already in the neighborhood, it seemed reasonable to stick around and follow up on Piper's hunch while waiting for some news about the trailer fire.

Jonathan Ashe had contacted some "professionals," so there were some loose ends to explore. With a redheaded Native American in mind, I intended to ask questions around the sparsely populated area between Phoenix and the National Forest.

Unless both parents carry a recessive gene, it is impossible for a trait such as Scarlett Taylor's red hair to manifest. Most likely, if the redhead in the newspaper photograph proved to be Scarlett's child, the father was the descendent of someone that had interbred with Europeans. Alternatively, was it possible that the recessive trait had arrived in North America thirty-thousand years ago?

It might not mean a thing to the average observer, but these are precisely the kind of speculations that I find fascinating. What did our early ancestors bring to the continent? Did myths and rituals accompany our genetic material on its arrival in the Americas? How about the gene mutations that accompanied the appearance of written language? The development of skills that define us as modern humans occurred almost simultaneously in cultures isolated on separate continents, similar types of advances with striking chronological parallels. What triggered these evolutionary events, and why did they occur in so many separate places around the globe at that particular time?

I called Piper to tell her about the laboratory fire and my intention to continue the investigation into Scarlett's disappearance while waiting for further developments. Piper was understandably stunned, but could shed no additional light on the incident.

After we had thoroughly discussed the destruction of the laboratory and the details Charley had provided about Dr. Donald Petersen, I asked Piper about what she had investigated in Arizona. Apparently, Jonathan had monopolized much of her time, but between visits to mystics, she had tried to find witnesses. I did not want to bother with going over ground she had already covered.

"I'm sorry about Jonathan. He really is a sweet guy, but he gets carried away. He told me about your conversation."

"It's all right. He obviously cares about you. Did the psychics provide any insight?"

"It's definitely amazing, the way they can piece things together from observing body language and so forth, but you can't take it seriously. The time would have been better spent looking for someone that knew where to find the redhead that appeared in the newspaper."

"So no one had any idea who it might have been?"

"It was unanimous. Everyone that looked at the picture suggested that the color was not natural; more likely ceremonial paint or dye."

"Is that common?"

"Not that I know of. Usually, the skin is painted; headdresses are decorated with feathers, or cloth braided into the hair."

"So dyed hair would be unusual."

"I would think, but all I got were shrugs. The article was about health care for Native Americans. It was a file photo; the editor apparently used it because he wanted something colorful to accompany the story. The staff photographer that took the picture told me that it was a chance shot; the riders had happened by one day while he was working on something else."

"Did you go to the reservation?"

"I guess it would surprise you to know that the reservation does not consist of a handful of tepees out in the wilderness?"

I laughed. "Come on, Piper. I have done other things in life than chase skirts."

Her skeptical "ha" made me smile.

Back at the University, Piper and I kept our part of the bargain, never mentioning what had really happened on the expedition. The meager data we had collected proved to be insufficient to support a definitive study; although I wrote a paper about the petroglyphs, it was too weak for publication. Around campus, we avoided being seen together, paranoid that our secret would become obvious. Our youthful lust ran rampant however, and the illicit nature of our relationship was tantalizing.

The school was relatively dormant in the summer months. We bumped into each other one quiet afternoon, and exchanged a discrete kiss in the hall. Hormones took over. We ducked into an empty lecture room, and embraced more earnestly. Piper's tongue was sweet, her arousal evident beneath the thin cloth of her blouse. I ran my hand up her leg, lifting her pleated skirt, surprised at how ready she seemed. Turning, she braced against the back of a chair. Her intention was obvious, those long legs providing the perfect height. I wasted no time, entering from behind, reaching around to stroke her. It was fast and hot, and we didn't get caught.

This became our modus operandi. We would steal a quick session here and there, novel locations and varied positions compounding the thrill. I didn't think it was a good idea for us to be seen entering each other's apartment. After several weeks of trysts in classrooms, closets, the auditorium, and the parking lot, I begged my friend Charley to let me borrow his bedroom.

Piper giggled, sounding for a moment like the awkward, giddy coed with whom I had explored the boundaries of intimacy.

"Sorry, Stephen. I know about your scientific achievements, but my memories are tainted." She cleared her throat and continued in a more serious tone, "The picture of the horseback riders doesn't reflect any modern-day reality. The traditional costumes must have been worn for a special event, but no one I spoke with in Phoenix could shed any light."

I copied down the names of the people left on her list, including Jonathan Ashe's "professionals," and promised to call back. After disconnecting, recollections of that strange summer lingered.

Charley had leered knowingly before leaving us to our own devices. The loss of secrecy disrupted the flow; our lovemaking had no urgency. Finally able to spend time alone sharing our thoughts, our magic disappeared. Piper was despondent over the disappearance of Scarlett Taylor, and became distracted, launching "what if" scenarios, imagining the worst. I felt it was unproductive to dwell on a disaster that marred my first professional outing. I was also broke, and needed to move on.

It was the beginning of August, and the end of our affair. Piper was going to New York to continue working toward her degree. Neither of us was ready to settle into a real relationship. The split was amicable, the inevitable termination of an insignificant summer romance, the memory of which would serve as a spicy garnish on our life experience.

My research partner, Pauline Denzer, was starting her first term as associate professor, teaching classes full time. I don't know whether having me around was distracting or she simply took pity on me for having nothing on my agenda, but once again Professor Denzer found an expedition for me to join. Fortunately it was in a warm climatic zone.

By September I was in the Cyclades trying to construct a model of a seafaring Neolithic society, based on artifacts dredged from the bottom of the Aegean Sea. I put the disaster in Arizona behind me, and tried to produce some work that would enhance my reputation and kick-start my wallowing career.

My next call was to Ingrid Luft. I made the mistake of telling her about the incident at the makeshift lab. She became upset. Trying to help with the finances of a bastard child was bad enough; risking my life to go to the assistance of another woman from my past was icing on the cake. I have no idea why I allowed the conversation to take this direction, but once the discussion began, there was no turning back. Ingrid's voice was dry ice over the airwaves.

"I thought it was so damn important that you earned the money for Magda's child! When you told me you were in Arizona, I thought maybe you were coming to your senses! Suddenly you run off to help a woman you claim to have not had contact with for fifteen years!"

"There is a new clue to a mystery that we have been trying to solve for a quarter of a century! I'm not abandoning the other project."

"Is that supposed to be the lesser of two evils? What happened to your sudden attack of paternal obligation?"

"Believe me, I have no desire to propagate a family, but there are factors…"

"Here it comes. Scientific reasons for your behavior. Go ahead, Dr. Shaw. I'm all ears."

I was unprepared for this line of attack, and stumbled while improvising, "There are logical rationales for the behavior of fathers."

Her tone of voice took on a pedantic superiority. "Ah. How so?"

"My friends that raised children seemed to change somehow, to age differently."

"Do I really want to hear this?"

"Disagree?"

"No, but I don't see what bearing…"

"It's all about testosterone."

"Why does that come as no surprise? All about the male hormone? Go figure."

"Seriously. A pregnant woman's pheromones have an influence on men, triggering the production of prolactin, a hormone that causes testosterone levels to drop significantly."

"Am I supposed to view that as a bad thing?"

I ignored the sarcasm, and continued, "In the case of fatherhood, it's a successful evolutionary tactic because it helps the man to focus on caring for his progeny, rather than on aggressively spreading seed."

"You talk about humans as if they were goats! Modern men don't need to 'spread seed' in order for the species to survive. They use the theory as an excuse for barbarian hedonistic behaviors."

"Despite our cognitive prowess, we are still animals."

"That which separates us from the rest of the mammals is the ability to transcend pure animal reaction through the power of intellect."

"We cannot deny the influence of our primordial instincts."

"So you should be free to copulate with every desirable mate you come across?"

"I'm merely pointing out effects that our innate physical nature have on our behavior. As we age, our hormone levels drop. After crossing the menopausal boundary, women are relieved of their procreative burden. The female brain is abruptly forced to deal with a completely alien chemical balance and a radically altered sexuality. A man's loss of virility is gradual, and for a long time deniable. The male brain compensates for the physical decline by boosting the ego. Sexual desire remains high, despite becoming disproportionate to actual potency."

"You don't seriously think I'm buying this, do you?"

"Have you ever heard the term 'angel lust'? Post mortem priapism? Even at the threshold of death, the human body will take one last shot at sex, a final desperate attempt at procreation. Not just men, women too!"

"That's the most ridiculous thing I've ever…"

"There is documented evidence to support everything I have just said."

"You're the one that complains about scientists searching for what they expect to prove, and finding only that for which they look."

"A problem that is exacerbated in another way when a professional initiates an inquiry that goes against a widely accepted theory."

"That's what you're doing now? Initiating a professional inquiry?"

"Give me a break, Ingrid. You can't really believe that I traveled all this way to chase a piece of...look, I could use your help, if I'm ever going to turn this thing around..."

After the phone call, I played things over for the umpteenth time. Magda had been seeking information on behalf of an idiotic vampire cult, and chose to seduce me in the process. I had no reason to resist a fresh-faced temptress in a little red cocktail dress. The affair had been a one-night stand; we never had a relationship. From my point of view, it had appeared that both of us were simply available, attracted, and tipsy enough to lose our inhibitions. I didn't discover her larger agenda for several days.

While I may have acted irresponsibly by having unprotected sex with a stranger, I was single at the time, not getting younger, and presented with a rare opportunity to sleep with a beautiful woman. I did not even consider anything beyond a night of casual consensual sex. Magda was the one aware of her cycle and the risks involved in her actions. I have to wonder if the pregnancy was in some way intentional.

While Magda was still carrying the child, it had been easier to pretend that the problem didn't exist. Once the baby was born, everything changed. Now it was a little person we were concerned with, altricial and dependent. Despite my rationalizations and delegations of fault, the planet had a new citizen, one that would convey my genetic legacy into the future.

I have no other offspring, at least as far as I know. My sudden solicitude came as a shock. It may be that my feelings of responsibility were being reinforced on a molecular level, survival being the prime function of DNA. I did not even know the baby's name, wasn't sure I wanted to. From a distance, cash seemed the best assistance I could give.

Would I someday wish to send greetings and birthday gifts? Visit? Although unimaginable at the moment, I was honestly unable to rule it out entirely.

March Twenty-six

Sheriff Blake stopped by my motel room in the morning and gave me an update. The two men from the trailer had turned up at the hospital in Safford. Dr. Petersen had sustained a minor gunshot wound to the wrist. When the hospital reported to the Police Department as required, the computer indicated that the scientist was endowed with high-level security clearance. This fact seemed to figure heavily in the determination of my alleged culpability.

The other man, named Carlton Jains, had suffered third degree burns. Apparently, Jains was the mysterious owner of the property, and intended to press charges against me for trespassing. The Sheriff implied that the outcome would most likely be the issuance of a restraining order.

The friendly officer asked about my plans. He did not formally restrict me from leaving town, but I agreed to stick around to "help" with the investigation. I was planning to stay in the area for a few more days regardless, but this turn of events did not seem like good news.

Phoenix was a little over three hours away. The metropolis is home to community centers of various tribes. I headed west to search for a native equestrian sporting long, wild red hair.

My amateur sleuthing had elicited a lukewarm reaction from law enforcement officials in the smaller towns bordering the National Forest. The big city cops would probably be even less impressed. Passing a hospital, I thought that a healthcare professional might be worth a shot.

It hadn't occurred to me that medical personnel would be too busy to take time to talk to me. The nurse at the admittance desk irritably informed me that red or blond hair was not as rare among Native Americans as I supposed. Her brief, unnecessary lecture on Mendelian inheritance pointed out that recessive traits could be carried for generations before being paired. I quickly escaped, to her evident satisfaction.

Piper had tried the newspaper with no luck. Where else would information be available? The library? A school? There was one milieu where I was likely to hear a tale or two, and the price for information would be agreeable. A taxi driver gave me directions to what he promised was "an authentic cowboy bar."

It was beyond hope that anyone at Tom Ryan's would have knowledge of Scarlett Taylor, but it appeared to be a venerable watering hole, a genuine honky-tonk, exactly what I was seeking. Locals might have some ideas for places to search.

The few regulars already in mid-afternoon attendance seemed somewhat hostile and indifferent. I wore no Stetson or snakeskin, an obvious outsider, the dreaded tenderfoot tourist. The bartender emotionlessly drawled, "Howdy, stranger," an apparent sarcastic approximation of cinematic cliché. I glanced at the tap handle, ordered a local draft and a round for the bar.

The patrons accepted the drinks, but the indifference continued. I hoped the tip was big enough to encourage the bartender to chat it up to keep my money flowing. Apparently the baksheesh was appropriate. She gave me the once-over, noting the obvious.

"Don't look like a lawman."

I tried to play along with the game, and drained half the glass before answering, "No. You're right, but I am looking for information."

This statement earned me a sullen glance from the weather-beaten local sitting closest. I finished the beer and signaled for another round. It was an obvious ploy, but the familiarity of the act took some of the tension out of the air.

I went on, "I know this is going to sound corny, but I'm looking for a Native-American with red hair." The cowboys stared, as if I had been speaking Greek. I paraphrased, hoping for a reaction. "About thirty years old, long bright red hair."

I had paid for the drinks; presumably the silence belonged to me. I began to recite the tale. By the time I got to the part about my suspicion of top-secret government experiments and the fire at the laboratory, the audience was giving me their attention. I described the newspaper photograph, and held out my open palms. The first reply was terse, but relevant.

"Been to Gila? Got horses down there. Put on a show." This came from the man at the end of the bar, and received nods of agreement from the others. "Sounds like Gila, with the horses and all."

Back at the car, I checked the map. Gila River was ten miles south. Plenty of time to get there before sunset.

It was a good suggestion, but I came up empty handed. The red earth at the equestrian facility reminded me of the postcard I had found in Mexico. I wondered how far south the color extended, and if it coincided with routes traveled by jaguars. The trip was not an entire waste, however; from the staff at the tourist attraction, I learned of a movement to establish contiguous zoological sanctuaries that will allow uninterrupted wildlife migration along the Rockies, stretching from Mexico to Alaska. The naturalists would have a database with information about the areas in question. At least my two investigations seemed to coincide. I headed back to Safford for the night.

March Twenty-seven

The early morning knock was a surprise. I opened the motel room door to three stern men in grey suits. I didn't bother to closely scrutinize their Department of Homeland Security identification cards; it was obvious that they were Federal agents. Their impassive faces might as well have been cast of titanium. Charley would have called them "very heavy cats," probably the most concise description. I allowed them into the room, and they took up practiced positions obviously intended to intimidate. It was to be a long morning.

They began by asking my reason for coming to Arizona. As I recounted the disappearance of Scarlett Taylor, the lead interrogator waved a finger at one of the other men, who immediately began manipulating a small touch-screen computer. Within an astonishing minute, he nodded in affirmation; my story checked out.

They went on to ask about the trailer fire. It seemed like they were using a hackneyed television detective technique, having me repeat myself while they tried to trip me up. When I inquired what was going on, the response was a typical, "We are asking the questions." Judging by the subjects that repeatedly came up, I assumed that the scientist, the gunslinger, or both, were involved in some clandestine operation, and the government was extremely concerned that the project had been compromised.

I omitted the details Charley had provided, not with any intention of defrauding the investigators, but I knew of my innocence and trustworthiness. There was no point in involving my old friend, especially considering that my suspicions were merely unsupported speculation at this point. If the agents wanted my opinion, they would no doubt ask for it.

After close to two hours, the session ended abruptly when a message came over the computer. The men conferred briefly and rushed off, leaving me a card with a number to call if I remembered anything pertinent. I assumed that either I was not a suspect in the incident, or they intended to watch for my next move. I phoned the Sheriff and left a message. It was a pointless effort; within minutes, Sheriff Blake knocked on the door. He had stopped by to apprise me of the latest developments.

Petersen, the researcher, had voiced the allegation that I was engaged in industrial espionage and suggested that I was trying to discover his top-secret progress and then destroy his laboratory in an attempt at gaining time to develop the process myself. At this point, I was not yet suspected of criminal activity, but my status had been upgraded to "person of interest." The admonition to remain in the area came in sterner language, but I was not under arrest. I located the number for a local lawyer, just in case.

The day was shot; if I drove off to investigate further, there was little doubt that it would trigger a suspicion that I was fleeing. The local delicatessen was happy to deliver a bottle of wine and a sandwich to the motel. My search would have to be confined to the telephone. I tried to fill in some gaps.

Before Piper's disappearing act, Jonathan Ashe had contacted a spiritual tour guide. Under the circumstances, the appointment had been foregone. My follow-up call went through on the first try. Greg Slater is one of those people that, in eagerness to impress, don't seem to hear what you say. His breathy voice intimates that he is your confidant, that every word is being whispered in secret. In answer to my question about a red-haired native came a barrage of spurious facts.

"As I recall, the year was nineteen thirty-one. An amateur archeologist discovered some tunnels in the western part of the state, near the California border. The excavation was forgotten during the Great Depression, and then came the war. The site remained untouched for over a decade. When the next explorers entered the underground labyrinth, they found mummified bodies of men who were between eight and nine feet tall! Giants!"

I tried to interject, "If there was scientific substantiation..."

"The remains were over eighty-thousand years old!"

"Documented evidence suggests fifty thousand years as the earliest..."

"The giants had red hair. That's why it's not unusual to find Native Americans with auburn locks; the genes have been in North America for thousands of years!"

That detail almost leant some credibility to the story. I assumed it would pointless to explain to Mr. Slater that the chemical for dark color in hair breaks down faster than the pigments that produce lighter hues. Any archeologist will tell you Egyptian mummies have reddish hair, despite the fact that black is the dominant coloration among the population of the region. Greg Slater was on a roll. I played along.

"If genes were inherited for hair color, what about for height?"

This got his attention for a second before he was off and running again.

"They were extraterrestrials! The gene for height was carried on the forty-seventh chromosome. Humans only have forty-six, so the trait was never passed down." I barely stifled a guffaw as Slater continued, "Of course the discovery was suppressed. They didn't want anyone to know."

"Who are 'They'?"

"The government, of course! They've been in contact with the aliens forever! They don't want anyone to find out, because the visitors from Zeta Reticuli are spiritual beings and would teach us to live in harmony. The government would lose its power!"

Mr. Slater began to explain about the "vortexes," and their connection to the cosmos. I pressed the star key, pretended the beep was an incoming call, and promised to phone back later. Small wonder that Piper had bailed on the appointment.

March Twenty-eight

Ingrid Luft pressed "End," and sat holding the phone unconsciously as the apartment grew dark around her. Magda's calls always left her depressed. Ingrid was not the jealous type, had always been self-confident, and had brokered a rapport with Magda as a way to help Stephen. Now she wasn't so sure it had been the right thing to do.

Ingrid and Stephen had fallen in love while dealing with a threat generated by psychotic bio-terrorists. With the enemy clearly defined, the two anthropologists were the guys in the white hats. The new couple felt united, as philosophical soul mates and champions against evil. As the danger passed, they explored deeper into their own beliefs. Distinct differences appeared, heightened by age and nationality. The disparity led to friction in everyday domestic issues.

Ingrid could easily forgive Stephen love affairs that predated their acquaintance. However, was that acceptance a good thing? Should she expect to tame his freewheeling ways? Would he one day betray her trust?

Now the problem had grown worse. The other woman had carried his baby; didn't Magda and Stephen deserve the opportunity to decide – as parents, as a team – the fate of the child? Was Ingrid's interference destroying that potential?

As liaison with the pregnant woman during Stephen's absence, Ingrid had developed a relationship with Magda, and she found herself constantly dwelling on the situation. It had begun to interfere with work, and nothing had been allowed to come between Ingrid and her profession since she first embraced the avocation.

Ingrid had to know; if she disappeared from the scene, would Stephen run to Magda? There was only one way to be certain.

First on my day's agenda was a trip to the Sheriff's office to be fingerprinted and give a DNA sample. The forensics team wanted to make a comparison with other evidence that had been found at the scene. The detectives were proud to possess the latest in crime solving technology. There were probably few opportunities for using advanced techniques in the rural precinct. The process ate up the morning.

I stopped at the Park Service station on my way back to the motel. The Rangers that had informed me of the demise of the last Arizona jaguar had promised to print out a list of scientists working for an organization called the Wildlife Conservancy Group, an ecological consortium supported by private donations. Apparently the United States Federal Government declared the issue of wild jaguars a lost cause, and halted all official attempts to rectify the situation. The animal loving Park Service personnel were grateful for a sympathetic ear, and happy to provide the information although there was not much I could promise to do. The list was an astonishing three pages long, close to a hundred professionals in thirty-six eco-zones.

I called Hector Ramirez to give him an update. I had turned up no link to Scarlett Taylor, and needed to return my attention to the search for the mask before the funding was cut. I assured Señor Ramirez that my visit to Arizona had been crucial, and that I was soon returning to Mexico. The Guatemalan seemed to accept my explanation of the glyph being a possible reference to a wild cat as opposed to a sign of an ancient king, but I knew his financial support would not continue indefinitely.

March Twenty-nine

Early in the morning, Sheriff Blake stopped by and informed me that the case was out of his hands. The Department of Homeland Security had seized the laboratory and sealed the files. I wondered what it meant for me.

"Am I free to go?"

"As far as I'm concerned." Disgust was evident in the officer's voice. "It's no longer my jurisdiction."

"They haven't contacted me."

"That's their problem."

"So it might be a ploy; to watch what I do?"

"I have no idea. That's the trouble with law enforcement these days. Instead of taking advantage of local resources, these greenhorn honchos come blustering in like the cavalry. As if I don't know beans after doing police work for the last twenty years!"

You could hardly blame Sheriff Blake for being insulted, but if Federal agents wanted to keep an eye on me, so what? Maybe if they thought I was headed for the border, it would force their hand and they would reveal their intentions.

Even if I stayed in Arizona to continue searching for signs of Scarlett Taylor, I needed something to tell Señor Ramirez. Jaguar habitat lay less than a hundred miles away. Fifteen minutes later, I was southbound on Route 191.

When the phone rang, I pulled to the side of the road. It was Piper, and I could tell by her voice that she was excited.

"Stephen! You won't believe it! When I got back home, I couldn't stop thinking about Scarlett. It occurred to me that things have changed; there are resources that didn't exist before. I posted an inquiry on a social networking website. Through the Internet, over the past few years, I have reestablished contact with a host of acquaintances from the past, including students and faculty members. I asked anyone that knew Scarlett Taylor to contact me."

It sounded promising. "And?"

"One of her old friends sent me a confidential message. Her name is Shannon McCarthy. We had a nice long telephone conversation."

"Don't keep me in suspense forever, Piper."

"She and Scarlett were taking drugs! Shannon didn't come forward at the time of the disappearance because she was afraid of getting expelled or arrested."

"What does that have to do with our expedition?" I flashed on the hike up the mountain. Scarlett had seemed a little spaced out, but I could not imagine a drug addict wanting to subject herself to an arduous wilderness trek in the name of science.

"Scarlett was meeting someone!"

"At a mountain peak on the Mogollon Rim?" It still wasn't making sense. "I didn't think narcotics were coming in through that part of the country until recently."

"Not that kind of drugs! Do you remember Carlos Castaneda?"

Suddenly the murky circumstances began to crystallize. As a student of anthropology, I had been thrilled when a field researcher published a treatise that became a national bestseller. As it was based on the religious use of peyote, the focus of Castaneda's work was well outside of mainstream thought, and this was also appealing. It gave me reason to hope that some of my questionable theories would one day prove popular. However, the book was troublesome from a professional standpoint. The writer had become caught up in mysticism. I couldn't take all the tales of superhuman feats of flight and astral projection seriously.

Piper continued, "Hallucinogenics were the rage. Through Castaneda, Scarlett got into anthropology to justify her psychedelic experimentation. In her mind, the Native American ceremonial use of mescaline somehow legitimized her own taste for psychoactive drugs. Scarlett told Shannon that the purpose of the trip to Arizona was to experience peyote with a tribal shaman. She promised to bring back some buttons."

"So while we were looking for petroglyphs, she was hunting for cactus flowers?"

"Peyote doesn't grow in Arizona. No, according to Shannon McCarthy, Scarlett used the expedition as an excuse to ask her father for a sizable chunk of change. She wanted to follow in Castaneda's footsteps, but going to Mexico alone was out of the question. When she heard about our expedition, she located a tribe of Yaquis living near Tucson, members of a church whose use of the drug was protected by law."

"Yaquis?"

"They are the tribe featured in 'The Teachings of Don Juan.'"

It sounded familiar, but I had read and disregarded the books so long ago.

"So what happened?"

"That's all Shannon knew. She never heard from Scarlett again."

"So Scarlett left the camp, and hiked off toward Tucson by herself? I still don't…"

Piper interrupted, "No, of course not. Scarlett was smarter than that. If she planned to recreate Castaneda's research, she would have gone after the whole mystical experience. I think she met someone on the mountain, and something went wrong."

"But there was no sign of her leaving, no footprints, no trail, nothing."

"In that terrain, Stephen? Rocks and shifting sand? By the time the four of us trampled all over creation looking for her…we probably spoiled any tracks that were left."

It was true. When we first noticed that the girl was missing, it didn't occur to us to look for evidence on the mountainside. We assumed that she had merely become disoriented in the dark, and couldn't find the way back to camp.

"By the way Stephen, where are you?"

"Still in Arizona, south of Safford. Homeland Security has taken over the investigation. It's another long story."

"I looked up the Yaquis on the Internet. As long as you're already in the neighborhood…"

I guessed the jaguar habitat would have to wait.

Piper gave me directions to Pascua Village, a Yaqui community in Tucson. On the road where I had taken the call, absolutely nothing interrupts miles of monotonous two-lane pavement. It was hard to imagine that the Federal Agents would waste time tailing me; there was no place to turn off. If they were really interested, they could call ahead and have someone else follow me at the next terminus. I watched the mirror closely for a while, but eventually country music radio began to bore, and a road induced trance set in. Absentmindedly, I picked up the chronological trail of my memories, and reflected on details I had not deemed appropriate to record in my diary.

The Greek sun had colored my skin a deep bronze, and my slender torso became fleshed out with muscle from loading dive tanks and swimming. I had assumed that the weather would begin to get cooler in October, but by the end of the month the temperature still rose above ninety degrees each day.

I won't pretend that I was an Adonis, but the radiance of glowing health gave me a confidence that may have developed into poise. Several young women left little doubt of their interest, but fresh from the affair with Piper, I was taking my time. The temperature was blistering, clothing was minimal, hormones were pumping; it couldn't last.

Her name was Dasha, a little spitfire if there ever was one. She worked on the boat along side the men, somehow doing an equal job despite her diminutive stature. The intense sunlight failed to lighten her coal-black hair even as her olive complexion darkened to the hue of oil cured Kalamatas. I assumed that competition for her affections was fierce, and was shocked when it became apparent that her advances were toward me.

Dasha had a sweet, heart-shaped face, finely balanced features, and a body that was, well...Greek. I would have basked in her aura forever except for one thing; when we made love, she would laugh.

At first, I thought I was tickling her; ruffling the fine hair below her bikini line caused a twitch as when teasing a cat's ear.

I probed further, and she giggled. The harder I worked, the more she chuckled. This was especially unnerving when mounting to consummate the act. Despite eventually learning to expect the sob-like guffaws that accompanied her climax, hearty laughter did not exactly stimulate my passion.

At the time, I had no idea that these moments were imbued with unique magic that would never be repeated. There would be other girls, but never another Dasha, sweet and wet with youthful heat and athletic vivacity. I guzzled from that fount in blissful blindness.

When I learned that my mother and father had been critically injured in an automobile accident, I immediately flew home to the States. I didn't maintain contact with my little laughing Lorelei, arrogantly assuming our brief burning-hot fling was merely an average sexual experience to be often repeated throughout life.

It was a rarely revisited memory with which to while away the monotonous drive to downtown Tucson.

The Pascua Yaquis believe in a curious syncretism, a blend of Catholicism and pre-Colombian oral history preserved from the clan's first emergence in Mexico. Unique elements of their original cultural heritage have been preserved, although the tribe seems for the most part to have been absorbed into mainstream America. I found the members articulate and willing to discuss my predicament, but none knew of a redheaded rider. Although they were not related to the Yaquis that use mescaline, they explained that the peyote cactus is now designated as an endangered species, and legal harvest is confined to several sects of the Native American Church in Texas.

The tribesmen suggested questioning followers of a "New Age" philosophy that had established an isolated retreat center in the vicinity of Scarlett's disappearance. Members of the group were known to practice an ancient tribal religion known as the "Red Road." The refuge, called Stone Summit, was located on the mountain ridge that traverses the Sitgreaves National Forest.

I drove a little farther north from Tucson before checking into a motel for the night, convinced that no one was following.

March Thirty

I was in for another long drive, back the way I had come. Slowly the mountains grew, and the road became treacherous. There was no shoulder, and the ground dropped away dramatically, first on one side and then the other as the pavement snaked through the bluffs and mesas. After overcoming a mild sensation of vertigo, I began to enjoy the ride, and became totally absorbed in maneuvering the rental car. Pity it wasn't something sportier.

No sign for Stone Summit had been posted on the highway, but there was only one turnoff in the area. I had been counting the miles from the town of Morenci, relying on the directions I had received at Pascua Village. As in most of the region, there was nothing around. One hundred feet from the highway, the asphalt gave way to dirt, and the dusty track angled skyward. Parts of the rudimentary driveway had been eroded by springtime run-off, but well-traveled tire ruts led uphill through a series of switchbacks.

I'm not sure what I was expecting, shacks maybe, or tents. The houses, and they did appear to be well-constructed houses, gracefully melded with the rock outcroppings and scrub pines. The grinding of my tires on the packed earth seemed to violate the placidity of the wilderness. I cut the engine and exited. The car door closing sounded unnaturally loud in the prevailing silence, certainly enough noise to alert the residents to my presence.

Surprisingly, the man that came to greet me was Caucasian. In a resonant baritone, he introduced himself as Samuel Clearwater. Intelligent grey eyes sparkled from the crinkled cheeks of a face steeped in sixty years of happiness, the tint of the irises almost matching a thick shock of unruly curls. The broad palm he offered was the texture of tanned leather; Samuel Clearwater worked with his hands but kept them clean.

I gave my name and explained that I was an anthropologist. Evidently the pace of life was leisurely at this altitude; instead of immediately asking the reason for my visit, my host offered a modest refreshment, and indicated a small house fronted with a wide porch. I accepted a glass of iced herbal tea and a seat in a wooden lawn chair. Mr. Clearwater began speaking as if taking up the thread of an ongoing conversation.

"It's all about sustainability, you understand. We simply cannot continue to rape the environment and exploit natural resources as if they were unlimited. I assume that a man in your profession must address this issue constantly, Dr. Shaw, or would that be sociology?"

I began to answer, but the question must have been intended as rhetorical. The gentle voice immediately continued, "This is what I asked myself: How are we, the species that is, going to survive if we carry on steadily and obliviously destroying our habitat? Ancient indigenous populations recognized this problem and devised means of coexisting with nature without upsetting the delicate balance. There had to be a way to convince modern man of the benefits of this way of living.

"Fortunately, I was not alone in this train of thought. Great minds were working together to forge an innovative method of looking at our world, a 'New Age,' as it eventually became known. Here at Stone Summit, we sought to bring the advantages of modern science into accordance with the ecological balance attained by ancient civilizations and enhance the new lifestyle with spiritual guidance. The theosophical tenets of the pan-Indian 'Red Road' became a rallying point for the like-minded."

While I'm sure the participants had the most noble of intentions, they were living in an idyll, preaching oneness while most of the world struggled in the harshness of a different reality. I had traveled a long way to ask about Scarlett Taylor. I tried to steer the conversation without offending.

"How long ago did the project begin?"

"Some of the precepts were originally proposed in the nineteenth century! Can you imagine? But it took a period of global reawakening, the nineteen sixties, before these progressive ideas began to gain widespread acceptance."

"I meant, here in Arizona. When did you first form a group up here in the mountains?"

"Oh, that would have been the early eighties. You see, back in the 'Summer of Love' when we became interested in these concepts, we were mere children. It took twenty years for us to acquire the wherewithal to mount the project in earnest."

"How many were you?"

"At first, only three. When our aims became known, the ranks swelled to over thirty. Some went on to found separate communities; others simply became too old for the self-sufficient life style. Currently there are five full-time residents here, although we are frequent hosts to retreat groups and scholars."

"This is in partnership with tribes in the area?"

Samuel Clearwater suddenly seemed to notice that I was asking questions.

"The tribal shamans are the source of ancient spiritual wisdom. Without native participation, the project would fail. But you never did tell me what brought you up here, Dr. Shaw."

"Yes, I'm sorry. Your project is so intriguing that I quite forgot. The Pascua Yaquis suggested that you might be able to help. I am searching for signs of a woman that disappeared in this area, back in nineteen eighty-five."

"Eighty-five? We were still camping then. Just in the planning stages."

"I understand, but what I'm looking for is something more recent, a Native American man with long red hair. A picture appeared in the Arizona Republic last year. The missing woman also had flaming red hair. Considering the scarcity of the trait in the local indigenous population…"

I had the sudden feeling that I had gone on too long. Samuel Clearwater's kindly crinkles became somehow sad.

"…I thought there might be a connection," I finished.

The broad hand came up in a stopping gesture, and fell slowly to a knee.

"I may know something, Dr. Shaw. I'm truly sorry if it turns out to be related."

Clearwater seemed to arrange himself, dusting off his trousers and sitting up straighter before continuing, "Drug use was a rite of passage in those days; actually much more than that, it was a confirmation of commitment, a badge of honor. To share in the psychedelic experience was a means of aligning oneself with the forward thinkers of the generation. At first, the alteration to the psychological process was productive; it helped one learn to think 'outside the box,' as the young people put it these days. After a while, altered consciousness became a box of its own. A small, stupid box."

I resigned myself to the fact that this was Clearwater's manner. I would have to endure the roundabout monologue before getting to the crux.

"An enormous amount of hype was ramping up concerning the impending harmonic convergence. We all desperately wanted to believe that humanity was poised at the cusp of a new era. The mountains are awe inspiring, a perfect setting in which to elevate the soul and senses. The hopeful, the naïve, and the opportunistic swarmed to the Rockies in droves. The young people adopted native beliefs, customs and dress. And they brought drugs.

"At that time, we were only able to live here during the warm months. Our camp consisted of merely a few tents. We were experimenting with temporary shelters, trying to define the elements of sustainable habitat. Developing renewable resources. Declaring independence from the municipal power grid. Building homes that were naturally cool in summer, warm in winter, those sorts of things.

"From time to time, kids would show up, mostly college students that had heard of the project. We never turned anyone away; it would have gone against everything we stood for. However, we did not condone the use of illegal drugs."

Clearwater seemed to steel himself, and went on.

"It was late spring or early summer in eighty-five. Our season was just getting under way. A young native man–I'm not sure what denomination–walked into camp, looking to buy food. He did not want to stay, only to pick up a few pieces of fruit or bread. I'm not sure who, but someone gave him what he wanted, and he went on his way."

"There were a few other stragglers hanging around, and that night they stayed up partying. The next morning, we made it clear that this was not acceptable behavior at our commune. It turned out that they had bought mescaline from the visitor."

"I probably would never have remembered-so many events took place during that time frame-but the next summer, the same boy rode up on a horse, carrying a newborn baby wrapped in a blanket. Surprisingly, the ruddy infant already had one red curl of hair.

"The young man was exhausted and despondent. We couldn't get much out of him, and gave him a place to sleep in a lean-to. One of the native girls volunteered that she knew a woman that was nursing. She took charge of the infant, to our great relief, and drove off in her jeep.

"In the morning, we found the young man hanging by the neck. The horse was wandering nearby. Sadly, suicide seems a frequent affliction in the tribal communities. The native members of our crew proclaimed it an 'Indian affair,' and took the body to the reservation for proper burial. They promised to care for the infant while searching for the mother. There were no clues, and little hope she would be found alive. We may have been misguided in not calling the sheriff, but at the time, in our lofty frame of mind, an Apache funeral seemed a noble solution.

"The memory has faded with time, due to a protective function of the human mind, I believe. I haven't thought about the incident for years."

We sat in silence on the porch. An unnatural stillness descended on the woods. Not an insect marred the quiet, no birdsong or rustle of leaf. I tried to read between the lines. Scarlett Taylor had gone to buy drugs, and either ran away with this boy, or was kidnapped. She became pregnant and couldn't return to face her parents. My guess was that she died during or shortly after childbirth, and the heartbroken young father had committed suicide.

Clearwater murmured, "What on earth?"

I looked up to see a gun aimed in my direction, for the second time in a week.

My interrogators had reappeared. One Federal agent stood guard over us, while the two others took a look around the area. The grim faced G-man gestured with his head while speaking. The handgun trained at my chest remained perfectly motionless.

"Where are the other residents?"

I had wondered that myself. Clearwater's voice was as calm as ever.

"It's shopping day. They've taken the van up to the grocery store in Eager."

"Leaving you free to take this meeting."

"I had no idea that visitors were expected."

There was no point in allowing the agent to bully Samuel Clearwater; I was obviously the one they were following. I interjected, "If you told us what this is about, maybe we could clear things up."

"Clear things up?"

"I had nothing to do with the fire, you must know that by now."

"Oh, we know all about you, Dr. Shaw. Lost your job and moved to Austria, where you were arrested for murder. Quick visits to East Germany and Serbia. Involved in the death of a biological terrorist."

Clearwater scrutinized me circumspectly as I interjected, "I was working with the police!"

The stern voice persisted with practiced innuendo. "A meeting with a wealthy radical in Guatemala. Side trips to Honduras and Mexico."

Was it remotely possible that the United States Government was behind the theft of my backpack, and the break-in at the hotel in Guatemala? The attempts had seemed so amateurish. There was hardly time to wonder before the tirade continued.

"Then you came to Arizona for a clandestine tryst with a renegade scientist. You stole his secrets and left him for dead! Now we find you in the company of a documented subversive!"

"Of all the cockamamie..."

"Cockamamie? You're facing a very serious accusation, Dr. Shaw."

"I didn't start the fire!"

"You're not being accused of arson, Dr. Shaw. The charge is espionage."

Hands cuffed behind our backs, Samuel Clearwater and I sat in the back seat of an unmarked van. Two of the federal agents accompanied us; one drove while the other faced us, his weapon still unholstered. The third man had remained behind at the commune. Our captors let us talk; probably hoping we would divulge something. We spoke loudly enough to ensure they could hear that we were not conspiring. I was curious why the Department of Homeland Security considered Clearwater a threat. Not expecting an answer from the agents, I asked the man himself.

"You're a known subversive?"

The silky voice answered thoughtfully. "Some members of the 'Red Road' advocate violence when other means fail. Stone Summit carefully distinguished itself from those factions. Of course the government must assess the threat posed by organizations that could be inciting violence against the State. The FBI interviewed us, and checked periodically to be sure we were in reality merely what we appeared, a peaceful group exploring ways to live in harmony with nature and each other."

"Why would anyone think I was selling secrets to Stone Summit?"

Clearwater shrugged, and the agent guarding us surprised me by saying, "Perhaps I can answer that for you, Dr. Shaw. Every clandestine paramilitary organization in the world has a civilian counterpart, an agency that poses as a legitimate concern for purposes of communication and fund-raising."

"So you believe I am selling stolen information to Stone Summit, which will then be used by violent factions of the 'Red Road' to attack the United States?"

"Something like that. The 'Red Road' is connected with tribes south of the border, who in turn are stooges of the radical socialists proliferating in Latin America. You, Dr. Shaw, travel freely amongst them all, disseminating information that puts the United States at risk."

"That is the stupidest thing I have ever heard! Do I really look like a spy to you?"

"A clever deception that has protected your deep cover for years."

"Deep cover!"

Clearwater spoke up, and for the first time I could detect concern in the sonorous voice. "I would like to contact my attorney."

"That is not currently an option," came the smug retort.

"I'm an American citizen! It's my right!"

"The world has changed, Mr. Clearwater. Under several different provisions of the Patriot Act, we can hold you incommunicado indefinitely if national security is at stake. I suggest that if you desire representation, you confess. When the formal charges are brought, then you can retain counsel."

Conversation came to an immediate halt.

We arrived at our destination after dark. It was impossible to discern anything about the surroundings, and even the location was a mystery. I'm not sure if you would call the facility a "safe house," but the modern ranch-style home was clearly not regularly inhabited. There were furnishings, but no evidence of personal possessions.

Clearwater and I were taken to separate rooms. My handcuffs were removed, and the agent exited. Checking the door seemed a useless gesture. I drew back the curtains; the heavy mesh screen sealing the window was no surprise. The bathroom had a sink and toilet, but no shower. This was a jail cell disguised as a cheap motel room. How many facilities like this one are spread out across the country?

I stretched out on the single bed, and tried to ignore the smell of disinfectant laundry soap that permeated the linen. You would not think sleep was possible under the circumstances, but some deep primal instinct allowed me to doze.

There was no knock, but I instantly became awake as the door opened. One of my captors entered. I had paid little attention to detail at the previous interrogations, and couldn't remember the man's name. The agent, who was apparently in charge, was happy to remind me. "Sanderson" seemed a complicated choice for an alias; presumably it was a real name. Now that I was captive, he seemed almost relaxed, or perhaps bored.

"You didn't think your little turnaround in Tucson was going to fool us, did you?"

"I went to Tucson to question some Native Americans about the disappearance of Scarlett Taylor."

"Come off it, Dr. Shaw. We've looked at your record. Every single thing you have ever been involved in is questionable. Admit it; you've been a courier for almost thirty years!"

"I am not, nor have I ever been, a courier!"

"We would expect you to say that. Your travel record reads like a shopping list for recruiting enemies of the state."

"My job is to mount expeditions. The study of humankind necessarily ignores borders arbitrarily imposed by modern societies."

"Countries like Syria are breeding grounds for terrorists!"

"They are also the location of the most ancient civilizations on the planet. I assure you that the purpose of my visits to the Middle East, Asia, South America, and Eastern Europe was to study humanity, the goal of which is to understand why we do what we do, not to foster terror or destruction. I love my country. Despite its many problems, America is the greatest society that has ever existed!"

"Yet when comparing your itinerary with the sites of acts of hostility propagated against the United States, there is a striking parallel."

"I think you could make that case with any traveler's record."

"Not to the degree that your history implies."

"Then why have you waited so long to arrest me?"

"Until you meddled with a Department of Defense physicist, you were flying below the radar."

"I think you are paranoid and delusional, Sanderson. Have you sought professional help?"

"Now, now, Dr. Shaw. We are going to be working closely for the foreseeable future. Do you really think it's a good idea to bait me?"

Agent Sanderson arrogantly rose and left the room, the click of the lock obvious and ostentatious in the silence.

After half an hour, I heard angry voices, the first time during my incarceration that any sound had come from elsewhere in the house. I pressed my ear against the door panel. A few audible words soared above the rumble of argument.

"...Single shred of solid evidence...probable cause...American citizens!"

I was surprised when Sanderson opened the door. The lead agent seemed irate, fairly spitting the words, "I must apologize, Dr. Shaw. Apparently I was...misinformed. Newly discovered facts have clarified the matter. You are being released."

I expected Clearwater would be raising hell, but like me, he was content just to be free. Sanderson returned our possessions and led us to my rental car, which they had apparently appropriated. We didn't speak until reaching the speed limit on the open road. As the threat receded behind, I broke the silence.

"What the hell was that all about?"

"Did you hear the shouting?"

"Yes."

"Apparently their superior showed up and questioned the lack of evidence."

"The car is probably bugged."

"So what? I've got a good mind to..."

"Make hell for them?"

"Exactly. See them in court. What a crock of shit."

There was little more to say. Clearwater offered to put me up, but I had no desire to visit any more hassle on the residents of Stone Summit. We rehashed the incident on the drive back to the commune. After promising to let each other know of any further developments, I unceremoniously dropped him off.

This time I really was intending to hightail it to the border.

Part Four

March Thirty-one

At the airport in Tucson I stopped to make arrangements with the car rental company. I was informed that I would not be allowed to drop off an American vehicle in Mexico City. I didn't see the point of flying South only to turn around and drive back up. The rental agent suggested buying a clunker and selling it upon arrival at my destination.

One thousand of Señor Ramirez' dollars later I was the proud owner of a decrepit compact Japanese pickup that was the "pride" of the counter attendant's brother. What a racket. The Mexicans might recognize me as a fool, but I would not be mistaken for someone worth robbing.

I didn't realize that I would be entering a combat zone. Straddling the border, the town of Nogales exhibits the trappings of East Berlin circa nineteen fifty-three: high fences, barbed wire, armed guards. The rancor is thick and putrid on both sides of the fence. If life along this international boundary is any indication of the state of our relationship with our close neighbors, something desperately wrong is taking place on a fundamental level. Faced with this battlefront, the jaguar doesn't stand a chance. They are not the only species being placed at risk; sealing the border could have a disastrous affect on the environment.

Modern man's attempts to sculpt the biosphere demonstrate his inability to take all variables into account. A well-documented scenario? We annihilate apex predators to protect our livestock. Population unchecked, wild ungulates devastate the vegetation. With no roots holding the soil, runoff from rainfall erodes the riverbank. Waterways become muddy, shallow and wide. Fish die off. Spring floods overflow the low banks and destroy homes. We build levees, dam up the rivers, redirect water, alter the landscape. Naturalists lobby the government for the creation of protected habitat for the very creatures we destroyed in the first place.

Samuel Clearwater had a point; this method seems a poor substitute for learning to live in balance with the original systems we encounter in nature. There is no telling how far-reaching the effect of fencing off large sections of the southern border would be. Moreover, there is little doubt that as long as massive profits are forthcoming, drugs will continue to flow north regardless.

I was an American heading south; although security was tight, there was no problem with admission to the country. Evidently, the Department of Homeland Security was no longer concerned with my whereabouts; no one tried to stop me. My passport was accepted at the border crossing and noted in the computer without question.

Continuing south on Mexico Route 15, in the distance to the left, mountains parallel the road. Small dusty towns passed in flashes. Having no way of knowing where the next gasoline would be available, I topped up the fuel tank at every opportunity.

The ancient Mayans did not build cities this far north on the west side of the Sierra Madre. I intended to visit the sites of recent cultures until finding signs of Mayan influence. At the northernmost point of this occurrence, I would start to search for clues, but for all I knew, the priceless jade mask was at the bottom of the ocean in the hold of a sunken Spanish Galleon.

My disposable "go phone" had been useless since shortly after crossing the border. As evening approached, I looked for lodgings that provided telephone service.

It was the middle of the night in Austria; too late to call Ingrid. I dialed Piper's number. My old colleague was understandably stunned by the news. She wanted more information, some kind of physical proof of Scarlett's demise. I explained my reason for leaving Arizona so abruptly.

"You do understand why I didn't want to stay and continue the search."

"Of course I understand, Stephen. Civil rights are taking a beating these days. But isn't there a chance that the events Clearwater described were unrelated to Scarlett's disappearance? I mean, it's not like you found the horseback rider, or made positive ID on a corpse, and none of it explains where she was during the pregnancy. Someone somewhere must have seen her."

"Under other circumstances, I might have investigated further, but apart from sheer inquisitiveness, the only reason I got involved again was to help you. Who else will benefit if I discover more proof? Her father? Brent Taylor can kiss my ass. If the child was raised in a Native American home, he won't have any recall of the incident. One day, Scarlett's bones may be found in the desert, or the mysterious rider will surface, request a DNA test, and make a claim for the Taylor millions. Other than that..."

"I have to know. I have to know that we were not at fault."

"Between the statements of Shannon McCarthy, and Samuel Clearwater, I think it's safe to say that things were beyond our control. Scarlett left the camp of her own volition."

"If that's what really happened."

Piper copied down Clearwater's contact information. If events warranted, I could return to Arizona after the hoopla died down. After Sanderson and his motley cronies found some other likely victim. For the time being I was satisfied. If Piper was too curious to wait, she could forward her own agenda.

April One

I tried Ingrid's number in the morning, but the phone rang continuously, never going to voicemail. Before continuing south, I decided to send an update by email, and coughed up the hourly fee to use a computer terminal in the motel lobby. One of the messages in my inbox was from Ingrid Luft.

> Stephen,
> I'm sorry, but I cannot live this way. You will never change; I was foolish to believe things would be different. Please try to understand.
> I boxed up your things and sent them, saving you the trouble of coming back here. Let's not prolong our incompatibility. Better we should remember the good times,
> Ingrid

The message should have come as no surprise, but I had been hoping that our relations would improve. The reason Ingrid's phone had gone unanswered became obvious. I replied immediately:

> Ingrid,
> Of course I don't blame you, and understand your anger. As it stands, we are apart anyway. I will contact you when I am free of this obligation. Maybe things will seem different then.
> All my love,
> Stephen
> P. S. I'm back in Mexico.

Similar situations have arisen in every relationship I have ever had with a woman. At least I had experience; I would have to take it in stride. Contemplating my role in the debacle would occupy my mind on the long, solitary drive.

I had been crazy about Stacy, my ex-wife; I was prepared to do whatever it took to make her happy. Conversely, she looked at me as a lump of raw clay that could be sculpted into something acceptable. The tools for this reshaping were emotional: anger, desire, refusal, distance, disappointment. As she went about the task, the domestic situation became unbearable. I sought escape.

That experience contributed to my reticence concerning the development of close relationships. Over the years, I found it easier to keep love affairs on a casual basis. Restructuring my life to include Ingrid Luft had required an enormous sacrifice.

I was determined to recover from the emotional letdown. Ingrid expressed anger because I refused to change. If you don't like what you see, why get involved at all? I had no wish to be manipulated; I had seen the results of that experiment.

Almost symbolically, I drove on alone.

The itchy suspicion that someone was following me might have been a result of the encounter with the agents from the Department of Homeland Security, but unwanted, the feeling tagged along. Continuously looking over my shoulder was tiresome. I wished I could shake the case of the creeps.

With the morning sun painting a blush on the distant mountains, I continued the journey south. As the cloudless sky took on a dark blue luster, the distant hills purpled against a foreground of surprisingly bright greenery. Traffic was light. It seemed doubtful that anyone was following, but that had appeared the case in Arizona as well.

After miles of emptiness, road signs began to appear on the approach to a rural town. There were more vehicles on the road, although I could not imagine where they would have entered the highway. Up ahead, something had brought traffic to a standstill. Drivers exited their cars and milled around the blacktop.

I pulled to the shoulder and walked. After fifty yards, I could see a ramshackle parade crossing the divided highway. Sensing my foreigner's curiosity, a nearby truck driver called down to me, "La Santa Muerte," the Saint of Death.

In the wake of the extreme violence perpetrated by drug cartels, many Mexicans began praying to various deities for assistance or salvation. New saints were conjured from a conglomeration of Catholic and Native beliefs. Apparently the mayhem had affected even this remote outback. The marchers were begging for help from the patron saint of the worst of sinners.

The procession passed, and I resumed the drive. Pondering the ramifications of this religious phenomena triggered a cascade of thoughts. A few short months ago, Ingrid and I would have happily debated the subject. We were good together when involved in science, but just when we both needed emotional support, our bond was disintegrating. Had she been concealing a darker side of her personality? Her sudden intolerance seemed cruel.

I continued south for the next four days. The little old truck proved to be a marvel of engineering, constantly on the brink of disintegration, yet unfailing (with the exception of the air-conditioner) to the point of disbelief. My diary lists the locations I visited, the uneventful entries becoming wearied and laconic. I remember my mounting frustration as the fruitless search led back toward the Mayan heartland. In an apparent attempt at keeping my spirits up, I noted in the margin that I lost some weight during my busy visit to Arizona.

April Two

Petersen's injury had not warranted a hospital stay. The buckshot wounds had merely required a topical dressing and a sling to protect his sore arm. Jain's burns were not so easy to deal with. The financier had been moved from intensive care to a private room. In the quiet ward, the men conversed.

"I swear Donnie, I am going to get even with that meddlesome prick."

"We still don't know what he was doing."

"Industrial sabotage, what else?"

"He really is an anthropologist."

"Anthropologist my ass. Whose side are you on, anyway? Now we've got to rebuild the whole damn lab!"

"I think we have demonstrated that distance is not an impediment to the entanglement. Instead of resurrecting the trailer, I suggest we move the project farther underground. Thanks to that intruder, Federal agents have been nosing around. I'm guessing they will try to get a look at what I do next. The DoD will want to make sure I'm not violating my nondisclosure, noncompete agreement."

"So we'll lose control of the technique?"

"Hardly. From the rubble left after the fire, no one will be able to get an overview. Hell, it would take them years just to re-create the gamma ray application."

"What about the rabbit? And the, what did you call it? Polarization?"

"Dismantled or destroyed in the fire. I'm sorry to say that even our little bunny got barbecued. After our success with the lab animal, there was no need for the long distance machines. I disassembled them and packed everything away until the new computers are ready. Until the explosion I had been concentrating on other factors. The investigators won't have a clue."

"So what's the next move?"

"Like I said, Carlton. We go underground. Someplace where we can build a center for our synthetic "brain," our command center of quantum computers."

"Where do you have in mind?"

"What's the most secure place you can think of?"

The Nation's Capital enjoys the protection of the mightiest military force that ever occupied planet earth. The city is also generally out of range for serious damage from natural disasters such as blizzards, hurricanes, floods or tornados. The safest place? Carlton Jains thought of his family home in Spring Valley, and the security he had taken for granted all his life.

April Three

Against the doctors' recommendations, Jains insisted on being released from the hospital. The two wounded men headed east in the motor home. Petersen had loaded all the gear that could be salvaged from the camp into the cargo space. Along the way they made several stops to procure used medical equipment that the physicist had located online.

Jains was able to take short turns at the wheel so Petersen could sleep, and they pressed on around the clock. Nonetheless, driving the cumbersome recreational vehicle to Washington, D.C. took two days.

April Four

Earlier in my career, before commercial satellites became commonplace, there were no alternatives; when out in the field, isolation was expected and received little consideration. Occasionally a little dalliance might develop between coworkers, but most times, off hours were consumed in study. These days there are plenty of options for communication. We've all become accustomed to nearly perpetual interaction, even from a distance.

I felt it fair to warn Charley that I would not be flying to Ingrid's side in Austria at the conclusion of my expedition; I was headed for his place whenever my search for the mask came to a head, so to speak, one way or the other. A bottle of Heradura Gold was the best available complement to a phone conversation with my drinking buddy.

Charley cheerfully informed me that a box addressed to me had arrived from Austria. I wasn't surprised by the impression that my old pal was secretly pleased upon hearing that my relationship was suffering dysfunction. Our friendship has outlasted countless optimistic partnerships with women, love affairs both his and mine. Heeding each other's counsel has not actually resolved any personal problems over the years, but it has been a means of support.

Charley tried to get my mind off of the situation by recounting ribald anecdotes from our younger years. The repartee bolstered my spirits. A serious dose of tequila also helped to fortify my attitude.

April Five

I had covered the west side of the Sierra Madre range, about fifteen hundred miles back to Mexico City, with no new clues for the effort. Referring to my notes, I tried to discern a pattern, a route the mask could have traveled. On a map of the Mayan empire, I drew lines connecting the sites where I had found evidence. The resulting geometric shape resembled a notepad doodle.

I had yet to explore the Yucatan Peninsula. In northern Guatemala, ruins are left from the Zacpeten, a culture that resisted Spanish domination until the end of the seventeenth century. The civilization was centered in the heart of jaguar territory. I decided to start again at Tikal and work northeast toward the realm of the Aztecs, searching the once-inhabited rainforest for traces of the legend.

On the list of scientists I had gotten from the Forest Rangers, a Dr. Les Berman was registered as the researcher responsible for gathering data on wild cats in that region. I sent an email stating my suspicions about jaguars occupying the same remote locations as they had in antiquity, and my desire to visit those areas.

I left the faithful little truck in the parking lot at Benito Juarez International Airport with the keys in the ignition. I wish I had known then how many flights would be required before I could land in Guatemala.

April Six

Carlton Jains' semi-attached garage boasted two interior doors that opened directly into the house. One led to the rear and the kitchen, presumably to provide a chauffeur or tradesperson access without having them traipse through the main living quarters. The other gave entry into a windowless vestibule that had been furnished as a small office. Beyond another doorway, the adjoining drawing room now contained a jumble of equipment that the two men had spirited in through the garage. The domestic help had no idea what was locked in the front quarter of the palatial home. Jains wasn't too sure either.

Petersen had run extra electrical wiring himself, unobtrusively snaking cables up from the basement. Several machines slowly taking form were the bastard children of cannibalized hospital equipment. Parts had been pirated from an X-ray generator, a magnetic resonance imager, and a fiber-optic surgical system. On a billiard table covered by a sheet of cabinet grade plywood sat a partially disassembled industrial laser and a pile of electrical components.

Two old oak desks had been pushed into a corner to accommodate the computers. Three large processing units surrounded a single monitor and keyboard. An incubator and an autoclave had commandeered the powder room. Loitering in the hall, a battered electron microscope loomed like an antediluvian ancestor of the sophisticated machinery. A bookcase had been set aside for the storage of chemicals, but to Jain's great relief, only a half-dozen innocuous containers currently rested there.

Petersen seemed perfectly content to spend sixteen hours a day working in the suite, with a constantly brewing coffee pot and the odd sandwich or piece of fruit. Carlton easily became bored with all the tinkering, and left the physicist alone. The private study down the hall was well equipped with creature comforts, where Jains nursed both his disfigured skin and festering hatred in solitude. The sooner Don built the infernal machines, the sooner Carlton could exact revenge.

April Seven

The Zacpeten temple ruins at Laguna Salpeten, Guatemala, face due west. Architectural anomalies at the site are apparently unique to the area. While different compass orientation of artifacts at the other Mayan cities had not led to anything of significance, I still believed the oddity could be a clue. This area has been alternately occupied and abandoned since around 300 BCE. I explored the Post Classic areas first, the handiwork of people that had settled here in the fifteenth century following the collapse of Mayapan, (from whence the term 'Maya') located to the North.

The Zacpeten constructed patio style apartments, and their pictographic adornments take the form of painted murals rather than carved basalt or animal skin books. At first, I found nothing that related to the jaguar hieroglyph, and continued on a tour of time by visiting the tall statues left by other inhabitants. On the edge of a pillar that had been carved sometime near the beginning of the Aztec ascension was an image that sent me reeling.

The work was rudimentary compared with the well developed art of advanced Mayan civilizations. The lines appeared jagged, as if made by single dull or inefficient blade. The etching that had drawn my attention was a crude rendition of the now familiar glyphic jaguar symbol. A spiral was carved beneath the graphic image, and chiseled above the rune was a sideways "V" with jagged protrusions into its interior.

I spat on my fingers and rubbed saliva over the faint lines. The grooves darkened and the carving became clearer. The coil below the figure sported a small protuberance with an oblong shape at its end. More spit revealed that the "V" had at one time been surrounded by additional details. As a result of my work on early petroglyphs and recent exposure to Mayan script, the implication leapt out at me; the symbol of the jaguar king was nestled by a snake, and lorded over by a gaping wildcat's maw. The mask had never been found in a likely temple, pyramid or tomb. Perhaps this treatment of the glyph implied that the relic lay elsewhere.

I had heard that small karst caves were scattered about in the heart the of El Peten rainforest, and that the ancients had frequented natural rock formations in the area. Presumably, many tribes would have visited these spots, perhaps even dating back to the first humans that explored the isthmus. Even if the mask was not in the vicinity, this was an opportunity for exploration that I was not likely to be blessed with again. I returned to the hotel in Flores to equip myself for a jungle expedition.

My inbox held a reply from the Wildlife Conservation Group. Dr. Les Berman concurred with my opinion that jaguars had been repeatedly using the same remote routes throughout the millennia. The researcher agreed to direct me toward the ancient trails provided my presence did not interfere with the collection of data.

I wrote back stating that I was already in the country, cited my experience at working remote sites in Central America, and asked to join the expedition. The jaguar habitat encompassed the area containing the limestone cave formations. To have an experienced guide would be a definite bonus.

April Eight

The return message from Dr. Berman seemed a little harsh, but correct under the circumstances:

Dr. Shaw,

I had assumed that you would arrive in El Peten between my trips to the field. However, I am leaving the day after tomorrow for a three-day hike into the wilderness. If you have been truthful about your experience in this environment, you are welcome to join the expedition. I must point out that there will be no assistance should things go wrong. You are entirely responsible for you own welfare. This includes your survival gear, water, food, weapons, etc.

My time is limited. Should you become a burden, I will not hesitate to leave you behind. I don't know how long you plan to stay in Guatemala, but I will be happy to consult with you upon my return from the rainforest should you deem that a better course of action.

If you decide to join the expedition, take the main road north from Tikal fifteen kilometers, and turn right on the old logging track. We depart April 9, 0400. You would be well advised to hire a local guide to show you to our base camp in daylight.

Yours,
Les Berman

Old Les sounded like a real hard-ass. I certainly couldn't blame him for the attitude. Weakness or inexperience can certainly create problems for a foreigner to any environment. The message did not intimidate me in the least; conversely, the implication of professionalism was encouraging. I replied:

Dr. Berman,

I understand entirely. My experience is as stated. Should your trek appear too arduous, I will bail out long before there is an issue. Expect me 1700 local time, April 8.

S. Shaw

I took Berman's warning seriously. One of the biggest problems would be water. Drinking from streams along the way was out of the question, although I did have a three-day ration of purification tablets for an emergency. I packed several bags of shelled nuts, a little beef jerky, some carrots and radishes; not exactly an epicurean tour de force, but the staples would not spoil or attract unwanted visitors. Eight quarts of water weighs sixteen pounds. A pint of rum along with the food put the load at about twenty. A light blanket from the motel, mosquito netting, DEET, a small machete, a key-chain flashlight; it wasn't too much. I added two more one liter plastic bottles of water. The burden would become lighter as the hike continued.

April Nine

I spent the morning packing and repacking. With all the water, there was no room for extra clothing or toiletries. I added a hat, and a kerchief that could double as towel or washcloth. My get-up began to resemble that of a hobo in search of a train.

On Ramirez' recommendation, I hired a local driver called Rolando. He brought along a back-seat copilot named Jose, whose main function was probably to keep me outnumbered in case I had an attack of insanity. We left around noon. It was only seventy miles or so to the base camp so this constituted an early start. I did not want any unforeseen circumstances along the way to interfere with my joining the expedition.

After circling Lake Peten Itza to access a bridge, the road became two-lane blacktop through heavy undergrowth. Occasional glimpses of the river glinted through the trees. A road sign signifying "Jaguar crossing" was charming. The black image of a cat was distinctly Central American somehow, although the yellow diamond shaped marker was identical to those seen on highways in the states.

The two men kept up a running commentary in Spanish, but their speech was so rapid and colloquial that only half of what they said was comprehensible. We were stopped and briefly questioned at the entrance and exit where the highway ran through the national park at Tikal. Having local guides made all the difference.

Some of the drive was on smooth and deserted asphalt pavement, but most of the thoroughfares were potholed and rough. It was almost five o'clock by the time we turned off the main road onto a sun-baked clay trail. At a campsite in a clearing one hundred yards along the path, the driver stopped. We all got out and stretched, and the lackey pretended to help me with my things. After confirming our rendezvous for the return trip, I paid the fare and tipped them both. Their final words were accompanied by wheezing laughter. As they were driving away, I pondered the meaning of the machine gun Spanish. As near as I could figure, Rolando had said, "Don't let the cat woman bite off your head."

The site was quiet. I called out hello, and receiving no reply from the surrounding woods, sat on a log by the central fire pit to wait.

After about fifteen minutes, a diminutive sprite with broad native facial features materialized from the undergrowth calling, "Buenos tardes, Señor Shaw."

Surprised, I stood, saying, "Dr. Berman?"

The man laughed, and continued in Spanish, "No, no. Dr. Berman is coming. I am Carlos, your guide."

We shook hands, and Carlos gave me the once over, checking my boots, jeans, shirt and backpack. Apparently I passed inspection. He gestured for me to sit, and began building a fire.

A fanfare of metallic rattles accompanied an old model jeep bouncing into the clearing from the jungle track. The driver was almost a twin to Carlos. The occupant of the shotgun seat exited the vehicle, attempting to tuck stray strands of hair into a straw hat. I was a little surprised at realizing it was a woman; her figure and attire had appeared quite masculine at first. She helped flip the seat forward for the passenger in the rear, a tall khaki clad man with photography gear hanging from straps around his neck.

I approached as they stretched and shook out the kinks.

"Dr. Berman?" I looked between them, hoping not to appear presumptuous.

"I'm Leslie Berman," the woman replied. "This is Mr. Cortland. Reggie Cortland, the photographer," as if that said it all.

This would have been a great time to say, "Love your work," but I had never heard the name. I stated my own, and extended my hand. Mr. Cortland seemed slightly amused, and clasped it firmly. He struck me as affable, strong, and confident, a good combination for a wilderness trek companion.

Ms. Berman continued, "We've just been checking that the trail is clear. The cats can hear a vehicle from a long way. We usually take the jeep to within hiking distance of the habitat corridor, and continue on foot."

As we walked toward the fire, she continued, "I see you have met Carlos." She gestured to the jeep's driver. "This is Armando, our other park guide. Before you ask, no, they are not related."

Armando grinned at the mention of his name, a little gold flashing in his smile. I wondered how well he understood English.

Dr. Berman went on to explain that we would be leaving at 0400 hours. She described the terrain, and what we were seeking. The area had been scouted by plane, and the coordinates of animal sightings had been noted via GPS. We would be visiting these specific spots, hoping to establish the number of offspring that had survived since the last survey. Jaguars breed year round, so there is no specific season when cubs appear. Only the females tend the young, and they will not tolerate male cats entering the area. We would be searching for skittish animals in a vast wilderness, without our quarry's advantage of an acute feline sense of smell.

In the gathering darkness, we sat around the campfire. Dr. Berman reiterated the perils of the expedition, and offered advice. Mr. Cortland smiled, and benignly tinkered with his cameras. Carlos and Armando took turns between dozing and feeding the flames.

Apparently a light snack constituted dinner. Each of us would stand a two-hour watch while the others slept. Smoldering leaves kept the insects to a tolerable number. Not having had time to prepare a place to drape my mosquito net, I lay next to the fire, my exposed skin smothered with insecticide. I was almost happy to rise before dawn.

April Ten

Dr. Berman expected the ride to take a little over an hour. The terrain was rough but fairly flat, and the rudimentary track wound around the larger trees and small pools of water. Apparently our route generally followed the course of a stream that remained out of sight. The forest was alive with shadows, fleeting apparitions dancing in the pale yellow cones cast by the headlamps.

Conversation was difficult over the racket made by the jeep, but I managed to glean an overview. All of our tracking would be done facing the wind. Carlos was the bush scout, searching for scat, footprints or other traces left by the animals. Armando would take the jeep and patrol the perimeter. Recent spates of violence committed by drug runners are making the area dangerous. Armando and Dr. Berman carried handheld VHF radios; there was no cellular service in the wilderness. We would be dependent on the walkie-talkies if a threat from smugglers or renegades became imminent.

The jeep trail dwindled into a barely recognizable path through the brush. Exiting the vehicle, we shouldered our gear and continued on foot. The native explorer went first, with Cortland following close, cameras ready. As the sun rose, following the primitive trail became somewhat easier.

Dr. Berman and I chatted as we brought up the rear, keeping our voices barely above a whisper. I started with the expected platitude. "I really appreciate your letting me tag along."

"Frankly, Dr. Shaw, I'm surprised that you found your way here at all, much less prepared for a hike into the interior of the rain forest. Honestly, I didn't pay particularly close attention to your email. Didn't think you'd actually show. Tell me again why an anthropologist is so interested in the migration routes of jaguars?"

I had given some thought to the inevitability of questions of this nature. Not wishing to divulge the true purpose of my quest, I replied, truthfully, "Human evolution has been influenced by a vast variety of environmental factors. Now we have become so prevalent and powerful that many of the creatures that contributed to our development have become extinct, or soon will. Earlier inhabitants of this area revered the jaguar. More recent cultures have...what's the word? Extirpated them. Humankind's destiny will be shaped in the world we are creating."

Berman's tone was ironic. "Without denigrating the importance of protecting endangered species, I don't quite see how the migratory route of wild cats pertains directly to the future development of humankind."

"That's why my question to you was 'Do the animals use the same paths as they did in antiquity?'" I borrowed from the philosophy of Samuel Clearwater. "If that paints an image of the natural world before changes wrought by modern society, it may also describe the niche that Homo-sapiens occupied in that period, an era in which we may have existed more harmoniously with the natural environment. Then the rate of the behavioral changes that have taken place since that era can be measured." I hoped this subterfuge was enough explanation to mask my true motive, and changed the subject. "What made you gravitate toward jaguar research?"

"Not just jaguars, Dr. Shaw. The 'Conservancy' monitors the condition of several hundred species as part of a broader effort at understanding precisely the effects you just described, although from our point of view, it is blatantly clear that mankind's effect on the entire biosphere is deleterious."

"Of course. We believe we are sculpting our world to suit our needs, but fail to recognize the complicated systems that keep nature in balance."

"Which is exactly what happens when the natural habitat is destroyed."

"Suddenly we realize that the entire macro-environment is in a state of collapse..."

Carlos motioned for quiet. Backing toward us, he spread his hands to the side and gestured several times. We sought cover in the brush, and waited in silence.

The creature that momentarily appeared resembled an oversized domestic hog with a long pointy snout. It came down the path about as far as the scout had progressed before stopping to sniff the air, deposit a gift, and head off perpendicular to the trail. Carlos reappeared and beckoned. Not a word had been spoken, and we continued hiking as before. I hoped we had all passed the wilderness guide's test.

Despite our views originating from the vantage points of different disciplines, Dr. Berman must have been satisfied that I was in her camp as far as conservation was concerned. At least there didn't seem to be any argument.

The trail became less navigable, and our little group continued single file, stifling conversation. We stopped a few times on Carlos' signal, but didn't scatter into the forest. The leaf canopy was thick; it was hard to tell if the sun was directly overhead when our guide finally stopped for lunch.

As we rested, Cortland showed us the digital images he had recorded of the tapir. The sighting was an unexpected bonus, as the animals are predominantly nocturnal. Carlos said it was a sign of some other activity in the area. I assumed he meant that the boar-like beast had been rousted from its usual daytime haunts, although it didn't look particularly stressed out to me. The guide warned that tapirs are instinctively aggressive toward humans, and at three to seven hundred pounds, best avoided.

We hiked several more hours before reaching our stopping place for the night. Southerners would call the structure a "Chickee," a platform built above the swamp, or in this case, raised from the forest floor. The framework of the shelter was ancient, with relatively fresh thatch laid on the surfaces. Ebullient despite hours of walking, Carlos explored the nearby forest while we checked for pests, and rigged mosquito netting. At dusk, he returned with news that he had found evidence of jaguars.

Dr. Berman explained that the feral cats are not technically classified as *nocturnal*; they are *crepuscular*, mostly active in the half-light of dawn and dusk. We too would approximate the animals' schedule. All four of us went to examine the footprints the guide had found.

After an uneventful search of the surrounding undergrowth, we returned to the Chickee. Cortland explained that the expedition had been scheduled to coincide with the full moon. The extra light was unnecessary for the cameras, but would help us find the subjects. So as not to frighten the animals, he was using a "dark flash," a powerful strobe using a combination of infrared and ultraviolet light from outside the visible spectrum. The data representing the images would be mathematically interpreted to create corresponding visual range wavelengths. The resulting pictures would appear as if taken in daylight.

Dr. Berman had volunteered to take the first watch. As the rest of us lay down to sleep, she sat on the edge of the platform and removed her outer garments to apply insecticide. In the intermittent shafts of moonlight, I could see that she was an attractive woman, her shoulders not so masculine as I had supposed. It was the first time I had seen her without the hat obscuring her face. She had a look of resigned weariness that I attribute to great sorrow or disappointment, a lovely fragile feminine vulnerability toughened by a stoic sense of duty. I wondered if she and Reggie Cortland were more than just colleagues, but they had seemed indifferent in that way throughout the day. Did that mean she was a free agent? I can't help it; after all my years spent in constant pursuit of female companionship, these sorts of speculations just come naturally.

I stayed with my parents to help out around the house while they recovered from the accident. I was in a funk, but Mom and Dad were thrilled that I was sticking around and didn't seem to mind my indigence. It had been my intention to return to Greece after their convalescence, but the dive season had ended, and for the moment I was not needed.

As a postdoctoral researcher, I now had two expeditions under my belt, and no definitive piece of work to show for the efforts. I was not yet thirty, already divorced, unemployed, with student loans to repay. The academic year was in its annual headlong rush to the winter holidays, not a great time to look for a job.

The slump extended into the area of personal relationships. High on the memory of my recent successes at casual intimacy, I plunged into the local dating scene with ridiculous expectations. I might as well have had "loser" tattooed on my forehead. I finally calmed down and stopped hunting like a hound. It turned out that beautiful women were all around. I had been so intent on my own imaginary world that I hadn't noticed.

The next thing I knew, I was being roused for my watch. Exhaustion had won out. I had been asleep for hours.

April Eleven

In the twilight of the approaching sunrise Carlos led the way through the undergrowth, showing us how to move soundlessly through the bush. Cautiously approaching a spring-fed pool, we found a place to hide with a view of some footprints our guide had discovered the previous evening. After waiting in silence for thirty minutes or so, we were rewarded with our first sighting. A mother with two cubs had come to drink. I was surprised to see the young ones jump in and frolic in the shallows at the edge of the pond. I thought cats hated water.

After we had observed for a few minutes, Cortland indicated that he wanted to get closer. If the animals sensed his presence, our viewing would be over. The jaguars did not immediately bolt for cover, but suddenly seemed uneasy. Perhaps they detected human scent, despite our carefully chosen downwind blind. Playtime was over, and the female marshaled the youngsters into the brush.

Dr. Berman stored the location in the hand-held GPS. Carlos beckoned, and we followed into the jungle. Several minutes later, we emerged onto what was presumably a game trail. Occasionally it was necessary to clear the way with a machete, but the path was fairly evident, marked by scars on the bark of the larger tree-trunks. As the sunlight angled higher through the foliage, we moved deeper into the rainforest.

The pathway unexpectedly opened into a clearing and a roughly triangular rock outcropping loomed into view. The sight was startling; blocks of pockmarked grey stone appeared to have been randomly strewn by giants at play, lintels indelicately balanced on plinths, dominoes toppled by titans. Had the scene appeared at the base of a pyramid, it would have easily been perceived to be the ruin of an ancient shrine.

The porous stones comprising the formations were tessellated; after centuries of erosion they appeared almost as evenly shaped as ceramic tiles. Coming across such regularity in the midst of a rugged landscape was startling. A traveler might easily assume that the oblong boulders were the work of ancient man. The long flat stones reminded me of the eroded sculpture at the Temple of the Jaguar.

As I turned from the path to approach the pile of boulders, Carlos called out a warning: danger, there are snakes! It hit me immediately; on the stela at Zacpeten, the glyph was surrounded by a serpent and watched over by a jaguar! We were in the heart of jaguar territory at a locally notorious snake pit positioned halfway between two ancient warring cities. If the mask had been hidden during a sectarian skirmish and the location later chronicled in stone, this was a logical place to look for the cache.

The trouble was, I couldn't search for ancient treasure in the present company without divulging my purpose. We paused to rest for a few minutes, and I surreptitiously stole a look at the coordinates currently being displayed on Dr. Berman's hand-held GPS unit.

Carlos told us that the mother jaguar's territory ended at a small stream about a mile ahead, and that on the other side we might find evidence of a different female. After that, it would be time to return to the "Chickee" for the night.

I fell in with the conservationist as the hike continued. "Seems like a whole lot of work for ten minutes of observation, Dr. Berman."

"You were lucky, Dr. Shaw. I might make five excursions like this one during a visit to El Peten. Sometimes I don't notch up a single sighting during an entire expedition."

"You know, the locals warned me about you."

"Really?"

I told her what the driver had said, adding, "You don't seem that dangerous to me."

This got a laugh. "Let me guess…Rolando?"

"Small world," I observed.

"I've been coming to the Peten Basin for five years. Usually there are other scientists besides me, but generally I arrive in Flores by myself. That makes me a target for Latin machismo. I put a stop to the advances early on. I guess Rolando has not forgiven me."

We had a chuckle over that. I wondered if she could be trusted with the secret of my real purpose for coming to Guatemala. I was going to need help when returning to search the snake-infested pile of stones.

Old maps refer to the hill as Mt. Alto. Despite the name, it's not much of a high mountain at three hundred fifty feet above sea level, but it's not located just anywhere. Accounts differ, but despite prior incidents involving electronic surveillance, the Soviet Union was somehow allowed to place their sovereign soil, the Russian Embassy, at the top of the third highest point of land in Washington, D.C. The site commands a direct line of sight to the Capitol, the White House, the Pentagon, and the National Mall. With a wrist rocket, you could just about lob a rotten egg into the National Observatory, where the Vice-president lodges during tenure.

On the opposite side of the installation is Tunlaw Road, two lanes following a long slope toward the Potomac River, named Walnut Hill until a blight destroyed the trees in the early twentieth century and the letters were subsequently reversed. To the North, hilly piedmont borders the Potomac River as it grows from fresh water feeders in the Appalachian Mountains. From the roof of the main building in the foreign compound, the Washington homes of diplomats and billionaires appear to poke through the treetops like so many dollhouses.

Donald Petersen recalled that as boys, he and Carlton would secretly climb onto the roof of the Jains' house. A third floor porch abutted a gable, and with a stepladder they could reach the eave. From there, ascending the main peak was relatively easy. Jains was surprised when his old friend emerged from the laboratory, and asked if they could go there now.

Scaling the terracotta tiles brought back the old conspiratorial thrill, despite there being no one to prohibit them from doing it. Jains knew there had to be a reason for the precarious ascent. "This is not just for the sake of nostalgia, is it?"

"You know me so well."

"So what about it, Don?"

"It's just an idea I've been tossing around. To transmit and receive my signal any great distance, I'll need a powerful antenna. So I've been thinking of a way to hijack one, rather than building something from scratch."

Jains looked around at a skyline littered with steel towers and tall buildings. Hundreds of antennae sprouted like weeds through the budding treetops.

Petersen pointed north toward a high-rise, saying, "That's new, isn't it?"

"It was just forest last time you were up here."

He looked to the Southeast. "What about over there, just to the right of the National Cathedral?"

"Russian Embassy. It was still under construction when we were kids."

"Ah." Petersen stared for a moment before saying, "All I need to see," and cautiously descending from the roof.

April Twelve

At dawn, we made one last search for jaguars before heading back to meet Armando and the jeep. Pulling into the campsite around noon, we discovered Rolando already waiting to take me back to Flores. Dr. Berman was going to Tikal with the native guides, but Cortland was leaving the country, and hitched a ride with me.

I still had not decided whom to take into my confidence. Cortland to document the search? Leslie Berman with professional contacts and GPS? Armando and Carlos with experience and an off-road vehicle? Bringing strangers in on the recovery of an object worth approximately six million dollars seemed like an invitation for trouble.

One thing was sure; none of them would be in the area of the stone mounds the next day. I began to think it would be better that way. The first thing I did when I got back to Flores was rent a beat-up SUV. I was a little shaky about returning to the rain forest alone, but sure I could find the way.

The hotel provided a thermos of iced cappuccino and a box lunch. I took a nap in the evening and left at midnight, intending to hide the rental vehicle near the end of the jeep trail at dawn.

April Thirteen

Where the tire ruts petered out, I pulled into the bushes and covered the exposed fenders with brush. I obliterated the telltale tread-marks, and continued on foot.

With the aid of a compass, I followed the crude trail through the surrounding wilderness. As we had cleared the path the previous day, my little machete was unnecessary. I found a stick with which to knock away cobwebs, and struck a steady pace. After an hour my sweat had evaporated and I became slightly more comfortable with the humidity. The path was mostly in shade, and I made good time.

Approaching the mound of boulders, the track wound through pieces of limestone that had been carved by the elements into shapes that in my imagination began to resemble bones. At the base of the pile, I looked around for snakes and prepared to climb.

A rattle stopped me dead in my tracks. Cold-blooded animals remain active all year in the tropics, but even after being warned, I hadn't anticipated much of a problem. Despite popular misconception to the contrary, pit vipers such as rattlesnakes do have the ability to hear. The first rattler's signal had apparently alarmed the entire community of serpents. As I slowly backed away, about a dozen of the creatures slid from crevices around the rock pile and took up positions along the path leading to the summit. I was afraid of being flanked from the rear, and retreated even farther. The posture of the new arrivals was not menacing; the snakes merely seemed curious, wishing to inspect the intruder.

It took a half-hour to collect sufficient dry tinder for a fire. I built a stack of wood as close to the mound as I dared, and began advancing upward by systematically carrying burning sticks up the rock pile. I took my time, and the rattlers did as well, reluctantly slithering to the sides, or disappearing into crevasses. The kindling was still a bit green and smoked considerably. I hoped the flames would remain lit long enough for me to clamber up and search.

At the pinnacle of the formation, three stones formed an alcove. I was able to slide one of the heavy slabs far enough to make an opening. Kneeling, I cautiously peered in, not wanting to disturb a sleeping reptile. A pile of what appeared to be decaying leaves occupied the dark space. I poked it with my walking stick, expecting to rile a nest of horrors. When nothing happened, I tried to screw up enough courage to reach in. The air held a static charge in the dry heat of stones that had baked under centuries of intense sunlight. My pulse increased with excitement and anticipation.

At the sound of a rattle close behind, my hand jerked back instinctively. I looked around; not only were the serpents returning, but a glint of light flashed in the nearby forest. Only a manmade object would cause a reflection of that quality. I had certainly created enough smoke to draw attention. Choosing to err on the side of caution, I quickly pushed the stone back into place, and began to descend the mound, trying to appear frustrated.

Upon reaching ground level, I was suddenly confronted by two small dark men entering the clearing. My assumption had been correct; a man made object had reflected the sunlight. The glimmer had originated from the polished barrel of a long rifle. The second man was armed with a pistol. Carelessly holding their firearms at the ready, the duo was smiling, their expressions particularly menacing due to a noticeable absence of teeth. The fiendish twin with the handgun spat out what seemed a question in a dialect I didn't recognize. I held my palms open as he violently gesticulated with the weapon. Having gotten through most of my life without facing one single threatening gun, it seemed that lately it was becoming an undesirable habit.

Petersen was obviously proud of his latest development. Carlton Jains commented that the electronic equipment appeared to be in even greater disarray than on previous visits to the improvised laboratory. Unperturbed, the physicist continued explaining the new idea.

"Remember that electromagnetic waves were going to provide the means of creating entangled particles?"

Jains distractedly looked up from typing a text message on his phone. "I don't understand. I thought you were using 'gamma rays.'"

"All electromagnetic radiation-radio signals, microwaves, visible light, ultraviolet frequencies, gamma rays-behaves the same way. The difference between them is their wavelength, but the phenomena are identical."

"So that's why you were asking about radio antennas? To broadcast gamma rays?"

"You got it. Actually, I need what is called an isotropic radiator. I found a way to tap into the power of someone else's microwave transmissions. I can hijack the energy to boost and relay the gamma frequency broadcast, and no one will notice that I am piggybacking on the signal. Best of all, using simple GPS coordinates, I can relay my remote signal directly back here."

"That's why you were checking out the Russian Embassy? You're planning to use their antennas!"

"Almost poetic, isn't it?"

The sharp report of a gunshot sent the birds skittering, and within seconds the forest plunged into silence. Although I was petrified, I was also strangely composed in my daze. My ears whistled. I looked down and realized that I was unscathed. The next interrogative was shouted in guttural but recognizable Spanish.

My answer was apparently unsatisfactory; the pistol spoke again, and this time an electric shock surged through my arm. A crimson welt appeared on my left shoulder. Almost immediately, the entire jungle seemed to explode with gunfire. There was no immediate pain, only a terrifying awareness that I was in deep trouble.

Suddenly the men were moving fast. I couldn't think clearly. Was I mortally wounded? Should I play dead? If I fell, would the snakes attack? I clutched at the wound and realized I had stopped breathing.

A half-dozen ruffians appeared mysteriously from the jungle like wraiths of death, far worse in aspect than the two little toothless brigands. The newcomers' weapons appeared to be sophisticated, positively sinister, oozing with the sheer evil of machines created for purposes of which only the devil himself could conceive. My original attackers fled into the forest, which further added to my confusion.

It was frustrating to go down without a fight, but I was facing insurmountable odds. I dropped to my knees to get out of the line of fire, applied pressure to the wound and waited for doom.

Part Five

"So I don't get it, Don. I looked all around; antennas everywhere. But there's nothing sticking up from the roof of the Russian Embassy."

"Their antenna is fractal, CJ."

"I've heard you use that word before."

"Like your phone. You don't need a long wire, or one of those ridiculous clothes-hanger jobs with different loops tuned to specific frequencies. Shapes that have been reiterated in a space-filling curve are conducive to both transmission and reception."

Petersen went on to explain that due to the fractals, a single antenna could accommodate multiple bandwidths. The thin flat copper configurations had been built into the exterior walls of the Russian building.

Jains preferred to remain ignorant, and shrugged it off.

"Whatever; just as long as it works."

I felt like the sky was going to cave in, but the gunfire ceased.

"The fuck you doin' here, Yankee?"

The words seemed odd at first. I had been expecting the explosion that would finish me off. Through a tunnel created by my swimming vision, my attention focused on what appeared to be a guerrilla soldier standing over me. Boots, fatigues, backpack. Was that an American-made weapon? An M16 rifle? Big gun at any rate. The man had a military appearance, camouflage, bush hat, sunglasses, and a kerchief over the mouth. Did people such as this really exist? A moment passed before it registered that the words had been spoken in English. At least there was some chance of communication.

My voice wouldn't cooperate, but I finally struggled to my feet and squeezed out a constipated "Mayan Artifacts." The response was a blank grin, so I tried it in my feeble Spanish, "Soy antropólogo. Estoy en busca de artefactos Mayas."

The man laughed cynically, and the rest of the entourage joined in. This would be the leader. He glanced around, and the levity ceased as if on cue. I tried to focus, but pain was setting in.

The big man continued in mixed English, "So you find the forest people, no es?"

"I'd say they found me."

The chuckles that followed this remark were not particularly reassuring.

The soldier spoke again. "The Uchben Itza take it serious the privacy. Pero, este not so good por my business when they kill the traveler, and is come the government. Comprende, amigo?"

Smugglers then. Not renegade militia. I nodded meekly, saying, "You are simply passing through. You want no problem."

"Tu es smart hombre, Señor Antropólogo." He took a flask from his belt, and held it toward me. Tequila. It was a gesture to be appreciated, no matter what my fate. I took a good long belt. Live or die, the liquor would help.

The group laughed hoarsely. I guessed it was in approval of my gameness. At the tall man's signal, the band of smugglers faded back into the undergrowth and disappeared into the jungle.

Is tequila antiseptic? I figured I could spare a little, and cautiously poured a good swallow onto the area around the wound. Thankfully, I no longer seemed to be losing a substantial amount of blood. I vaguely remembered something about not lying down after sustaining upper body punctures. Makes it too easy for the blood to pump out.

Even light cotton cloth is incredibly hard to tear with one hand. It took considerable effort to wad up some strips from my shirt, and plug the gash in my shoulder. The skin covering the deltoid muscle had been torn. It looked to me as if a small caliber bullet had grazed the surface. I stood resting my back against a tree trunk, applying compression to the wound until the bleeding stopped completely and my pounding heart slowed to a relatively normal rhythm.

I assumed that the first attackers would return as soon as the smugglers were out of the area. I wasn't getting any stronger. Resisting the urge to belt down more liquor, I furtively hustled down the trail, hoping that my vehicle was still hidden in the bush. If the car was not still parked where I had left it, regaining the main road on foot would take an entire day.

Maybe it was the liquor, maybe the shock or fever, but I have almost no memory of finding my way out of the rain forest. It seems clichéd, but faced with death as the only alternative, one foot follows the other automatically. As long as the will to live remains, the body somehow finds the strength to go on. After finishing the leftovers from the hotel lunch, I tried to use the tequila to generate energy. Beyond that I merely kept moving. There would be no rescue, no cavalry, no miracle.

By late afternoon I reached the place where the SUV was stashed, and was not surprised to discover the space empty. I staggered on zombie-fashion. Before it got completely dark, I had the presence to note a compass heading before leaving the trail to find a hiding place. I could follow the magnetic needle back to the tire ruts in the morning, but I had nothing left for this day. Gigantic tree roots confounded my feet, indicating their wish that I fall among them. I nestled in a seated position between the Mahogany arches and slept fitfully through the night.

April Fourteen

At first light, my march resumed. After washing the wound with more tequila, I ripped the sleeves of my shirt into strips, and tied them around my armpit and shoulder. The rutted dirt track made for slow going, but the hike didn't seem that bad considering I had been shot. Continuously bearing the entire weight of a pack intended for two arms, my right shoulder ached almost as much as my left. I guessed the distance to the road at ten miles; it took a little more than five hours before I reached the highway.

I managed to hitch a ride all the way to Flores on a truck already overloaded with men that appeared to be local laborers. Thankfully, the hotel staff recognized me; my clothes were in shreds, and I stank of sweat and liquor. I could easily have been mistaken for a drunken bum. Mid afternoon, I was soaking in a tub of scalding water.

The bullet had missed the bone. All my vaccinations had been updated before undertaking this trip, including one for tetanus. Provided no infection set in, I didn't see the point in seeking medical attention locally. Practitioners of Western Medicine are difficult to find in that part of the world. In any event, I planned to return to the States immediately. The search for the mask was going to have to wait until I was ready to sling a backpack again. I booked a seat on the next day's flight to Miami, ate a rare steak to replenish my lost blood, and slept the rest of the afternoon.

When I called Hector Ramirez in the evening, he insisted on sending a car for me. After accepting his profuse apologies, I followed again through the house to the garden. I recounted the tale with more detail than I had given him over the telephone. He was thoughtful, and extended the courtesy of his fine old rum.

"Please understand, Señor Shaw; to my knowledge, the Uchben, or 'old order' Itza are a modern myth, a fabled tribe that inhabits the rain forest."

"Why would they be concerned about me exploring the jaguar habitat?"

"To understand this, we must go back to the early civilizations. Long before the term "Maya" came into existence, there were many tribes, many cities, many rulers, and they waged wars against each other.

"When the Spanish came, some local sects allied themselves to the invaders to help vanquish native enemies. In some locations, the Mayan religion became intertwined with Catholicism.

"The Itza civilization had spread north from El Peten into the Yucatan for five hundred years, becoming a powerful nation before finally submitting to Spanish rule near the end of the seventeenth century. The "Old Itza" are alleged to have never succumbed to the Spanish, and kept the aboriginal religion pure."

Ramirez stopped abruptly, crossed his arms and pondered.

"Do you believe the Uchben Itza are interested in the mask," I prodded, "or was this just a coincidence?"

"Until now, I did not believe in their existence. Just because a smuggler used the term isn't proof…still…I know that the modern Itza population still flourishing in Guatemala today can be traced directly back to pre-colonial cultures, even though their language is almost entirely extinct. The mask represents the means of returning to power, a physical connection to the gods of the mythology. Is it possible that a faction of the Itza is aware that a search is underway…? This I have no way of knowing."

"It doesn't make sense that a group that is so fastidious about preserving their pre-contact heritage would be carrying modern weapons."

The Guatemalan shrugged. "This is true. I had not considered…Perhaps the smuggler was in error. It could easily be an entirely different group of rebels."

I had almost forgotten the dull ache in my arm. I must have winced when shifting positions; with a concerned expression

Ramirez poured more rum, and went on, "I fully understand your wish to recover at home Señor Shaw, but again, I will be more than happy to see to your comfort here in Flores."

"I'd only be a burden. Back in the States, I have things to take care of that don't require traipsing around jungles. I think the time off will give us a chance to review the clues. Do you think that while I am gone you can find out more about the Uchben Itza? Someone has been following me. If they are involved, it would certainly be pertinent."

"As you wish, Señor Shaw. I will of course compensate you for medical expenses. I will try to find the truth about the Uchben Itza. I believe you have accomplished much, and hope you will not give up on the search..."

I had not confessed that I believed the mask was hidden somewhere in the snake infested rock formations, or even hinted at the limestone mound's exact location. It was obvious that something had drawn me to the area. If Ramirez recovered the artifact himself, why would he bother to pay the reward?

"Believe me, Señor Ramirez, I'm as hooked as you."

April Fifteen

I managed to get a window seat over the port wing, ensuring protection for my throbbing shoulder. While everyone on the plane was made to turn off their electronic devices, I was still free to continue with pencil and paper, and began organizing my notes. I had been telling Ramirez the truth; reward notwithstanding, from a scientific standpoint the possible existence of the Uchben Itza was extraordinary. No way was I going to turn away from the search for the mask.

Isolated "primitive" populations exist in cultural pockets all over the globe. The Lacandon people of Mexico are one such group, direct descendants of pre-Colombian Meso-Americans that purposely remained segregated from the rest of the world. They were successful at maintaining their distance until the middle of the twentieth century. Cultures such as this provide an opportunity to look directly into the developmental stages of civilization. The problem is that as soon as contact is made, the evidence is tainted.

The Uchben Itza, if they really existed, had resisted the influence of European settlement in Central America. Although completely aware of the modern society surrounding them, these Mayans have allegedly chosen to live in the manner of their ancestors. If they could be found, the situation would be unique.

I had no desire to fend off the inevitable questions regarding a bullet wound that would arise at a hospital emergency room. Back in high school, I dated a girl that now practices veterinary medicine in Miami. I called from the airport, and she agreed to meet me at the nearby Sheraton. My injury was not going to require surgery. The animal doctor cleaned, stitched, and rebandaged my shoulder. With a handful of antibiotics to ward off evil, I finally felt safe enough to let down my guard. I pulled the heavy drapes and slept for eighteen hours.

April Sixteen

By the time I dragged myself out of bed it was too late to book a commuter flight. I took a cab to the airport and rented a car.

Miami rush hour. Zero to ninety and back to zero as fast as you can manage. At the first opportunity, I got on the turnpike, took the exit for Alligator Alley and headed across the Florida peninsula toward the sunset.

April Seventeen

I had arrived at Charley's in the evening, and briefly recounted the details of the adventure in Guatemala before retiring. When I awoke in the morning, Charley had already left for work. I integrated my few belongings with the indeterminable items that reside in the corner of my friend's spare bedroom. I unpacked the box from Ingrid and stared at the paltry contents. I hadn't left much behind. Maybe she had too little physical reassurance that I planned to return.

In the late afternoon, Charley came roaring in with armfuls of bags, eyes ablaze. I knew something was up, but he refused to tell me until after we put away the groceries, fired the grill, and sat down with a couple of beers.

"Been scopin' out this 'Petersen' dude."

"And?"

"Check this. You remember I said the cat was into intercellular communication? His work's been published in a couple of journals; I finally had time to flick through the articles. Interesting stuff, quorum sensing in macro-cellular structures."

I felt a sense of accomplishment upon realizing that I comprehended. Cells have a means of communicating to each other the point at which enough of them exist before they collectively begin performing their ultimate functions. Charley went on, "Next couple a years he's quiet, and then up pops an article in a journal called 'Quantum Optics and Electronics,' an analysis of frequency resonance in fractal media."

Now I began to get lost. "What does that mean..."

"Hang tight, slim. There's more. A piece on quantum entanglement appears a year later in a national publication. So he changed fields again!"

"So you put all this information together with what I overheard..."

"...And a pretty good guess is that he's somehow affecting cell development with controlled radiation, and there's some quantum level connection. So I check out his last known employer, the Defense Advanced Research Projects Agency, expecting to find a bunch of mumbo-jumbo, or top-secret subterfuge. What a hoot! They make no bones about what they are up to, almost as if they are daring you to invent weird technology before they can, knowing that you couldn't possibly command comparable resources. Matter of fact, if you have an idea, and can present it in a scientific manner, they might even do the research themselves! Some of the wild stuff they have actually created originally appeared in old sci-fi novels!"

"This is all out in the open?"

"The details of some specific experiments are classified, and there are doubtless projects underway that never appear to the public. I'm guessing that Donald Petersen's work falls into that category; apparently he was on their payroll but his proposal was not publicly mentioned on their list of projects. Before going under the Defense Department's umbrella, he wrote a letter to the editor of a peer-reviewed publication suggesting that he was 'leapfrogging' over technical advances; that is, projecting where the next phase of technology could lead, after quantum computing becomes commonplace, after the so-called 'God particle' is better understood. Following that, his published contributions ceased. Evidently at some point he stopped working for the government."

"That's when he turned up in the desert in Arizona."

"Not so fast, Jack. Dude secretly did more work at a privately owned weapons systems lab before he skedaddled. Apparently unauthorized."

"Which is why Homeland Security said I was meeting with a renegade!"

"Which brings up the next question: what is the illustrious Dr. Petersen up to now?"

April Eighteen

Piper called on my old cellular number, agitated and excited. I had not checked the messages since leaving Mexico for Guatemala.

"Stephen! I've been trying to reach you for days! Where are you?"

"I'm staying with Charley while I recuperate from..."

"You're in Florida? Thank heavens! I need to see you."

"I didn't realize you still felt so strongly..."

"Cut it out, Stephen. I am serious. Is Charley still at the same old place?"

"No, he has a house now, believe it or not. What's this all about?"

"I don't want to talk about it over the phone. I'll come right over."

I gave her directions, and she promised to meet me in two hours.

The machinery at the mansion seemed more complete than it had a few days before. Jains was eager to start the cure, and tried to pressure Petersen.

"You don't need much of an antenna to transmit the entanglement to me."

"No, you're right, CJ. I realize that patience is not one of your more prominent virtues, but repairing your injuries is a complicated procedure. If something goes wrong with a distant target that's one thing, but...well let's just say I'd hate for something bad to happen to you. There are a few things I need to check first."

The scar tissue looked a lot worse than it felt. The burns had left red marks and mottled scars on Carlton's neck and shoulder. The plastic surgeon had recommended skin grafts, but Carlton was depending on the quantum procedure.

"It worked on the rabbit."

The scientist cracked his knuckles. "I have a small confession to make."

"Don't fucking tell me that this whole thing is a crock of shit!"

Petersen laughed. "God, no CJ. I'm not that cruel. No, do you remember asking me if we were going to manipulate the intruder's molecules?"

"The woman at the camp? No shit! You did it, didn't you!"

"Not the entire genome. That's still extremely questionable. However, since her DNA was available, I was able to create an emergence event using information contained by a gene on chromosome fifteen."

"So fix my burns."

"Your situation is far more complicated. This was a slight variation in a simple polymer chain. I want to see the results before I go any further."

"How are you going to do that? Cut her open?"

"You are so extreme! No, when I see her, the effects will be obvious. I should be back in a few days."

Jains knew it was pointless to argue. A few days. Then the cure. After that, a quantum disarrangement of the DNA of one certain meddlesome anthropologist by the name of Stephen Shaw!

I was sitting on Charley's screened front porch when Piper arrived. It amused me to see her run from the car, the same gangly sprint that I remembered from so long ago. She wore a long-tailed shirt over a simple black tank top and skimpy khaki shorts. The ensemble gave the appearance of a short dress with little underneath. This too struck a resonant chord in my memory. A felt beret on her head seemed incongruous, and somewhat impractical in the Florida springtime heat.

Her hug was brief, but expressive. I could sense relief, as if she was finally letting down her guard after a long conflict.

"It's the weirdest thing..." she began, and then seemed at a loss. She doffed her cap and bowed her head so that I could get a closer look at something that was plainly evident; in stark contrast to her long gray tresses, the first inch or so of hair next to her scalp was growing out in the pale honey color of her youth.

"Wow." I instantly assumed it was related to the experiment in the desert.

"It started when I got back from Arizona. My hair is not the only thing that is different; I feel happy about the most insignificant things. It seems like food tastes better, my vision and hearing have improved, but it's not all good, either. I also seem more susceptible to certain allergies and irritants, stuff that's never bothered me before."

"It sounds as if you're getting younger."

"That's what I thought at first. No, look at my skin." She extended an arm. "Parts of it seem to be getting lighter, but the age spots are still there. I still have the same sags and wrinkles, the same old aches and pains. This is something else."

"You believe it has something to do with those scientists?"

"It almost has to, don't you think?"

I recalled the words of Carlton Jains, "Shoot your quantum gizmo at me."

I took Piper's hand, and patted it in the impotent universal gesture of reassurance.

"Charley should be home soon. You should explain it all to him."

Piper eyed me skeptically. "Just what do you think that beatnik can do?"

"You don't know about Charley? He's been working at the forefront of biotechnology ever since school. A little goofy maybe, but the guy is brilliant. He knows all about the latest breakthroughs and therapies."

Piper respected my opinion enough to reluctantly agree to tell Charley about her predicament. I suggested the most therapeutic thing I knew. We concocted a pair of large Mojitos, and recounted the events of the previous weeks in detail while waiting for my eccentric buddy to arrive.

Charley pulled into the driveway, and we went out to meet him. He had to have been surprised by Piper's presence, but it didn't show. Instead he seemed mildly amused.

"Are you two at it again?"

I was hoping to keep him serious, saying, "Piper wants to show you something," but he was already staring at her hair. He took a step forward, exclaiming, "Woot! Dude! I've seen 'blondes' go dark at the roots, but never..."

I tried to rein him in. "Woot? What the hell is 'woot'?"

Charley made a dismissive motion. "It's a figure of speech."

Piper shook her head in resignation, and shifted from foot to foot. She obviously felt that consulting Charley was a waste of time. I tried again.

"Charley, Piper has come a long way to see me. I think that scientist in Arizona caused this. It's a serious problem, and she needs help."

I could see the transformation on his face; his focus narrowed, and his eyes took on a dark intensity. Charley's powerful intellect was shifting into gear.

"Let's go inside." These simple words were spoken with a quiet tenacity that even Piper could feel. Her look of apprehension became one of hopefulness.

Almost as if the separate facets of his personality grudgingly share living space, Charley divides his house into dedicated areas. The kitchen is open to an informal den that reflects his passion for jazz. Thousands of vintage record albums line shelves along one wall. Posters, old musical instruments, and memorabilia decorate the room. Down the hall, the open door to his bedroom reveals austere décor. No books or television; this is a space reserved solely for sleeping.

At the back of the house is the room I was currently sharing with his collection of odd machines, boxes of wires, tools, spare parts, and exotic devices that appear to be specifically designed to confound any notion of their practical use. Across the hall from this is Charley's office, similar to the guest room in all respects except it lacks a bed.

Charley cleared some things away from a boxy machine that I did recognize, an electron microscope he inherited and modified when his lab had determined the machine to be obsolete. Much of his home setup had been furnished in that manner. He pulled on a pair of latex gloves and turned to Piper as she inspected the bizarre contents of the room with astonishment. For a fraction of a second, his expression softened.

"I'm sorry, but may I have a few hairs, please?"

The genteel demeanor startled Piper, having previously interacted with only Charley the jive-talking prankster. She complied distractedly, and I detected a sense of wonder. The exchange seemed to linger for a moment, as if they had just noticed each other for the first time.

Charley gingerly took the long strands with a pair of forceps, saying, "This will take a few minutes."

We watched Charley mount the hairs onto the specimen stub. Apparently, Piper knew something about the process; she was asking about fixatives and coatings. They began to discuss chemicals with which I am unfamiliar. I was suddenly struck by the thought that they were of an ilk; two lanky ectomorphs peering intently at their work like peculiar wading birds focused on the same school of minnows.

While I continued to notice similarities between my two friends, the fine texture of their hair, their long noses, their mental prowess, at the edge of my awareness, I registered that the specimen was being placed in the vacuum chamber. An image began to appear on the computer screen as the scanner collected data.

Charley manipulated the picture until finding the area he wished to explore. He reset the magnification, and a closer view appeared. As the image took shape, I assumed we were looking at the border between the blond and gray segments of Piper's hair. I asked, and received one of Charley's typical dismissive grunts in reply.

Charley made two more passes over the samples, one for each section of color. This time the magnification was so great that nothing was recognizable to me. The shapes, appearing as so many grains of sand, had an eerie three-dimensional quality. After enhancing the images with software, he made prints, and with an odd "Hmn," carried them to another computer. Piper silently shadowed him, looking over his shoulder. While the machine booted up, Charley muttered, "Just want to confirm."

Piper looked at me and I shrugged. With a smile and a nod, she redirected her attention to the screen. Images flashed, and then a match appeared. The similarities were obvious, even to me. Charley said, "Melanin. Could have guessed that."

Piper repeated the word "Melanin," questioning, "the pigment?" Charley turned and addressed the room at large, while his eyes never left her face.

"Throughout life, production of pigment changes, increases, decreases, or ceases entirely. But your hair doesn't turn gray due to a total lack of colorant; otherwise it would become transparent immediately. Black eumelanin gives it the gray until production of that stops too, and finally the hair appears white. On the other hand, without the presence of other pigments, closely related brown eumelanin will tint the hair yellow."

Piper wondered aloud in a timid voice, "So somehow my black pigment has become brown?"

Charley laid the pictures on the desk where all three of us could see them clearly. With a pencil, he pointed out the differences between the molecules.

"You can see that in this close-up of the gray segment, there is one configuration of shapes. In the blond section, this formation is different. Brown instead of black."

I was feeling relieved. This didn't seem so sinister. "That's it? They turned her from gray to blond? Are you kidding? People would kill for this technology!"

"Not so fast, Steve." Charley resumed watching Piper's face. "The function of melanin is not well understood."

Piper interjected, "I thought that the latest evidence demonstrates that northern people evolved light complexions to facilitate the absorption of vitamin D from sunlight."

"Right. Certainly an advantage in the higher latitudes, but a reaction to sunlight does not explain the presence of concentrated pigmentation elsewhere in the body, places that never see the light of day, like the inner ear and the brain. Melanin is also related to other chemical processes."

"So all the pigment in my body may have been affected?"

"Like Steve said, people would kill for this technology. I have no idea how such a change could have been effected, or what it would do elsewhere in the system. We could take a look at some other cells."

"If the pigment has been changed, what kind of affect will it have on me?"

Charley shrugged, "Some people have black eumelanin, some have brown. I don't think there's a fundamental distinction, but who knows? Studies suggest that there are varying perceptions of pain associated with a person's specific natural colorations."

"Well, I have been feeling...different lately. Can we do that? Look at some other cells?"

Charley seemed pleased with Piper's wish to continue the investigation. I was thrilled that my old friends seemed to be hitting it off under the circumstances, and volunteered to fix something for dinner while they continued to work.

It did not take much to persuade Piper to stay the night. There was plenty to talk about, and she was facing a long drive. After accepting the invitation, she made no move to contact anyone at home. I asked if anyone would be missing her.

"I have an independent lifestyle; there's no one I need to call."

"What about Jonathan?" I wondered aloud.

"Ah, Jonathan," she shrugged. "The trip to Arizona did us in. We got along in many ways, but fundamentally, we were light years apart. Metaphysical naturalism is about as close as I get to a religious belief. Jonathan practices some convoluted form of New Age Zen. I drink iced tea because it's refreshing; he drinks it to put more yin yang in his Feng Shui. It couldn't last. Eventually the relationship imploded."

Charley seemed tickled. I couldn't tell if it was Piper's brief levity, or the fact that she had recently become single that lightened his mood. Passing up his usual intense saxophone music, he tuned in some mellow Van Morrison on the satellite radio.

As we sat down to dinner, the conversation briefly turned away from the problem at hand. Charley continued to speak English like a normal person.

"Steve says you're a consultant these days."

"Yes, for a firm that designs systems for business."

"For that they need an anthropologist?"

"To predict how humans will interact within a designed environment."

"Such as?"

"Well, a bank for example. After the processing systems are developed, they need to be implemented in a manner that is efficient for the tellers and officers. Workplace design influences productivity. Every detail, such as paint color or ambient temperature, exerts an effect. Then there are the customers, traffic flow, waiting time, and so on. Do the patrons feel secure? At what height should the countertop be situated? I analyze cultural trends to provide this sort of data. That reminds me; I'm giving a presentation this week. What am I going to do about my hair?"

"Color it?"

"Believe me, my firm also turns its analytic eye inward. Our presentations are well rehearsed. Preconceptions provide useful leverage for manipulation. When I show up with long gray hair and an outfit that subliminally suggests a safari, my credibility is much more readily accepted. I resemble a preconceived image of an anthropologist; therefore what I say is likely to be correct. My boss will have a conniption if I don't show up in character."

"Dye the roots gray," I suggested.

"Then I won't know what is happening underneath."

"How about a pith helmet?"

"Perfect. I'll carry a bullwhip and a buck knife while I'm at it." Piper let out a long sigh. "What am I going to do? Just the idea of that creep pointing a 'quantum gizmo' at me freaks me the fuck out."

Charley's eyes widened upon hearing the colloquial profanity. Apparently he took it as a cue that the atmosphere had become more casual. His reply was worded in a more customary idiom.

"We gotta check the dude out, suss what's goin' down."

"You would do that?" Piper seemed surprised.

Charley turned his palms upward. "Who else you gonna call?"

April Nineteen

Charley had insisted on sleeping on the couch, leaving the bedroom for Piper. In the morning we sat around the kitchen table drinking coffee. I voiced a few thoughts that had come to me overnight.

"Pigmentation is one of the most powerful engines of evolution, and operates in a variety of ways. As you observed yesterday, northern races seem to have evolved pale skin to better synthesize vitamin D at latitudes with less sunshine."

Piper encouraged, "Go on."

"Lighter pigmented people may have been able to survive in habitats for which they became adapted, but they certainly did not choose polar climes for their comfort or the bounty of the land. Currently accepted models suggest that all humans originated in Africa. Starting with the "Out of Africa" or "Recent Single-Origin" hypothesis, and the fact that genetic diversity in the human genome decreases the farther the population is from the equator, I submit that the natural selection process could quite possibly have worked in reverse."

"Another of your left-handed theories?"

"Does it make sense that northerners would develop pale complexions as an advantage while simultaneously losing the obvious benefit of adaptability that the preservation of a wider array of genetic possibilities provides? Given the nature of groups, I'd say that it is just as likely that individuals displaying particular traits were ostracized, formed their own societies and interbred. The recessive traits became reinforced, and the outsiders were pushed farther away from the core group. This resulted in survival of the least fit, or rather the genetically least diverse, certainly a long term disadvantage."

"So our ancestors didn't wander out of Africa, they were chased?"

"While that is an interesting concept, it's not where I am headed. What I'm getting at is this; Charley said yesterday that the various functions of melanin are not well understood. If the evolution of pigmentation is propelled by the sense of sight, then the levels of melanin available to the brain are being determined by processes that are unrelated to the chemical's neurological function."

"So changing the molecular structure of the pigment in my hair may have affected the melanin my brain?"

"It would explain why you have been feeling different lately."

Charley started typing furiously on his laptop, and paused to relate that melanin is a precursor chemical in the body's production of dopamine, the powerful neurotransmitter and hormone.

Piper's despair was plainly evident. Charley and I promised that we would get to the bottom of things. When Piper left to return home, I had the impression that our reassurances had failed to bring any cheer.

Petersen's web search had revealed professional listings, but not a home address for the woman. No matter. Harmodyne, her place of employment, was easy to locate. If he did not spot Ms. Locke in the employee parking area, he would certainly be able to find her at the weekend symposium where she was listed as a speaker. Attending the event would increase the risk of being seen, so he hoped to catch a glimpse as she entered or exited the workplace.

The physicist sat in his rental car as the parking lot filled in the morning, without success. Not wanting to become obvious by staking out the building all day, he went to the beach after the morning rush, and enjoyed a break from his routine. It gave him time to contemplate without the usual self-imposed pressure. In the late afternoon he returned to watch the exits. As the flow of homebound workers thinned out, he spotted Piper Locke walking to her car. Except for the long gray ponytail, a hat covered her hair. It was inconclusive evidence, but a positive sign that the process was likely to have worked.

On our own again in the evening, Charley and I enjoyed one of our extended, convoluted discussions. At one point we touched briefly on the particulars of Piper's situation. I was curious what neurological effect might result from the alteration to her melanin, but we easily became sidetracked.

"So pigmentation in the brain is developed in an evolutionary cul-de-sac?"

Charley seemed amused by the analogy. "More like a dead-end, Chief. But dig; neuromelanin is a different beast."

"So you were yanking Piper's chain?"

"Not at all, dude. If this Petersen cat screwed with the molecular structure of a basic polymer, what's to say how far it goes? It could have a profound effect."

"I got the impression that you and Piper found each other... interesting."

"Yeah?"

"Hey, I'm not jealous or anything. I've got my own relationship complications. If Piper and I had a thing for each other, it would have happened long before now."

"Honestly, Steve, working with the chick is a ball. She's brilliant, but the cool thing is that we are old enough now that the 'sex thing' didn't get in the way. And what a wild situation! Unraveling this one's gonna be a bitch."

Charley always did enjoy a good puzzle, but I didn't believe him about the sex.

April Twenty

In the morning, I drove up to Tampa to watch Piper give her presentation. Although she seemed grateful for the presence of a friend, I did not make the two-hour trip for entirely selfless reasons. Piper earned a good salary working as an anthropologist, and I was still unemployed. She had offered to introduce me around. An environment where a jacket and tie are required didn't interest me much, but perhaps after completing my assignment in Guatemala, I could find work doing consulting, statistical analysis, or related research.

I did dress to make a decent first impression. The air-conditioned breakout room was freezing. It made me almost glad to be wearing my aged but seldom used navy blazer.

Petersen seemed right at home as he scoped out the convention center. A sandwich board indicated the conference room where Harmodyne, Inc. was having its meeting. Across the lobby was an open lounge area. He took a seat with a view of the entrance and waited.

The woman appeared, head still covered, and at her side was the man from the trailer fire. That explained things, but now there was just too much chance of being noticed. Petersen covered his face with his hands. He would have to assume that the experiment had been a success.

As the pair of anthropologists entered the lecture room, Donald Petersen furtively headed for the exit. He would be aboard an evening flight to Washington.

Quantum Voodoo

Driving back to Charley's that afternoon, I realized that the sensation of being watched was still nagging me. I found myself reflexively looking back to see if the same car was always in the mirror. At the grocery store, I searched the faces of the other shoppers. Carrying the bags to the car, I paused suddenly to look behind and see if anyone else did the same. Tourists are common in Florida; cameras are everywhere. Were they pointing at me? Was I suffering from paranoia as a result of being shot?

Charley laughed at me, but I pulled the blinds and double-checked the locks before crashing for the night.

April Twenty-one

While Petersen had been in Florida, Jains had been studying the equipment. After all, he was footing the bill; the technique belonged to him as much as to his partner. Petersen was being far too scrupulous. After hearing about the change in hair color, Jains intended to learn how to do the process on his own. The two men met in the laboratory room.

"Give me some good news, Don."
"She's still above ground, CJ."
"So we can get started?"
"If you're sure you want to be a guinea pig."
"I have faith, Donnie. Let's do it."
"The first thing we need to do is culture some cells."

Carlton Jains had been establishing an agenda and intended to advance it without interference. He observed the proceedings with rapt attention.

I met several interesting people at Piper's convention, and had high hopes that some form of employment would come from the introductions. My calls to Ingrid still went unanswered. With Charley gone during the day, it was easy to concentrate in the silent house. I dove into writing up an account describing the search for the mask and putting the clues in chronological order.

After work, Charley came rolling in with a case of beer and a new idea. It took a few minutes to decipher what he was babbling about. The gist was, while Piper and I would be identified immediately, Dr. Charles Pulaski could investigate the quantum conspirators incognito. What he was suggesting was a road trip.

April Twenty-two

Jains was watching Petersen tinker with the gamma ray generator. The scientist re-calibrated the machine for close-quarters implementation.

Carefully taking note, Jains asked, "So now that we have cultivated the cells, what's next?"

The physicist answered without looking up. "The only reason that things are going so fast is that I've done this before. Don't be in such a hurry; we still have to test the machinery before we do the procedure."

Petersen seemed satisfied with the adjustments, and began closing up the housing.

"Help me get this on the table."

The two men wrestled the heavy contraption onto the plywood surface. Petersen aligned the machine to point at what looked like a glass satellite dish on the other side of the room. A third apparatus completed an equilateral triangle between the devices. Petersen began describing the procedure.

"The signal is generated here." He pointed at the metal canister housing the modified vacuum tube. "It enters the linear accelerator, and passes through the crystal," he continued, gesturing at a long cylinder. "Some of the photons become entangled and split into separate waves. One of these waves is absorbed by the target."

"Me."

"Right, in this case, you. The corresponding half of the stream is picked up in the dish, and sent to the receiver," pointing at the third machine, "where it is absorbed in the cloned cells."

"And now the cells are entangled?"

Petersen rolled his eyes. "Particles, not cells, but for the sake of discussion, let's say that they are entangled. As the particle stream continues to flow, healthy skin stem cells are introduced to the damaged ones in the model. The cells contained in the model join to form a community, and micro-DNA begins to issue instructions, causing emergence. Your cells receive information from the newly altered companion particles. The exchange of information induces a corresponding reaction in your body, based on the new paradigm. Stimulated by the low-dosage radiation, your cells take over the process, reproducing in the new configuration. In effect, this causes a mutation of the granular scar tissue. 'Normal' skin regenerates and displaces the fibrous healing matrix."

Jains stared down at the mottled scars on his arm. "How long before I see results?"

"A skin-cell cycle takes about a month, give or take a week or so," Petersen could see that his friend thought that was too long, "so let's get this test up and running."

Charley had packed up some boxes, and enlisted my help to load them in the car.

"Wouldn't you rather fly?" I wondered.

"Dig, show up at the airport with this shit?"

"What is all this stuff?"

"I'll clue you on the ride, bubba. Besides, your boys might not be hangin' at the crib. We got to go mobile."

I had easily found the address of Carlton Jains' Washington residence, but had no idea if he was back at home. There had not been any sign of Petersen, so this was our only lead. Charley said that by alternating turns at the wheel, we could drive straight through, and arrive in Washington within sixteen hours. He was gung-ho, and I had little on my dance-card. If nothing else, it would give me something easy to do while my wound healed.

Charley took the first stint at the wheel. I tried to doze so as to be fresh when my turn came. We were still several hours south of the Florida border when I awoke.

"So Charley, what is all that stuff in the boxes?"

"Everything I could lay my hands on quickly that might be used to detect electromagnetic radiation. A hand-held Geiger counter. Unexposed film. Different bandwidth radios. A microwave receiver. An infrared rifle scope."

"Because they were talking about gamma rays?"

"You got it. I also brought along a few toys, in case we need to play games."

"Such as?"

Charley just laughed. Eventually I gave up. With his sense of humor, toys and games could mean almost anything.

April Twenty-three

Approaching the Nation's Capitol, Charley insisted on taking over at the wheel. At the beginning of the evening rush hour, he exited the interstate. From the densely wooded two-lane byway he had taken, we could see bumper-to-bumper traffic stalled on the highway overpasses as we rolled along unimpeded. I was impressed.

"How did you know to take this road?"

"While you were gallivanting around the globe, I did a stint in Washington, remember? I drove a lot while carrying samples to different labs, got fed up with the traffic, and discovered alternate routes. It probably takes just as long to get anywhere, but the aggravation you save is worth the extra miles."

On the dash-mounted GPS, I followed our progress into the city. Even in the descending dusk, the area looked lush with new growth on the trees and banks of blooming azaleas. The road climbed from the riverbed into rolling hills. We found the correct street and turning onto it, I was astounded. Expecting a cityscape, the winding asphalt lane parting perfectly manicured lawns came as a surprise.

Charley drove slowly past the address, saying, "No way to stake this joint out from the car."

The house was gargantuan, set back from the road at the top of a hill. Stone sculptures graced the sloping lawn leading to the mansion. A serpentine driveway led through the front of the property, and exited on the other side. The garage alone was two stories, as large as the house where I had spent my childhood. Charley was right; no cars were parked on the suburban style street. We would be painfully obvious sitting there.

"I guess this is where I take over," he continued.

We drove around to scope out the neighborhood for a while, and pulled into the deserted parking lot of a nearby church. Charley took the handheld Geiger counter from the trunk. I got into the driver's seat, dropped him at the top of the hill above the mansion, and returned to find an inconspicuous parking space on the congested street near United Methodist. I walked back toward Carlton Jains' house, thankful to stretch my legs.

Charley strolled along slowly, watching the Geiger counter. The neighborhood was beautiful in the blue-gray of evening, but no pedestrians were out and about, no one walking a dog, not even any cars going by.

A few lights were on behind the curtains of the big house. Pretending the little radiation detector was a phone, Charley put it up to his ear and faked a conversation. He paused and gestured, putting his foot on the curb and then pacing in circles. After a good look at the house, he finished the "call" and ambled on down the hill.

There had to be some other access; surely people that live in such palaces do not haul their trashcans down the driveway to the street. Charley continued down a long block, took the next turn, and circled around. Backing the house was dense forest; the mansion was not even visible. Getting closer was going to be tricky.

As I passed a wooded area, someone behind me growled, "Nice night." It gave me a start, but I recognized the voice immediately.

"Very funny."

Charley stepped out of the bushes, saying, "Ain't a soul on the street."

"How about radiation?"

"Can't get close enough to test."

"We don't even know if they're in there, Charley."

"Gonna have to find a hidey hole."

"What say we find a hotel and some dinner?"

The lights flickered ever so slightly when Petersen threw the power switch. Before the brain could register the occurrence, the treatment was complete. The physicist said, "OK," and powered down.

"What's wrong?"

"Nothing, CJ. That's it."

Jains suspiciously inspected his shoulder. "That's it?"

"The initial event is over. It will take a while to document the results."

"That fast?"

"The speed of light, CJ."

Jains drew back the lead-lined curtain that Petersen had hung in the corner. The physicist had assured that the protective cover was necessary. There would be repeated exposure to potentially harmful radiation during the procedure. A little was tolerable, and in fact essential to the process, but multiple treatments could cause cell damage. Jains had said, "So what? We can repair the destruction, can't we?" but Petersen assured that it was a bad idea.

"Now what?"

"Now we wait until some new cells grow."

April Twenty-four

When I awoke, Charley was gone. We had checked into a motel in nearby Bethesda, Maryland, about four miles from the Spring Valley mansion. Even though my shoulder seemed to be healing nicely, I was still a little weak, and the long drive from Florida had worn me out. I had hardly been able to keep my eyes open long enough for a pizza delivery to arrive. There was a note on the table instructing me to call when I got up. I made coffee and showered first.

There was no answer at Charley's number. After a minute, the chime tone sounded on my phone, signifying receipt of a text message. The note was short: "3250 Nebraska Ave. Call from there." Assuming he had taken the car, I summoned a taxi.

The cab driver seemed confused by the directions; on the avenue where the address indicated, there was an open area of park, but no building. I recognized the surroundings, paid the fare, and called Charley's number again from the sidewalk. By way of reply, Charley momentarily appeared down the road. Placing a finger to his lips, he beckoned. I silently followed him over a small chain-link fence, into a densely wooded area. He led the way through the trees to a spot commanding a view of the Jains mansion.

Charley was well prepared for a stakeout, with binoculars, a digital camera, the Geiger counter, and a bag full of snacks. I thanked him for letting me sleep in and gratefully accepted a package of trail mix. The morning slowly slipped by.

My mind was wandering when an elbow in the ribs gave me a start. I followed Charley's gaze up toward the roof. Two men were scrambling toward the peak, pulling what appeared to be a satellite antenna up behind them. I snatched up the camera, and zoomed in. There was the confirmation we needed. Carlton Jains was at home all right, and Petersen was with him.

"Dude with that kind of bread don't hang his own satellite dish," Charley observed.

Jains and Petersen descended from the roof and led a cable down to the first floor.

"Now that the antenna is up, who's first on the list?"

"What list, CJ?"

"Come on, Don. Whose particles are you planning to rearrange?"

"Until we run this test, I don't even know if the antenna is going to work."

"Don't give me that. You used the method on the woman. You used it on me. Even if the antenna doesn't work, the entanglement does. You said so yourself."

"I also said that I only approached this invention from the point of view of a weapons system as a way to get funding."

"And so you did. Funding from me. Now I want to see the results of my investment."

"For which you have to wait and see if your skin grows back."

"But in the meantime, I want to know what else it can do."

Petersen dreaded what might come next. "What do you have in mind?"

Jains gestured with forefinger and thumb. "You manipulate the molecules, Donnie. I'll manipulate the people."

We crept from the woods and returned to the car. Charley opened the trunk, and handed me the keys, saying, "Ride around and find a hill, someplace where we can hang without drawing attention."

"A hill?"

"A rooftop might work too. Somewhere we can cop the signal."

"How are we going to do that?"

"Inverse square law, dude."

"Is that supposed to mean anything to me?"

"If they are using a 'Gamma ray to rearrange somebody's molecules,' then I'm guessing that's some sort of transmitter up on the roof. The farther we get from it, the greater the beam's width, and the weaker the signal. If we can measure the angle, maybe we can figure out what the target is."

"What if you're wrong about the gamma rays?"

"Then you had a nice little sight-seeing tour."

"What are you going to do?"

"Now that the antenna dish is in place, I'm betting they will test the so-called 'gizmo.' I'm going down to the house to check for radiation."

"What if they catch you?"

Charley pulled a hard-hat and a clipboard from one of the boxes we had loaded. "Abnormality in the pressure line, dude," he grinned. "Checking the natural gas meter for leaks. Want to convey authority? A clipboard beats the shit out of a badge!"

Piper Locke looked in the mirror one last time before donning the beret, crossing her fingers, and heading to the mall. Almost twenty-five years had passed since her last disastrous attempt at a different hairdo. When the gruesome disco-era shag cut had grown out, she had resigned herself to trimming the frizzled ends of her long ponytail, and keeping the style forever. She had gone completely gray before her twenty-eighth birthday.

Piper had rehearsed a lie about a dye job gone wrong. The fresh blond had spread to her eyebrows and lashes as well, but the chatty beauticians did not seem to notice. The stylist cut away the gray, shaping the contours of a short bob to de-accentuate the length of Piper's nose and highlight her steely gray eyes.

Exiting the beauty parlor, Piper looked at her reflection in plate glass windows as she passed the rows of shops, startled by the image. The khaki shorts and long-tailed shirt that had for so long seemed a casual indication of scholarly professionalism suddenly exuded a provocative classiness. Piper could feel the heat of men staring as she strode to the parking lot. She hated to admit enjoying the ego boost, but damn it felt good!

Charley sent a text message, and I met him at the bottom of the hill. He was chatting with an older woman and surreptitiously gestured for me to drive on. I waited around the corner. As it turned out, the woman was Carlton Jains' neighbor. The man from the "Gas Company" had created a cover by checking the house next door first. Relieved that there were no leaks at her own home, the neighbor lady had accompanied Charley up the Jains' driveway, reinforcing the flimsy alias.

Tossing the hard hat on the floor, Charley slid into the passenger seat, saying, "Positive for gamma frequency radiation, Stevie."

"You're sure?"

He showed me the readout on the little yellow plastic device. I questioned the accuracy of the instrument.

"Take my word, dude. This thing is foolproof. Every real estate agent should cop one of these babies. Can't be selling houses full of Radon gas. The average home in this kind of neighborhood does not emit radiation. They're up to something all right. You find a spot?"

"I didn't realize it, but this house is at the top of a large hill. The next rise is a long ridge a couple of miles away, and it's covered with buildings."

"Wonder if that's where they're aiming?"

Petersen was soldering capacitors into a new power supply designed to make the gamma ray system smaller and less cumbersome. He looked over the top of his reading glasses.

"I don't know what you think we can do, CJ. If you want to reap a profit, we have to offer the method to the government, and we can't do that without more extensive testing."

Jains' reply was terse. "Well, I for one have no desire to spend the next five years farting around with rabbits. If you don't have any intended targets, I can think of a few. The kind of profit I am after is not simply monetary. There are other ways to use this."

"Such as?"

"I could exact cooperation from some influential people in exchange for miraculously curing mysterious symptoms that abruptly afflict them."

"You mean extortion."

"Extortion seems like such a harsh word. How about 'persuasion'?" Petersen recalled his friend's lust for vengeance and dominance in the schoolyard. "I guess some things never change. Well, you can count me out." He went back to concentrating on the electronics.

"I don't think so, Don. Where will you get funding to continue your work? I own all your equipment. You might walk out of here with your files, but you'll have no physical proof to offer the next investor. Coming to me was your last resort; we both know that, but hear me out. I'm not planning anything that will compromise your precious integrity."

Petersen remained silent, knowing there was little choice. It was Carlton Jains' turn to explain.

"The way I see it, Don, the democrats are throwing up blockades, interfering with business, running up the national debt, raising taxes. We could do the country a great service by persuading some of the noisiest liberals to stand down."

The physicist paused while considering the ramifications, finally answering, "While I certainly approve of less interference from the government, on a scientific level the conservatives would plunge us back into the dark ages. I'm a physicist, CJ. Without government funding, we would lose our technological edge. You want to help empower creationists? Allow the church to influence the business of running the country? Continue to promote an ideology that was developed when the world was flat?"

"Get real, Don. Wealth and education are privileges of the upper caste. The rest of the masses are happier with religious tradition and timeworn superstition. You don't have to give up science. You merely need to accept that it is practiced by an intellectual elite, just as capitalism is."

"The day is coming when the world will have to embrace reality."

"Perhaps, but to prevent a potentially catastrophic mass epiphany, that taste of reality must be doled out in palatable increments."

"While just coincidentally providing a conducive environment for your capitalistic endeavors?"

"Sometimes, Don, things just work out perfectly. Now, I'm thinking we can start close to home. The senator from Virginia, for example."

April Twenty-five

Charley and I returned to our lookout post in the woods near the mansion. I pointed out that unless a radical event suddenly occurred, we could spend forever spying on the silent house. Charley tried to think of ways to force a confrontation.

"We gotta make something happen, Steve. Radiation is some seriously dangerous shit. A sudden attack of blond? I ain't buyin' it. What about callin' your boys at Homeland Security?"

"The trouble is, Dr. Donald Petersen has Top Secret Clearance. That's why the Feds first got involved, and they seem to be protecting him."

"Yeah, but they don't know about gamma ray transmissions in downtown Washington."

"So we call them in and wash our hands of it?"

"We can't sit up here playing spy forever, Steve."

"What about Piper?"

"I hate to say it. If they somehow used radiation on her, she should have tests to screen for cancer, but unless we promenade up to the door, and these jaspers fess up..."

"So I'm supposed to call a Federal agent, tell him my friend is turning blond, and I suspect a terrorist plot?"

Choking back laughter, Charley coughed, "Turning everyone into a blonde? Now *that* could be a serious threat!"

Part Six

Carlton Jains paced the room, absentmindedly examining various objects while explaining his plan. When he selected a small vial, he noticed his old friend stiffen, and deduced that the bottle contained sensitive material. Putting the contents in jeopardy added a little weight to his politely worded demand. He waved the container carelessly, saying, "So this is how it's going to work, Don. We'll do the same thing you did to the woman, but in reverse. I will inform the subjects that they are going to see visible signs of aging. After the phenomenon has been confirmed, I will 'cure' them, and make some…suggestions concerning their upcoming activity. Trust me, they will comply."

Petersen's eyes remained fixed on the bottle in Jains' hand. "Why are they going to believe that you have that kind of power?"

"They are going to receive messages from a Voodoo priestess."

"Nobody's going to buy that."

"Trust me, Don. Politicians are vain. When their hair starts turning gray, I'll have their attention. When I 'rectify' their premature aging, they'll be mine."

Petersen balked, despite knowing there was little chance of dissuading Carlton. "I'll need a sample of the Senator's DNA."

"No problem." Jains gingerly set the vial back on the shelf and looked his friend in the eye. "Tonight I am attending a state dinner where Senator Radcliff will be pressing the flesh. You will provide me with an inconspicuous kit for collection."

"Got it all figured out, eh CJ?"

"Donnie, this is going to be the most fun I've had in years!"

At ten o'clock that evening, Jains produced the samples from the pocket of his tuxedo. Petersen reluctantly began the process. Reproducing and altering the genetic material would take several hours. Jains was in an exuberant mood and retired to his private office to conduct the next phase of his plan.

April Twenty-six

In the early hours before dawn, Senator Tim Radcliff was catching a scant few hours of rest on the day bed in his office. While he slept, a subtle alteration was occurring in his cellular regeneration, a change mostly designed to influence the way the Virginia politician would vote.

After spying on the mansion for most of the day, Charley said he had a plan to get inside and take a look at what was causing gamma frequency emissions to register outside the home of Carlton Jains. I was not thrilled by the idea. Jains had been brandishing a shotgun at the camp. There was no telling what kind of weapon he might be keeping in the enormous house, especially frightening considering the atomic radiation emanating from within.

I also didn't like the gleam in Charley's squint – it usually means he has something crazy in mind – but he promised that the scheme would work. Back at the hotel, he suckered me into going out to buy a six-pack of beer, during which time he apparently did some prep work. When I returned from the convenience store, he declared that we were ready.

Just as the evening sky turned gray, we parked at the church near the Jains mansion. Charley asked me to bring along a couple of bottles of brew. He carried one of his mysterious boxes, and we walked back to the woods. At our familiar site, he asked for a beer, so I opened two, and we drank while the sky grew completely dark.

Looking at the house, he muttered, "Damn newfangled cigarettes."

"You don't smoke."

"Yeah. Nasty habit. Great fuses, though. But the butts they sell these days go out if you're not puffing. Fire safety requirement." Producing a pack of sandalwood incense sticks, he said, "Best I could do."

"Now, wait a minute…"

"Oh, don't be a ninny. Check this out!"

His expression was a mixture of pride and mischief as he folded back the cardboard flaps. The box was filled with fireworks; I recognized M-80's and cherry bombs. There were several packages of bottle rockets. No sparklers.

"Charley…"

He was already twisting the fuses of the miniature explosives around the incense, partway down the sticks. His voice became a hoarse conspiratorial whisper. "OK, listen. Here's the plan. I'm gonna light these, and hide by the back door while the incense burns down and sets fire to the fuses. When they come out to investigate the explosions, you shoot off the bottle rockets. They'll come after you. In the confusion, I'll sneak through the door, take a quick look around, and run out the front."

"Are you crazy? They'll call the cops!"

"They're not going to call the cops. Who's going to call the cops?"

I didn't have a quick enough answer. Charley relishes opportunities for cloak and dagger activities; I think the excitement makes up for all the hours he spends doing mind-numbing research.

He charged on ahead, saying, "Look, if we do get caught, we'll tell them we saw some kids running away, and we were trying to catch them. They won't think adults are engaged in this sort of prank."

"They don't know you."

"Precisely." He handed me a disposable lighter.

I protested a little more, but Charley was on the move. I realized that he had asked me to bring the beer so we would have empty bottles for launching the rockets. As he set the charges, I knew there would be no stopping him and prepared to ignite the tiny missiles to provide a distraction.

Charley's improvised fusillade went off like corn in a popper; first one kernel, then several, then a series of ricochets. Lights came on outside, and a door opened. I fired a rocket straight up. This brought someone out of the house. I heard cursing, and lit off another, trying not to look at the flashes. It made no difference; I was snow-blind from the flames and couldn't tell if anyone was giving chase, or if Charley had gotten inside. I picked up the box and ran.

I stuffed the remaining ordnance in my jacket, stashed the empty box behind the fence, crossed the road and strolled nonchalantly in the direction of the car. Two police cruisers came flying up the avenue toward me, and turned into the neighborhood at the intersection ahead. I picked up the pace. Back at the car, I locked the incendiaries in the trunk, and drove around for a while.

A text message gave me the address where to pick up my lunatic partner. We were getting good at this part of the game. Unfortunately, the ploy had failed to gain Charley entry. Conducting our surveillance was going to be more difficult now that we had drawn so much attention.

April Twenty-seven

Charley and I had agreed to give the stakeout one more day. Figuring it was safer to keep our distance after the previous evening's pyrotechnics, we tried to detect radiation from several vantage points farther away, but without knowing when a transmission was taking place it was impossible to tell if anything was being broadcasted from the house. Eventually, we settled for a spot farther up the hill with a direct view of the front door, and took turns with the binoculars.

In the late afternoon the physicist emerged alone from the garage, driving a mid-size Mercedes-Benz. At the bottom of the driveway, the sedan turned right. Charley whispered, "Come on!" We took off running.

Vehicles exiting the neighborhood in that direction must pass through a controlled intersection. If Petersen got caught at the red light, there might be enough time for us to make it to Charley's car and follow. It seemed like the perfect chance to isolate the scientist from gun-happy Carlton Jains.

We got to our parking space just as the light changed. Petersen's car came in our direction, and we lagged behind until a few other vehicles separated us before pulling out into traffic and following. Less than a mile down the road, the Mercedes turned left into the parking lot of a hardware store.

As Petersen parked and approached the entrance on foot, I dropped Charley at the front of the building. I could hear their conversation through the open passenger's window.

Charley rather politely asked, "Dr. Petersen? May I have a word with you?"

The scientist was noticeably startled. "Who are you? What is this?"

"I'd like to talk about radiation, Dr. Petersen. Specifically gamma radiation."

Petersen turned away from the entrance, and headed back toward his car. Charley followed, saying, "I'd also like to talk about eumelanin." I got out of the car and approached the two men.

Petersen pressed a button on the remote key to unlock the car, but Charley placed his knee against the door. The physicist turned away and stalked off, saying, "I'm calling the police."

"I don't think so, Dr. Petersen," Charley called to the retreating back. "I'm a friend of Piper Locke. You do remember Ms. Locke, don't you?"

A look of recognition crossed Petersen's face as he noticed my approach. He bolted and ran toward the wooded border of the parking lot. I was closer than Charley and chased, grabbing a handful of Petersen's jacket. He half-turned and lashed out backhanded. I took a glancing blow and reflexively turned my wounded shoulder away, still clinging to his sleeve. Taken off balance, the scientist twisted an ankle and fell, forcing me to let go and sidestep the sprawling body. An instant later, Charley was on him like an enraged Doberman.

With Petersen pinned to the pavement, Charley said something I didn't understand, and it triggered a rapid exchange of incomprehensible foreign-sounding scientific jargon. Donald Petersen seemed to lose his spunk as it became apparent that Charley had a good idea what was going on.

The two men stopped struggling as the conversation continued. It became my old buddy's turn to look stunned. Charley later explained the esoteric details of the discussion, mouthfuls like spontaneous parametric down-conversion, cross-linked DHI polymers, and radiation hormesis. At the time, my friend seemed dazed by the replies, and willing to let the other man go on his way. As Petersen dusted off his suit and walked toward his car, Charley muttered, "Unbelievable. Fucking unbelievable."

"What happened?" I wondered aloud.

Charley was shaking his head. "He took phenomena from unrelated fields, events that can be reproduced but are not wholly understood, and strung them together. Piper accidentally walked into a concentrated stream of radiation. As she had already been unwittingly exposed to the potentially harmful rays, he felt it fair that she be given some benefit that would coincidently confirm his theory. According to him, her hair will remain blond until natural production of pigment ceases. He claims the mutation will have no effect on neurological functions."

"Do you buy it?"

"It certainly explains what happened to her hair, but the implications are astounding! The technique could be used as easily to heal as to destroy. Despite his allegedly benign intentions, Piper felt other effects. What he did was unpardonable. No one is monitoring the experiments going on in that house, and who knows what that other maniac might be planning."

"What do you think we should do?"

"I say call in the Feds. The process could turn out to work the miracles this guy claims are possible, but obviously the fucking genius needs some adult supervision. Maybe the Department of Defense will take him back."

We sat in the car and I searched between the pages of my journal for the card Agent Sanderson had given me at the first interrogation.

A letter arrived at the Senator's office by certified mail. It appeared to be an invitation, a crisply folded note in an embossed RSVP envelope.

Senator Radcliff,

You are going to notice sudden signs of aging. To reverse this trend, you must comply with my wishes. You may not believe in the power of voodoo, but you will.
I will be in touch.

La Mambo

Senator Tim Radcliff chuckled as he carefully returned the card to the envelope, set it aside and continued with his correspondence. As standard procedure, his secretary would turn the letter over to the FBI. A week would pass before the legislator thought again of the peculiar message.

Petersen was too embarrassed to admit to Carlton Jains that he had been cowed so easily. He implied that the two men had already known the details of his technique. Jains became enraged at the mention of the name Stephen Shaw.

"I fucking knew it. You should have let me rearrange his molecules when I had the chance...with a twelve-gauge shotgun shell up the kazoo!"

"There's nothing they can do, CJ. No one will believe such a wild story. Besides, there's no law against conducting scientific experiments in the privacy of your home."

"I should have guessed that those fireworks last night weren't set off by the neighborhood kids. Fucking cops. If they'd have been doing their jobs..."

"Maybe we should pack up the gear and wait until things calm down."

"No fucking way, Don. Your scientific advances are important to you? Well, my agenda is just as important to me. I have a plan to initiate some goddam fiscal responsibility and put the reins of government firmly back in the hands people who are qualified to guide this nation."

"What you are doing is clearly illegal. It will do you no good to have the FBI come busting in here and expose your little scheme."

Jains was breathing hard and starting to sweat. Even in his fury, the logic of Petersen's statement was clear. The physicist calmly continued, "All right, listen. As long as we can tune in to the Russians' antenna, we can transmit from anywhere in Washington. It won't hurt to hide the equipment somewhere else. They obviously know where it is now."

"What about the Senator?"

"He'll have a few extra days to stew. Come on, CJ. We need to get this stuff out of here."

"I suppose it's just as well," grumbled Jains. "Maggie's coming home this week."

I left a message at the Department of Homeland Security number and after several hours Agent Sanderson called back. He voiced surprise at ever hearing from me again after the debacle in Arizona. I reiterated that he had gotten me all wrong from the beginning.

As I explained the situation, Sanderson expressed disbelief and questioned every detail. I had intended to keep Charley and Piper out of it, but the agent wanted more proof before acting on the tip, so I told him everything, citing my friends as witnesses. In the end he promised to look into the matter and cautioned me to stay out of it further. I came away with the impression that Petersen's clearance provided some sort of immunity, and that all I had accomplished was to draw attention to the fact that I was still nosing around where I had no business.

Charley and I would have preferred to know for sure that the situation was under intense scrutiny before calling off our little stakeout, but this was the best we could do short of becoming obsessive vigilantes. We packed our bags and left in the middle of the night, to avoid the worst of Washington's impossibly heavy traffic.

April Twenty-eight

On the long drive south, I asked Charley about a project he had been working on in his spare time over the last few years.

"Whatever happened to your experiment to cure the common cold?"

"Worked like a charm."

"Are you serious?"

"Completely. Matter of fact, it worked too well. I finally had to destroy everything related to the experiment."

"*What?*"

"There was too great a chance that the viruses responsible for cold symptoms would have been completely eradicated."

"Why would that be such a bad thing?"

"The evolution of viruses has accompanied that of humans. Certain endoviruses even entered the human genome hundreds of thousands of years ago, and reproduce along with the DNA in our cells. Not all the effects are bad; they became an integral part of our development, sometimes even an agent of genetic change. A symbiotic relationship."

"But the cure for the common cold...," I protested.

"Cold viruses occupy a niche. Who knows what pathogen might take their place if they were eradicated. It was too risky."

"Haven't other viruses been successfully wiped out? Things like smallpox?"

"The full repercussions of which may not become apparent for thousands of years. Specimens are maintained for unforeseen contingencies, deadly samples stored under extreme security. If smallpox was inadvertently released into the environment, there would be no vaccine, no antibodies or antidote. Same thing could

Quantum Voodoo

happen with cold viruses; they would run rampant if we lost our built-up immunity. Stick with plenty of liquids and staying in bed. You're not going to die from it."

I was secretly hoping that Charley had retained a small amount of the cure for personal use.

April Twenty-nine

I called to let Piper know we were back, and she drove down to join us. Her hair was now completely blond, spiky and short. I had never seen her looking better. She immediately went to Charley for the news. By their interaction, the mutual attraction was obvious. Charley tried to be gentle and reassuring, but Piper was understandably upset.

"So I've been exposed to radiation and there's nothing I can do? They're going to get away with it?"

Charley explained, "A small amount of radiation was part of the process and probably did no harm. Electromagnetic particles hit you every day, from sunlight as well as cosmic rays from the far reaches of space. The atmosphere filters out most of the radiation in the gamma bandwidth, but small amounts are actually beneficial. You should probably have a blood test, but chances are the levels were so low that it had little effect."

"The bastards should be arrested!"

"We can't prove anything. The entire notion is so outrageous that no one will believe us. That's why the creep was willing to talk about it, and don't take this the wrong way, but if you walk into court looking as good as you do today, everyone is going to wonder what you're complaining about."

If this was intended to calm Piper down, it had the desired effect. Embarrassed, she looked down, saying, "Well, I suppose it could be worse. I can't thank you enough for all you've done. And you, Stephen," she added, politely turning to include me. "But what happens now?"

Charley answered this question too, taking Piper's arm and leading her toward the porch. "Well, I was thinking that as long as you came all this way, for lunch, we could..."

I didn't hear the rest. I was already thinking of an excuse, just in case they invited me to join them.

Tim Radcliff had been putting in the long days so frequently required of a United States Senator. Being from the state of Virginia, situated in such proximity to the nation's capital, was both boon and bane. He could live at home with his family at the farm in bucolic Front Royal, but it made for a long commute. During periods of intense activity, as these past few days had been, he simply stayed overnight at his office in downtown Washington.

After splashing his face with cold water, the Senator took out the electric razor he kept at the office for freshening up between shaves. Preparing to cut off two day's growth, he stopped, stunned by its appearance. Instead of his usual chestnut-brown shadow, his cheeks were covered in slate colored stubble. Staring up, it became apparent that his eyebrows too were graying; even the hair close to his scalp had become discolored.

"Sudden signs of aging," the Senator recalled. Voodoo. It was simply not possible. Radcliff felt prickly all over. He dropped the shaver and went to call the FBI.

In the C&O Canal area of Washington's Georgetown neighborhood, brick and stone structures originally built as warehouses paralleling the long-defunct commercial waterway now form a labyrinth of high-end shops and offices on narrow streets lining a steep slope. Under the name of a dummy corporation, Jains had rented a fifth floor suite with a direct view up the hill to the Russian Embassy.

Entering through a bay door at the rear of the building, the two men ferried the now completed equipment up in the elevator. Without all the stray spare parts and remains of cannibalized machinery, the installation was neat and simple, a half-dozen sleek machines resembling those one might expect to find in an efficiently furnished dentist's office. The unused electronic components had been divided between a dumpster and a storage unit. Jains' house now contained no evidence of anything related to the experiment.

Petersen explained that they would not need a line of sight to the Senator to reverse the emergence. From the Embassy's fractal antenna, the transmission would irradiate the target area. Since communication channels had already been established, the quantum-linked gamma radiation would resonate with only the politician's unique configuration of particles. The entire operation could be controlled from the little cubicle on the top floor of the office building.

While Petersen fine-tuned the gear, Jains went about concocting a scheme for delivering his next message.

April Thirty

Charley arrived home long past his customary hour. I knew without asking that he had gone to visit Piper after work. It was also obvious that if I stayed on, my presence would cramp their style. The idea of my two old friends striking up a relationship had my complete approval, and I had no intention of inadvertently interfering.

I tried calling a few professional acquaintances, looking for a short-term project to work on during my convalescence. After this proved fruitless, I decided to rent a car and get away for a week or so, to relax and finish recovering from the gunshot wound while deciding my next move.

At the Senator's insistence, the FBI had expedited the threatening message through the forensics process, and called to report finding no evidence whatsoever. The paper's manufacturer was identifiable, as was the brand of printer, but there were thousands of possible origins. No fingerprints were evident. The delivery certification had not been processed by the Post Office. The adhesive-backed form had come from a kiosk at the main branch downtown. It had been filled out, attached, and simply deposited in a regular letterbox. As there was no return address and the correct postage had been affixed, the envelope had been routinely delivered. The card had passed through a security inspection at the Senate mailroom, apparently posing no chemical threat.

The investigator also explained that "La Mambo" is a name given generically to Voodoo priestesses. The agent had obviously read the note, and implied that Senator Tim Radcliff was making a fuss about nothing.

May One

I drove south along Florida's gulf coast, past a seemingly endless procession of shopping malls intermittently interrupted by golf courses and housing developments bearing precious names. Eventually, the highway turned east into the everglades. Swampland stretched for miles into the distance. I gratefully left behind the sensory assault of man-made landscape.

I had no firm destination in mind, but approaching the congestion of Miami, I turned south again. Beyond the farmland lay the Florida Keys. Almost like "cruising the strip" in small town America, I decided to drive to the end of Route One. Upon reversing my direction of travel, the southern terminus would become the beginning of the road, an apropos location considering my current desire to start anew.

Senator Radcliff's secretary had been instructed to screen the mail stringently for possible messages from the mysterious blackmailer. She handled all the incoming correspondence with latex gloves, opening each envelope methodically so as not to taint potential evidence. The painstaking process was adding hours of aggravation to the administrative assistant's workday, but the importance had been made clear.

The second letter arrived with the regular morning mail, this time scrawled by hand in flowery old-fashioned cursive.

Senator Radcliff,

By now I have your attention. The symptoms will disappear. Should you choose not to cooperate with my next request, you will be returned to your current rate of rapid aging.

La Mambo

Tim Radcliff would not have admitted it, but a sense of relief washed over him. The symptoms would disappear. Thank God. When the voodoo priestess made her demand, the FBI could use the motive as a clue with which to track her. For the moment the Senator was safe.

May Two

Petersen was finishing the gamma ray transmission to normalize Senator Radcliff. Carlton Jains watched closely. The scientist shook his head, saying, "I can't believe you didn't tell your own wife about your injury, CJ."

The klystron continued to emit a hum even after the physicist flicked the switch to the off position.

Jains did not seem particularly apologetic. "You know Maggie, Don. I'd never hear the end of it."

"What's she going to say when she sees your scars?"

"She hasn't seen me without a shirt for ages."

At Petersen's questioning look, Jains went on to answer the unspoken question.

"You know Maggie and I don't have that kind of relationship, Don. We did our duty and had the kids, but the whole reason we got married was that our parents wanted to unite and protect our families' assets. Maggie can't have any more children; our daughters will inherit the estate. It's a done deal. So we go through the motions, keep up appearances. As long as we're discreet and don't incur the families' wrath, we can do whatever we want."

Petersen had passed up several chances for a suitable mate, and sometimes harbored regret for having chosen to remain a bachelor. At this moment, however, he wondered if it hadn't been for the best.

Sanderson was perplexed by the phone call. After being released, Stephen Shaw had gone to Mexico and simply explored the ruins of ancient civilizations; pretty much what might be expected of a member of his profession. There was no indication of any threat from Dr. Shaw, and the agents had stopped watching him.

Back in Arizona, Sanderson had found no evidence of wrongdoing, and released the impounded laboratory. The physicist Petersen, along with his partner, had taken the undamaged equipment and the camper and cleared out. A trucking company removed the semitrailers, and the desert acreage appeared abandoned. In Sanderson's opinion, the entire investigation had been a fool's errand intended to keep him and his partners occupied. The incident had been dutifully logged and filed. The national security task force had moved on to other pursuits.

Granted, a possible security breach concerning Dr. Petersen's classified experiments had presented enough threat to draw the attention of Sanderson's superiors at the Department. Questionable activity by the physicist could not be ignored. Moreover, why would the anthropologist bother with making contact again, unless there was something to his wild tale? Then again, Geiger counters? Gamma rays in the Nation's Capitol? Blond hair?

The information sounded ludicrous, but Dr. Shaw stood to gain absolutely nothing but trouble by playing foolish games with federal agents. Already in Washington on another assignment, Sanderson finally decided to personally visit the home of Carlton Jains.

May Three

Tim Radcliff happily shaved the brown stubble from his chin. It was too soon to tell about the hair on his head, but at least the gray had disappeared from his beard. The discoloration near the scalp was not all that noticeable. By his next haircut, the color underneath would be normal.

For the past five days, the Senator had obsessed over every tinge that could be construed as a sign of aging. Was it harder to stand after kneeling? That cough, could it be the onset of some chronic condition? The aching lumbar; surely it was worse than it had been at the age of thirty-something. The distraction made it nearly impossible to concentrate on his duties. There it was again; doesn't it become harder to focus as you age?

Voodoo. Putting the threat out of mind had become increasingly difficult. His rational side scoffed at the very idea, the power of a United States Senator was beyond the influence of anyone, much less a practitioner of some ludicrous ritualistic superstition. The other side of him was terrified at the thought of being destroyed in the prime of life with so many things unfinished, voters depending on him, and a family to support. Senator Radcliff was already drawing lines in the sand, weighing the cost of compliance against the price of defiance.

Margaret Jains was in no mood for hijinks when she opened the door to two crusty suits. Carlton had not bothered to be at home to greet her, and it had been a long, trying day dealing with airport security and travel industry employees that seemed determined to ensure that despite her vigilance and intervention, the woman and her luggage would not arrive in Washington on the same airplane. Moreover, that bastard of a husband should have at least had a limo waiting. Standing with the common rabble in line for a taxicab after the trying journey had pushed her over the edge.

Sanderson was not prepared to deal with a powerful and already irritated society matron accustomed to getting her way. When faced with Mrs. Jains, he thought back fondly to an incident involving the apprehension of an international terrorist. At least the roles in that case had been clear. Regardless of the beleaguered agent's immediate desire, there would be no justification for precipitating violence upon the person of Margaret Jains.

Maggie's reaction to the questioning, however, spawned a truce. The focus of her anger returned to her husband. After disparaging her mate as being incapable of companioning himself with quality acquaintances, she assured the federal agents that Mr. Jains lacked both the imagination and initiative to become involved in anything sinister, and indignantly insisted the men come in and take a look around.

The brief inspection was both embarrassing and pointless. Not a single object in the house seemed even remotely capable of producing gamma radiation. Chagrinned, the agents begged pardon, and retreated.

The pool and gardens at the guesthouse provided a perfect environment for doing absolutely nothing, but I began to feel guilty over my self-indulgence and went for a long run to explore the island. To cool off, I waded out into the ocean and floated on my back.

The warm salt water felt soothing on the scabs from the bullet wound. After a shower at the hotel, I felt invigorated and walked out to find some lunch.

I remembered that the locals were friendly on my previous visits to Key West, but they were downright polite as I headed for downtown, calling hello and greeting me as "Captain." One rather charming but obviously down and out fellow respectfully took off his cap to speak, saying, "Afternoon, Cap'm. I aint gonna lie to ya, I need a beer. Can ya loan me a dollar? I'll pay ya back." I gave him a ten and planned to avoid that block on my return trip. The results of his good fortune would probably not be pretty.

My next encounter was with a lissome young woman wearing a bikini top and cutoffs. She muttered familiarly, "Hey." I replied with the same, and by her next utterance, it was obvious that I was being mistaken for someone.

"Goin' to work?"

I took off my sunglasses, saying, "Excuse me," or something equally witless.

Surprised, she said, "Oh, I'm sorry. I thought you were somebody else."

"I am."

We both laughed at that. Her beachwear left little to the imagination and I tried to keep my eyes on her face. She mumbled under her breath and giggled. I asked if she would like to join me for a drink, and there was an awkward silence. Then she said thanks, but she had to go, and I wished her a good afternoon.

I walked on and found a bar with cold beer and a view of the old town's perennial sidewalk parade. I spent a couple of pleasant hours at an outdoor table, drinking conservatively and people-watching. A magnificent cross-section of society passed along the crowded walkway, without the baggage of their professions or personal lives to reinforce their identities. Under no time constraints, they wandered somewhat aimlessly, interacting amongst their own group in a hierarchy established under quite different conditions than those that probably ruled daily life in their home environs.

Working locals flitted through the meandering crowds like real-time shadows invading a slow motion movie scene. Barkers hawked wares and services, bums panhandled, crafters offered handmade art and jewelry, basket-weavers sold hats and trinkets made from coconut fronds. Ambling along the main drag, the tourist throngs hesitantly shed detritus of silver and gold.

Several individuals I found particularly amusing; I dubbed them the "Tree Shakers." These hustlers have no apparent agenda, don't ask for anything. Their goal is merely to strike up conversation, and see what fruit can be persuaded to fall. Perhaps a

Quantum Voodoo

cigarette if the quarry lights one for themselves, a drink for a thirsty stranger spouting a charming line of bullshit, maybe a dollar or two for a deposed executive, a war veteran, a literary genius, or an out of work roadie that personally routed Elvis' microphone cable.

I was absorbed with watching the dynamics of this freewheeling tableau when a voice to my right said, "Hey." It was the woman with whom I had spoken earlier, now wearing street clothes. Gesturing to the stool beside me, I asked, "Would you like that drink?"

"Please."

We shook hands and exchanged the usual pleasantries. Her name was Jillian, on vacation from Scranton, Pennsylvania. Mid-thirties, recently divorced, no kids. Decent figure, cute face. I couldn't decide if it was plain dumb luck, or if a high percentage of her demographic group frequented the southernmost city. We continued to observe the crowd and speculate about their real lives, laughing at how they chose to present themselves when traveling amid total strangers.

Late afternoon, the general flow along the sidewalk seemed to reverse direction, almost as if a whistle had blown. I suddenly realized that I was hungry, and suggested dinner. With a giggle, Jillian requested sushi. She later confessed that it was only the second time she had tried Japanese cuisine. We hailed a cab, and told the driver to take us to the best place in town.

Both the restaurant atmosphere and the fare were world-class, and we lingered for hours over fine sake and a series of bite-sized ambrosia.

After dinner, we walked slowly back toward the downtown, window shopping and peeking into galleries. By the time we reached the heart of the nightlife I had worked off the sluggishness of the meal, and suggested a nightcap. Jillian excused herself, saying that she was tired, and we had reached the street upon which her hotel was located. I invited her to come with me to the beach the next day, and we agreed that I would pick her up around eleven. She gave me a quick goodnight peck on the cheek, and disappeared into the guesthouse garden with a wave of her hand.

Jains was tired of waiting. A week had passed and there was no visible improvement to the scar tissue. Despite what he had told Donald, he could not avoid Maggie's scrutiny forever. Don had gone out for the day, and Carlton was restless. With nothing better to do, he went to the lab.

Petersen had said they would repeat the procedure after a rest period following the previous exposure. Positive that he could re-create the treatment, Carlton retrieved his altered DNA sample and set up the machinery. There was no protective curtain, but what the hell. If things went wrong, Petersen could repair the damage. Right now, what he needed was a large enough dose to get things moving.

With the klystron powering up, Jains crossed the room and stood in the target zone.

May Four

I bought a disposable Styrofoam cooler and a bag of ice, along with junk food snacks and adult refreshments for the beach. Knocking on the door of room sixteen, wearing hastily purchased baggy swimming trunks and an open denim shirt, I probably looked as goofy as the tourists we had laughed at the day before.

For her part, Jillian was decked out in a black bikini. She stood riveted in front of a wall length mirror, repeatedly putting on and taking off a straw hat while silently staring at her reflection. The quiet seemed a bit awkward after the previous evening's chatter. I moved behind her so that she could see us together, and put a tentative hand on her shoulder. That seemed to be the icebreaker, a sign that I was interested on a physical level. She closed her eyes, turned to face me, and wrapped her arms around my waist. Lifting her gaze, she looked at me questioningly and I kissed her lips.

With our bodies pressed together, I'm sure she could sense my rising desire. She moved back a little, saying, "Are we really going to do this?"

"We're adults. We're entitled."

She reached up to untie the neck-string of her swimsuit. I moved my hands over her sleek torso, enjoying the reflection in the mirror. I undid the second knot at the center of her back, and the skimpy brassiere fell to the floor.

Once her top was off, Jillian had crossed the Rubicon, and the hesitancy vanished. Our kisses were all tongue, and she eagerly pushed the shirt from my shoulders. I wriggled free of the denim without breaking mouth contact. Our hands began to explore, and in the process, we were naked in minutes.

We moved to the bed, and the foreplay continued. Eventually she took a hold on me to her evident satisfaction and my deep gratification. At that point I remembered that I was unprepared. Worse still, unprotected sex was the primary cause of my current state of affairs. Jillian apparently sensed my uncertainty and reached into a bag sitting on the nightstand. She made a game of putting the condom on, teasing me as she slowly unrolled the latex.

Sex may not be a substitute for love, but the intimacy goes a long way toward filling the void left after the end of a relationship. Both of us had recently become single. Our lovemaking seemed to be a release for all the fluctuations in emotion that we had endured.

Jillian got on top and rode wildly at first, as if to get out all the aggression and anger. After that initial burst of energy, she flopped forward, and I began gently massaging her body. She arched like a house-cat, and her breasts hung in my face. A soft bite on the swollen nipple produced an agreeable moan. Without separating, we rolled over, and from the missionary position I drew her leg across my chest and moved into a scissors, taking the weight off of my sore arm. In this posture I could continue to nibble at her breast, stroke deep inside and manually stimulate her, simultaneously.

The lovemaking became a relaxed, languid exercise. I was determined to enjoy it for as long as possible. Imperceptibly, the pace increased, and Jillian seemed almost overwhelmed by a sudden rush of excitement. Her body shook and her facial expression portrayed the convulsions as pain.

For a long while afterward we lay locked together that way, gently touching each other, reassuring. We never made it to the beach. In the afternoon we went out for oysters, refilled the cooler with fresh ice and carried it back to the room. The next eight hours were spent drinking rum cocktails, soaking in the hot tub, making love, and nursing each other's bruised ego. The snacks I had brought along were enough to sustain us through the evening, and we fell asleep in a tangle of limbs.

May Five

Jillian was booked on a late morning flight, and I offered to drive her to the airport. Although the chances of my showing up in Pennsylvania were minuscule, we exchanged telephone numbers. As I went to enter hers in my phone, I discovered that the battery was dead and had to write her contact information on a sheet of motel stationery. My smart-phone had not rung for days. I had assumed that no one was trying to reach me, and did not realize that the new device would discharge so quickly when not in use.

Back at my motel, I plugged in the charger. There were several voice messages waiting. An irate Agent Sanderson warned me about making sport with a federal agency. Apparently they had found no evidence at the Jains' mansion. I wanted to point out that our scare tactic in the parking lot probably caused the scientist to relocate, but from the agent's tone it was clear that he did not wish to hear from me again unless I had incontrovertible proof of an imminent threat to the nation's security.

Charley had also called, "Just to check in." I'm sure he was wondering how long his house would be free. He was probably at work; it wasn't urgent. I left the phone to finish recharging and went out for lunch.

Bedding Jillian had instilled in me an exhilarating vibrancy, the confidence that despite my years and failed relationships I was still a viable contender in the great pageant of human sexuality. This added an exciting prospect to my otherwise indistinct future. I ordered a healthy salad and fruit juice, intending to channel this newfound energy toward maintaining youthful fitness.

Ready to tackle the rainforest again, I drove to Miami in the afternoon, watching in my rearview mirror as the sun slowly sank into the aquamarine water.

Another handwritten note had mysteriously appeared in the pocket of Senator Radcliff's blazer. The contents of the message were distraction enough, but the fact that La Mambo or her agent had been physically close enough to slip the envelope into his jacket was simply terrifying. On top of that, the demand required that the democratic Senator vote in favor of legislation that he had already publicly denounced, a republican-supported tax break. Affirming the measure would probably cost him not only his reputation, but reelection as well.

The Senator retreated to his private office and refused all calls. He gulped a couple of painkillers and washed them down with a shot of bourbon.

I caught up with Charley on the phone that evening. He told me it was just as well that I was leaving for Central America. The spare room was unavailable, but not for the reasons I had previously suspected.

"Dig, Bro.' The chick was wiggin' out. Had to get her to chill."

"I take that to mean that you are trying to calm Piper down?"

"Thought if we re-created the dude's experiment, it might take away some of the mystery; make it less frightening."

"Don't tell me you built a quantum gizmo!"

"It was Piper's idea. Made her feel better to do something."

"You have got to be kidding! You're going to shoot her with this thing?"

"We haven't finished building it yet, but the guest room is full of equipment. We're having to improvise some of the components. Besides, I don't think she wants to reverse the effects of her other exposure; she just wants to understand what happened, allay her fears."

"Are you sure you should be messing around with this 'quantum' stuff? I mean, it's not really your field…"

"Sorta is, dude...there've been some recent breakthroughs. Quantum biology's a whole new thing. We been doin' some serious woodshedding..."

"I don't know, Charley..."

"Come on, Steve. You know me well enough by now. I'm not going to precipitate anything rash."

"Yeah, but you've switched to plain English, and that's always a worrisome sign."

We shared a chuckle, but I was more serious than not, and he knew it.

May Six

I took the midmorning flight to Guatemala City hoping the third time would be the charm. I had finished the course of antibiotics. My arm still ached, but no infection had set in and the skin had healed over in pinkish-purple flesh. The little vacation had restored my constitution, and I was eager to return to the search for the mask.

On this trip, I would not be entering the wilderness alone. Ramirez had enlisted a couple of bodyguards. I was reluctant to accept; there was always the possibility that the hired crew would simply confiscate the artifact and leave me dead in the jungle; but I had come to believe in Ramirez and it seemed the simplest solution. Over the phone, we had gone over the ground rules and requirements for my safe return to the remote regions of the rain forest.

Petersen flew to Massachusetts, ostensibly to consult with his colleagues at MIT. Part of the motivation for the trip was to see how far the competition's teleportation research had progressed, but the real reason was to get away from Carlton Jains for a while. Petersen had no desire to become an extortionist. He had only undertaken the quantum teleportation experiments to satisfy his curiosity about the fundamental nature of existence. Between the military applications and Carlton's manipulations, the ethical price of funding the program was turning out to be far greater than the physicist was prepared to pay.

At the Physics Reading Room in Cambridge, Petersen caught up with one of his mentors. Surprisingly, the old man already knew a stunning amount of detail concerning his ex-student's

Quantum Voodoo

current experiments. The professor explained that a scientist had contacted the physics department looking for Petersen, and described the remarkable advances Donald had made. The caller had been raising some interesting technical questions.

There was only one person with both the intimate knowledge and technical savvy to have made that phone call. Petersen copied the number, correctly assuming this "Dr. Pulaski" had to be the man that had accosted him in the hardware store parking lot.

May Seven

Due to the extra gamma ray exposure, Carlton Jains' skin was now healing at an astounding speed, but other processes had also been stimulated. The radiation-induced immune system response began in areas that had not been intentionally targeted. The rate of cellular reproduction accelerated. As nutrients were burned away, body fat became fuel for a runaway metabolism. Hormone production was disrupted. Jains began to crave cholesterol and sugar. He could not seem to drink enough Scotch.

At first the effects of the metabolic surge were mild, even invigorating. As more tissue became involved, chemicals in the brain went out of balance. Jains' mental processes were steadily becoming impaired. Feeling energetic, he did not realize that things were off, and secluded himself in his private rooms enjoying the binge, drinking heavily and only opening the door for deliveries from the deli and liquor store. Mrs. Jains was perfectly happy not to be burdened with her husband when he was partying, and abandoned Carlton to his own devices.

Ramirez had wasted no time in setting up an immediate expedition. A terrifying duo had been engaged to accompany me into the wilderness. Veterans of Guatemala's protracted civil war, the two former guerrillas bore the scars of combat, the lined faces and distant stares of fighters well inured to the atrocities of battle. Santiago was robust, stern and assured, and would act as bodyguard. His partner, our scout, was thin and skittish, offering only the nickname "Gaucho." Having been soldiers all their lives they knew no other trade, and took work in their profession where it could be found. Señor Ramirez assured me that the mercenaries were faithful and trustworthy.

Despite my nervousness at traveling in the company of such hardened cases, I headed again for the jaguar habitat. At least there would be some people on my side that were a match for the renegades and smugglers I had stumbled across during the previous expedition.

We left early in the morning and drove until reaching the end of the jeep trail. Considering my bad arm, I was not expected to carry a heavy load; Santiago packed enough water for us all. Also traveling light, Gaucho ranged ahead as scout, appearing occasionally as an ethereal phantom glimpsed among the trees. Communication between the two soldiers took the form of convincing birdcalls. We spoke to each other in a mixture of Spanish and English.

These guerrillas were well trained for the rain forest environment. Despite the sullen heat of the midday sun, we moved silently and rapidly along the trail. Even unencumbered by a heavy backpack, I had to hustle to keep pace.

The limestone mounds were unsettlingly quiet, like piles of sun-bleached bones lying interred in the otherwise dynamic jungle. The place seemed undisturbed since my previous visit. The paramilitary escorts scoffed at my intention to smoke out the snakes. With their rifle barrels and high jackboots they merely brushed the critters aside, and we climbed the mound without much ado. I wrenched the boulders apart, and peered between them with a flashlight.

Even in the tropical humidity, the space was sere and dusty. No serpents or scorpions were evident, and I carefully removed scraps of decayed material from what appeared to be a heavy object. Anticipation turned to disappointment as I pulled a plain chunk of limestone out into the sunlight. The chamber was empty.

As if to reinforce the failure, a loud thunderclap accompanied our return to the trail. Within minutes we were soaked, despite the thick canopy of treetops.

At the beginning of the telephone conversation, Petersen was dismayed to discover how far Charles Pulaski had advanced in reproducing the experiments, especially without the support of a scientific institution or the backing of a budgetary benefactor. The two men analyzed the procedure Petersen had performed on the rabbit. Charley began to accept that the teleportation been undertaken with benign intentions.

They continued to talk, their differences forgotten as mutual insatiable scientific curiosity drove an in depth discussion. Charley's expertise imparted a bio-molecular perspective that complemented the physicist's knowledge of the subatomic milieu. Petersen's comprehensive explanations clarified the dynamics and impediments lurking in the quantum world.

Formidable adversaries make for powerful allies. After an hour, the compulsive researchers agreed to stay in touch.

Excited by the possibility of finding the mask, I had not planned for any other contingency and had to rethink things. If the jade face was indeed hidden in the region, the locals could have knowledge of it. Naturally, I was reluctant to pursue the Uchben Itza after my first meeting with the tribesmen, but there were few other clues to follow. The attackers had been scared off before their intentions had become apparent.

Back at the little island city on the lake, Ramirez and I reviewed all the information we could find about the mythical sect. It seemed likely to both of us that if the old order did exist in the wilds of Guatemala, they could be in contact with the likewise cloistered Lacandon across the river in the Yucatan. Either of the groups could have knowledge of the myth.

Searching in the rugged isolation meant that the next expedition was going to be a much more serious undertaking. We would be leaving the last signs of even ancient civilization behind, heading north toward the Mexican border through dense road-less forest seeking possibly hostile inhabitants on their own forbidding turf.

May Eight

This was not the first time I had marked my birthday alone in a foreign country, but I kept the celebrating to a minimum. In the heat and humidity of the rainforest, a hangover would be about as welcome as a bow-tie. As there was no definite time limit for the upcoming excursion, I packed as much as I thought I could reasonably manage.

May Nine

We left Flores before sunrise and drove north toward the Mexican border. The pavement gave out by late morning, and we followed another logging trail until this too dwindled to a rudimentary path. Fortunately, the previous bout of wet weather had been a fluke; the rainy season was still a few weeks away. Cloudless skies of pure cerulean slowly disappeared behind the dense treetops as we forged deeper into the wilderness.

We followed a stream, a tributary of the Usumacinta River that separates this part of Guatemala from Mexico. The Lacandon people live on the north side of this natural border; my guess was that the Uchben Itza would be lurking to the South.

The Senate was in session Monday through Friday during May, and Senator Tim Radcliff stayed in Washington through the work days. Returning to rural Virginia for the weekend, he spent time with his family, and strolled the rolling hills taking inspiration from the burgeoning green of spring. This was the land he had chosen to serve, the home of his ancestors, the country he loved. With the stress of the voodoo threat playing heavily on his mind, he reached a decision. The Senator called his probate lawyer and made an appointment to review his last will and testament.

Petersen returned to the Jains mansion in Washington to discover his boyhood chum in the throes of a serious jag. Shockingly, Carlton's scars had healed completely. In stark contrast with the freckles and age spots of the opposite shoulder, the new skin was fresh and young. The physicist knew immediately that something had gone drastically wrong. Upon discovering the rate of Jains' consumption of calories, Petersen insisted on taking blood and conducting some tests.

As if his friend's disturbed mental state was not enough to contend with, Petersen was distracted. The scientist, Pulaski, was conducting tests of his own, using an extraordinarily ingenious array of substitute devices. After so much time in a creative vacuum, it had been exhilarating to come across someone with whom a scientific dialogue was possible. Despite the sensitive nature of the experiments, the two men had agreed to exchange data. But what if the woman – whom he now thought of as "Piper" – was suffering the same metabolic catastrophe as Carlton Jains? Petersen would be crucified for the deed!

May Ten

In his current state, Jains had become unmanageable. Petersen began avoiding his old friend while waiting for the results of the blood work.

Alcohol ceased to provide Carlton Jains with a release; there was not enough time to feel the effects before the sugar was processed. After frantically burning so much caloric energy, Jains was exhausted. A handful of Seconal tablets had bought a few hours of sleep.

Despite the deepening psychosis, or perhaps because of it, Jains felt clear-headed and energetic after getting some rest. He left the house early before Maggie and the help awoke, and drove his high-dollar SUV to Georgetown before the plaque of rush hour clogged the arteries of the city.

In the quiet fifth-floor laboratory, Carlton poked around the machines. Three quarters of a million dollars for these pieces of shit. They were sitting there doing nothing. He turned some of them on. Zilch. Not even a buzz to let you know if they were even functioning!

The gamma ray generator sat interfaced with the linear accelerator. Jains thought back to the weeks of boredom in the desert. Donnie hadn't wanted him to play with the contraption. What was it he had said, "...In the red range, the radiation will burn holes in your eyes?"

Sniggering contemptuously, Carlton separated the linked machines. "Fuck that sanctimonious asshole," he muttered, wheeling the klystron over to the window.

We spent a restless night in lightweight macramé hammocks suspended between thick branches high off the ground. One of us constantly kept watch; this region of the jungle was wilder and more seldom traversed than even the remote jaguar habitat. We had continued to follow the tributary, and were now at least thirty miles from the last sign of human activity. It might as well have been another planet. The stream bed provided access through otherwise impenetrable undergrowth. I had the eerie feeling that thousands of feral beasts were silently watching our intrusion into their zoological sanctuary.

In the middle of the afternoon, we reached a promontory overlooking the creek. It seemed as defensible a campsite as any that was likely to appear farther along the banks, and we decided to stop there on our second night in the wilderness.

Jains continued to talk to no one in particular. "What this fuckin' thing needs is a sniper-scope." With the aperture pointed uphill toward a large willow oak, he switched on the electric power. There was no vibration, just a faint hum, but Jains could sense the power as the klystron built up a charge. The tree remained unimpressed.

"Maybe it's too far without the accelerator thingy."

Jains aimed at some geraniums in a flower box across the street. The blooms swayed unperturbed in the breeze. Quietly cursing, he found another target. A pigeon landed on a nearby window-ledge. Jains pushed the slider into the red zone and let him have it. Indifferently, the bird flew away.

In a fit of frustration, Jains sighted the roof of the Russian Embassy and pretended to fire a couple of hundred rounds at the commies, stuttering, "Pow, pow, pow, pow, pow," and shaking from the imaginary recoil of a machine gun as radiation streamed directly toward the hidden antenna.

Lowering his hands, he mumbled, "Ah, fuck."

At the lack of a visible reaction, he lost interest and powered down. Pushing the tripod-mounted klystron back into its previous location, another idea came to him. What about the Senator? With the distractions of unbalanced metabolism and rapidly healing skin, Carlton had almost forgotten. The voodoo project required some attention, and there were plenty of other fish to fry. After he dealt with the politician, he would collect more DNA. That would get the ball rolling. With the equipment back in place, Jains locked the laboratory door and headed for his car.

By sundown, the pigeon was decomposing in a gutter. The geraniums had wilted. Several branches of springtime buds were blackening on the tree, and Carlton Jains had three new DNA samples multiplying in the thermal cycler.

May Eleven

Our exploration continued to follow the water's northward flow. By siesta time we had reached the confluence of our creek and a larger river. We piled our belongings at the edge of a small clearing, intending to wait out the intense noontime heat. The mercenaries wandered off to perform ablutions, bathe in the muddy stream, or doze in the shade. I sat on a fallen log and took advantage of the opportunity to write in my journal. We had been waking with the sun and turning in at dusk to conserve our resources such as candles and batteries. There had not been much chance to record our progress.

In my peripheral vision I caught a movement, and reflexively looked up. The forest appeared quiet, and I returned my attention to the page. Immediately, I sensed motion again, but turned too late to detect the source. I pretended to concentrate while watching out of the corner of my eye.

A child's head appeared from behind a tree, a broad Mayan face with huge dark eyes. Hiding behind my notebook, I stole a peek-a-boo and ducked back. This earned me a giggle. We repeated the same exchange a few times, and I heard the laughter of several other urchins. From their voices I guessed their age to be six or seven years. This meant that they were not far from home; a settlement had to be somewhere close.

The children were getting bolder by the minute. Apparently I posed no threat. I stood and moved slowly toward them, hoping they would lead me to their camp. This prompted a little game of hide-and-seek in the trees, and slowly we made our way through the forest.

We reached an opening in the leafy canopy, where the river had cut a deep winding bed through layers of limestone. The erosion had left the sculpted remains of jagged peaks composed of harder rock. Flora spilled down the banks, growing over these peculiar shapes like so many giant Chia Pets bending to drink at the water's edge.

The kids, three boys, ran around the formations and teased me on. At one partially denuded stone they scrambled up and called from the top. Suddenly the jovial taunts became screams of terror; one of the boys had disappeared. The other two became quiet as I approached to have a look, but they didn't run away.

The boulder was perched on a fissure at the top of a deep empty cenote. The boy had slipped on the hard surface, and fallen into the chasm about fifteen feet before becoming snagged on a rough ledge. His screams had become whimpers. Bits of loose gravel fell ricocheting down the jagged edges of the shaft and I could not hear them hit bottom.

Turning to the other boys, I pointed at my mouth, and tugged on my ears, saying, "Mama," in hopes that the rudimentary syllables conveyed some universal meaning. One child seemed to understand, and took off running into the bush.

There wasn't any choice; I slid down from the boulder, tossed my notebook aside and scrambled into the hole. With my back braced against one side of the limestone crevasse and my feet on the opposite wall, I began painfully lowering myself into the seemingly bottomless solutional cave.

Due to the hormone imbalance, Jains had not been able to sleep for much longer than an hour at a time and spent the night working in the laboratory suite. He had discovered that fresh fruit kept his rapacious appetite satisfied longer than anything else he had tried. Armed with a bag of apples, peaches, sliced cantaloupe, and figs, he researched his latest idea. The hours passed unnoticed while the molecular fructose fueled obsessive concentration.

As his thinking continued to deteriorate, Jains believed his idea was logical; it was just a matter of finding the right information. Donnie was fanatical about his files, and Carlton located what he needed almost immediately. He had a satisfactory potential match-up within an hour. After another sixty minutes, nothing more appropriate had appeared, so he settled on a plan. What came next was to isolate the particular section of genetic code that would produce the desired results.

Petersen had taken his friend's constant presence for granted, thinking that Carlton Jains paid little attention to matters that were difficult to comprehend. While that was largely true, Jains excelled at things to which Petersen paid little mind. One habit the investor had cultivated was the theft of passwords. From the physicist's mailbox, he sent out queries, signing Petersen's name. Using the scientist's auto fill pass codes, he entered a secure website and requested access to a member-restricted file.

The fruit supply was running low, and after a glance at the index, the complexity of the next phase of the research suddenly seemed insurmountable. Although his mental energy level was high, the physical toll was beginning to affect his vision and stamina. Leaving the genetic sequences for later, he prepared a kit for taking DNA swabs. Distractedly remembering to take the remains of his food along, Jains closed up the laboratory and drove to the National Zoo.

I crab-walked to a narrow space underneath the trapped child and rested for a moment against a tiny ledge. The boy was wearing a simple loincloth cinched by a leather thong around the waist. This thin strap had caught on a protrusion. The only other thing preventing a fall into the abyss was that with one hand he had managed to grasp an eroded fracture in the wall. It took some coaxing to persuade him to give up this hold, wrap his arms around my neck, and allow me to pull him free. With the tiny child astride my stomach, I began the ascent. My recently injured shoulder was throbbing, and one of my legs was cramping. I wedged in and rested wherever there was the slightest chance. I couldn't tell if the liquid dripping from my back was sweat or blood.

As I slowly inched toward the sunlight, faces appeared over the rim above. In a foreign tongue, they seemed to be cheering our progress, and gasped at every slip. I couldn't understand the words, but apparently the little boy was assuring the onlookers that he was all right.

It felt like hours but was probably less than ten minutes before we were safely out of the cenote. Three women were waiting, and one must have been the boy's mother. From her tone it was obvious that she didn't know whether to admonish him or celebrate his safety.

My shirt was in shreds and my upper back riddled with nicks and abrasions. My stomach muscles felt as though I had done a thousand sit-ups. As I checked to see how bad the bleeding was, two native men arrived at a run. They were armed with long wooden spears, and did not look happy.

There was a rapid-fire exchange of language, which I of course could not translate but had a good guess about. Abruptly the tone changed and the weapons were lowered. One man thumped his chest and extended his arm laterally in what seemed a brotherly gesture. I nodded and smiled, and retrieved my notebook.

With the children leading the way, the group began walking along the embankment above the river, looking back at me, apparently expecting me to follow. I stayed where I was, pointed at myself, held up two fingers and gestured back the way we had come. The message was apparently understood; there were two others with me. After the men had a quick conversation with the little boys, all of us worked back through the forest toward the clearing.

The area appeared deserted as we stepped into the open. My guides must have hidden when they heard our approach, and silently materialized at the edge of the glade with their weapons ready. Seeing my bloody condition, they moved aggressively toward the natives. This caused some rattling of arms, and I hastily tried to defuse the situation. After hearing my explanation, the tension eased.

The mercenaries tried to communicate with the natives. Gaucho spoke a little Nahuatl and tried his luck, but only a few words seemed to be understood. The term "Uchben Itza" produced a repetition of the word "Itza," and little else.

I turned back in my notebook to the page with the drawing of the jaguar glyph in the nest of snakes, and held it up to be seen. The native leader's eyes grew wide and he took a step back, saying a Mayan word that even I had previously heard. "Balam." Jaguar. He turned toward the river, and gestured for us to follow.

We had not been expecting to encounter a purely aboriginal population. I knew there was a grave danger of our transmitting infectious pathogens against which an isolated tribe would have no defense, but contact had already been made. Silently, we walked with them beside the muddy water.

Even after seeing it closely, I would have been hard pressed to find the "Itza's" camp again. The living spaces appeared to have been sculpted by the same designer that created the rainforest itself. Sheltered from the weather, areas for sleeping, storing food, and cooking had been randomly placed – at least to my eye – in branches and rock formations. I could not tell if our immediate area comprised the entire settlement, or if we were at the leading edge of a larger community.

Santiago and Gaucho helped rinse off my wounds, and I put on a clean shirt. Along with the two native men, we sat on some gnarly tree roots while the women served tepid "tea" in cups made of polished gourd.

I took the little digital camera from my pack and aimed at the underbrush so the device would not be mistakenly perceived as a weapon. No one paid any mind, and I clicked off a series of photos of the group. The man that was presumably the leader rose and spoke, and I again recognized the Mayan word "Balam." He began reciting a narrative, while acting out a ritualistic dance or series of gestures, periodically inciting reciprocation from the rest of the clan. I recorded as much video as the flash card would hold.

At the conclusion of the performance, the man abruptly disappeared into the underbrush. I retrieved an empty memory stick to replace the full one. The silence seemed awkward for the next few minutes, until the native man returned and gestured, repeating the only word we seemed to understand. We followed again, into the dusky shadows of the deep jungle.

Leaning against a boulder stood a chest-high four-legged effigy constructed of twigs bound with colorful yarn. From on top of the neck stared a polished jade face.

"Balam Koh," the tribal leader reverently intoned. "Balam Koh."

May Twelve

Having little desire to hang out at the Jains' mansion with Maggie presiding, Petersen went to the laboratory to kill some time. Everything seemed normal, but he could tell that Carlton had recently visited the suite. Looking carefully, he could see scuff marks leading from the klystron to the window. He went to the machine and turned it on. The digital potentiometer had been adjusted and set in the red range. The physicist closed his eyes and shook his head no in exasperation.

In his current state, Carlton could not be trusted. Petersen began examining everything in the rooms. The computer was in a standby mode. Petersen was certain he had shut the machine down completely before leaving for Boston. He checked the most recently opened files, but they were not the ones he had last closed. Was it possible that Carlton had access to the password?

Still wondering, Petersen resumed his examination of the suite. The thermal cycler was displaying the ready light. There were three new strips of plastic vials in the tray. The pairs of unknown initials on the labels were enough to put Donald Petersen in a panic.

We stayed the night with the "Itza," slinging our hammocks near the little settlement. One more man and a little girl joined the group in the evening, but apparently the entire clan consisted of three couples and their four children. We exchanged food for dinner; they offered potato-like root bread and a sort of dried game jerky or pemmican in exchange for our fresh vegetables, nuts and sweet flatbread champurradas.

The Mayan leader, whose name I approximated as "Exl," allowed me to photograph the mask in the revealing light of morning. It was doubtful that he understood what was taking place. I even got a close-up of the glyph, where it had been carved on the inside surface.

Returning to the camp, I realized that the little clan was packing up and leaving. We would not find them here if we returned. The tribe had avoided contact with outsiders for five hundred years. This visit had only been permitted because I had rescued their child and referenced their deity; otherwise we would have never discovered their existence.

My guides suggested capturing the idol by force, which I could of course never allow. If Ramirez wanted to send his guerrillas after the tribe, he could do it without my assistance. I was satisfied that the face of the jaguar king was exactly where it belonged, in the hands of the Guatemalan Maya as Nana wished.

The little band of natives turned east along the river. After a few minutes the clan had totally vanished. We walked west to rejoin the stream we had followed on our way in. As it was a late start, we skipped siesta and marched on through the heat of the day, covering the first third of the distance back to the jeep before stopping for the night.

Carlton did not answer his mobile. After his messages went unreturned for two hours, Petersen tried the home number. The day-maid informed him that Mr. Jains had been away since dawn, but was expected any time. Despite his wish to avoid Maggie Jains, Petersen locked up the laboratory and went to wait at the house for his friend to return.

Maggie insisted that Donald join her for tea. This involved a cup of Earl Grey and a short lecture before giving way to a bottle of Bollinger and a mound of iced wild sturgeon caviar. The champagne took the edge off, and Maggie became jocosely talkative. Charm being an innate talent endemic to her social station, the entertainment was infectious. Petersen was soon under the influence of the heady bubbles. A second bottle of different vintage was brought out, "for comparison."

Quantum Voodoo

Carlton had still not returned by dinner, and Maggie implored Petersen to stay, as it was "so uncivilized" to eat alone. The solid food absorbed a little alcohol, and despite a sizable goblet of claret with dinner, Petersen felt fit to drive after coffee and dessert. Promising to stop in and join Mrs. Jains for a glass of port before bedtime, he returned to the laboratory to look for his friend.

To his astonishment, the suite was empty; every last piece of equipment was gone.

May Thirteen

Jains had not moved far. Using his holding company, he leased warehouse space on the same block as the original laboratory, farther down the hill, adjacent to the pillars supporting the elevated Whitehurst Freeway. By peering between the buildings from the skylight in the upstairs loft, he still had a line of sight up Mount Alto to the embassy. Downriver in the other direction, the National Mall bordered the water.

In contrast with the immaculate brick office buildings higher on the hill, the warehouse was covered in soot and graffiti. Under the highway and close to the water, vermin prowled with proprietary immunity.

Jains didn't notice or care. His vision was skewed and out of kilter. Everything seemed sparkling and new. Obsession was the sole motivation now; Jains had forgotten the reason and purpose for his actions, and went through the motions functioning as an automaton.

During the previous evening, he had spirited the machinery out of the office suite, and the bizarre equipment now sat on an iron catwalk accessed by a fixed forklift. A hatchway accessed the roof, and Jains braced a stepladder beneath, making it easy to temporarily install the antenna when needed.

High voltage circuits ran throughout the empty storage chamber, remnants of a previous industrial installation. Potomac Electric Power Company had reconnected the juice that morning.

Carlton Jains' was under the thrall of a sleepless, burning dementia. Following his trip to the zoo, the genetic material in the thermal cycler had been joined by a fifth sample. Working feverishly, he got the machinery set up for when the DNA was ready. As his supply of fruit ran low, the residual barbiturates in his system began to assert their addictive attraction. Craving the hypnotic buzz of the drugs, Jains chewed a handful of tablets as if they were jellybeans. After twenty minutes, the manic drive had been repressed and sedation took effect. The wild man passed out on a pile of cardboard boxes left by a previous tenant.

Jains had not bathed or shaved for six days. Fruit juice and pulp had spilled from the corners of his mouth during his frenzied feeding. His clothing was sticky with sugar, and beginning to stink of rot. Fruit flies hatching from the discarded banana peels descended on the fetid ripeness exuding from his body. Closely following, houseflies came to lay thousands of little white eggs that immediately hatched into maggots on the promising host. Cockroaches were next, cautiously aware of the inert body's mammalian heat. River rats congregated in dank recesses to wait their turn, while in the dusky half-light of the decrepit hall, dozens of bats awoke, and swarmed from the heights to feast on the hordes of insects.

We continued hiking in our customary formation, Gaucho skulking ahead, Santiago watching my back. As we followed the gentle water of the stream, the day was slipping into sultry noontime drowsiness when the spattering of nearby gunfire shattered the stillness. While the point man continued forward to investigate, Santiago and I quietly slipped off the trail and found cover. There was some shouting up ahead, too distant for me to make out the words, and then all was quiet.

After about five minutes of silence, my companion motioned for me to stay put, and headed back toward the trail. Within minutes, he called and I rejoined him on the path. His explanation resolved many questions.

During the war, thousands of Mayans fled the violence, hiding in the dense jungle of the Peten Basin or crossing the river into Mexico. In the deep forest, groups of refugees and guerrillas formed collectives and hid from the government until peace accords were signed. These isolated communities were then relocated, leaving the area open to invasion by criminal organizations.

Pockets still exist where the CPR-Communities of Populations in Resistance-remain in the jungle, distrusting of government and determined to protect their solitary way of life by any means necessary. The gunshots we had heard were warning us away from one such settlement. Our scout had made it clear to the rebels that we were not a threat, and we were allowed to pass quickly on our way.

I had been troubled trying to reconcile the gun-toting marauders who shot me with the primitive family men who had reverently shown us the mask. It made more sense that the assailants whom I first believed to be members of the ancient tribe were in reality modern refugees. The smuggler's mistake of identity had provided a false, but ultimately vital clue. Now what remained was to get out of the wilderness alive.

Carlton Jains was still missing and there was little Petersen could do except wait. The results of the blood work had not been returned. He tried to deduce what his friend might have concocted. On his laptop computer, the scientist reviewed the information that Carlton had accessed at the lab, hoping something would leap out at him. The map of the human genome was surprising, an enormous file, and difficult to decipher, even for an expert. What the hell did Jains hope to gain there? What the tycoon knew about genetics would fit on the head of a chromosome.

Arriving at no logical conclusion, Petersen gave up, and checked his messages. Email was waiting from an acquaintance at the National Human Genome Research Institute, inquiring whether Dr. Petersen had been able to access the information that had been requested. Petersen had not contacted the Institute. It was proof that Carlton had been using Petersen's pass code.

The attachment had been downloaded and saved. Remembering what he had said about the porcine genome when persuading Jains to finance the experiment, Petersen blanched. The file in question contained the entire gene sequence of the rhesus macaque.

The mercenaries left me at the little hotel on the lake. They would report to Ramirez immediately, but I figured I could wait and meet with him in the morning. I felt as though the jungle had chewed me up, and finding me unappetizing, had spit me out. The beer I had stashed in the mini-fridge tasted better than I could have imagined. After three fast bottles and a shower, I went to bed.

While Jains had been unconscious, his body had been feeding on its stores of fat. His hair and nails were growing at four times the normal rate. He awoke dehydrated and ravenous, cheeks pallid and sunken behind a now bushy beard.

Standing, he reflexively dusted off his clothes, not realizing that what he thought was dirt was really maggots clinging to the reeking fabric. He staggered to the bay door and flung it open, got in his car and drove out into the evening.

At the grocery store he didn't notice that everyone wrinkled their nose and turned away in disgust. He loaded an entire shopping cart with bananas, apples, and strawberries, grabbed two gallons of orange juice and rushed to the checkout. The counter suddenly became free of other shoppers as he approached. In the parking lot, he crammed his mouth with fruit, washing down the pulp while barely chewing.

As the sugar entered his blood, Carlton Jains perked up and began to become aware that people were staring. Pushing the basket to his car, he piled the remaining fruit in the passenger's seat and hurriedly exited the parking lot before running into someone he knew. It would not have mattered. Covered in filth, sporting the wild hair and thick beard, the wealthy Washingtonian was unrecognizable.

The lights were still on in the warehouse, the door gaping open. After pulling the car inside, he remained behind the wheel gulping fruit. For a while, there was somewhat of a balance between the energy from the food and the lingering tranquility produced by the sedatives. Jains was able to map out a mental picture of the next part of the plan. He slammed the bay door, and climbed to the loft carrying bags of bananas.

For the next few hours Jains remained coherent, periodically topping off his energy supply with juice and fruit. Intensely focused, he raced between the machines.

Just as Petersen had demonstrated, Carlton cloned material from the first sample of human DNA into a multiple host range vector. He prepared the site for cleaving at the locus where the foreign DNA would be inserted. After the new sequence was assembled, the material was placed back in the thermal cycler to reproduce.

The acumen Jains drew on for this procedure was a direct result of the accelerated chemical processes afflicting his system. As the out of control metabolism burned the huge supply of fructose that he was taking in, the clear-headed intelligence morphed into mania. Frenetic behavior began to recur.

May Fourteen

Ramirez was thrilled. To my surprise, he volunteered to pay my commission even though he did not physically possess the treasure. I had located the icon, all I had been hired to accomplish. Nana would agree that the artifact should stay where it was. Ramirez intended to keep track of the clan and provide them with protection. We copied my photographs and video of the separatists onto the Guatemalan's computer.

Concerning who had shot me and why, we could only assume. There were a host of factions operating in the jungle, and I had been attributing actions to one that quite likely had been instigated by another.

The "Itza" who possessed the mask had not responded to the word "Uchben." Perhaps they had been a branch of the Lacandon after all. I had not studied the isolated clan enough to learn their unique characteristics. The photographs would certainly be enough to interest a university. Perhaps I could return to El Peten one day to do research. In my field, an opportunity to study a "lost tribe" firsthand is akin to finding the Holy Grail. Not surprisingly, it appeared that actual events had spawned a long-standing myth.

Petersen had the impression that the Metropolitan Police were not taking Carlton's disappearance seriously. There was no reason to suspect foul play, and admittedly, Jains had been on a bender before vanishing. No reports of anyone matching Jains' description had been filed at area hospitals or jails. Petersen felt that "be on the lookout for" was hardly an important enough status for the case; however, filial loyalty prevented him from disclosing the true threat that Carlton presented, which might have upped the ante.

Having known her husband during his partying years, Margaret Jains remained unruffled. She was saving her energy for giving Carlton a piece of her mind when this latest bout of foolishness was over.

On the eve of the vote, Senator Tim Radcliff received another message. His driver had noticed this one clipped under the windshield wiper of the politician's limousine:

Senator,
Don't forget me tomorrow,
La Mambo

Radcliff carefully retrieved the card and dutifully forwarded it to the FBI. The statesman intended to uphold his oath to the office the following day, ignoring the ultimatum come what might. However, he hoped the voodoo threats would be taken more seriously when the symptoms of rapid aging began to reappear.

May Fifteen

Hector Ramirez accompanied me to the Banrural Bank branch in Flores, and made the promised funds available. I transferred most of the cash directly to a Swiss bank, without it ever legally belonging to me. The numbered account had been set up so that Magda would be able to withdraw only the interest. In Bosnia, the income would be equivalent to roughly half of an average annual salary. It was not enough to make her rich, but she was young and beautiful. Having a "dowry" would not hurt her prospects of marriage. The eventual disposition of the capital could be decided once the child reached maturity.

I was scratched and bruised and sore, and had set aside sufficient funds to keep the wolf at the door while writing a paper detailing my experience in Central America. In the little town, word of a large bank transfer would get around quickly. I did not want to become a target for robbery. Exiting the bank, I immediately headed for the airport. Ever gracious, Señor Ramirez even covered the cost of these last return flights. By late afternoon, I was on the ground in Miami.

Despite his increasingly impaired mental state, Jains remembered to check the news. Online from his phone, he discovered that Senator Radcliff had resisted the demands. Enraged, he immediately went to get revenge, only this time, it wasn't going to be gray hair. He had something better for the bastard.

He ran the antenna up to the roof, pointed the dish at the Russian Embassy, and focused on the wall that Petersen claimed contained a "Fractal Radiator." He removed the newly spliced DNA from the cycler, and placed it in third machine in the gamma ray loop. The Senator's DNA went in front of the klystron to tune the frequencies and match the target.

Jains boosted the intensity a hair, just to make sure, and engaged the switch. Radiation filled the airwaves. Carlton Jains began to cackle.

May Sixteen

I was eager to see Charley and Piper's quantum experiment. My eccentric buddy was mysterious and seemed amused on the phone, adding to my curiosity. I caught an early morning puddle-jumper across the state and drove over from the airport in Fort Meyers. If I didn't find a new project soon, it would make sense to rent a furnished apartment for a few months while I sorted things out. For the time being, I checked into a cheap motel and headed to Charley's house.

The guest room I usually stayed in was occupied with gear. Cables lay across the floor, leading to and from Charley's office and on down the hall to the living room. When I arrived, Piper was happily ensconced on the only available couch cushion, reading through a sloping heap of technical treatises.

Charley had a metal box – he referred to it as a "Drift Chamber" – open on the kitchen table, and was constructing a mare's nest of multicolored wires inside. Neither of my old friends seemed to notice that machines had invaded the living space and simply stepped over the mechanical intruders or distractedly pushed them aside when necessary.

They proudly led me through the morass of equipment, describing each piece and its function. Charley finally began to explain the experiment's purpose.

"What Petersen did was transmit information on a quantum scale, but the actual motivator of the action was radiation. The gamma rays stimulated certain cells to reproduce, and their neighbors began to mimic the activity."

"Using the transmitted information?"

"Correctamundo. Displaying the programmed characteristics. We re-created that experiment, albeit on a considerably simpler basis, but we wondered," Charley and Piper conspiratorially locked eyes for a fraction of a second, "if specific molecules of DNA are targeted, could the entanglement be used to locate an individual?"

"We're also wondering if it could be done without irradiation being a factor," Piper interjected.

Charley shrugged. I wasn't surprised that Piper had studied the technology and come up with her own ideas. Considering the disappearance of Scarlett Taylor, I could certainly understand Piper's motivation for inventing a way of finding a missing person, alive or dead, but the idea of one's precise whereabouts being traceable at all times and distances was terrifying. I looked at the jumble of equipment with new respect.

"Did it work?"

Charlie fielded that one in his inimitable style. "Ain't got that far yet, dude. "Petersen thinks it could, but he used other techniques to locate his targets. He warned us that in the wrong hands, the technique could have devastating consequences."

"Petersen? You talked to him?" Now, this was news!

"Wanted the cat to realize we were hip to his shit. Actually, Steve, he doesn't seem like a bad guy, just scientifically inquisitive and maybe a little unrestrained. He was very apologetic for what he did to Piper," my friends exchanged a reciprocal glance again, "and reassured us that eumelanin was the only molecule that was targeted. He must feel guilty; he keeps calling to make sure she's okay."

"From what Charley told me, I get the feeling Petersen was excited to find someone who understood his accomplishment," Piper speculated. "As long as this is all there is to it," she tousled her hair, "I'm not really that mad any more."

Charley grunted, "Hmm. I want to know what he's up to, just the same. I'm building the multi-wire chamber so I can learn enough to keep up with his experiments. If I can come up with some way of measuring the qubits being transmitted, he will immediately detect that I am observing."

"How's that?"

"Any measurement affects the entanglement. Knowing that someone is monitoring the activity might help keep him in line. Just as importantly, if anyone else gets in on the action, we will both be able to tell there is a third party involved."

"Speaking of third parties, what about the other guy? Jains?"

"Ah, the money man. Apparently has designs of his own. Piper thinks that if we catch up, technologically speaking, we can coax Petersen away."

Piper took up the conversation. "I've met Jains in person, and I didn't like what I saw. He's got a sadistic streak."

"Not to mention a penchant for shotguns," I contributed.

While attempting to get revenge on the Senator, Carlton Jains had exposed himself to radiation for the third time in a week. The transmission had more effect than he had bargained on. The changes manifesting in Jains' body continued to accelerate as increasing numbers of cells reproduced in emergence. The new and rapid growth was fueled not only by recent caloric intake, but also drew on the tissue of the vital organs themselves.

With all of his metabolic functions racing, Jains was sweating away what little moisture remained in his body. The kidneys could not operate without more liquid, and the heart struggled to pump the thickening blood. Intense pain wracked his lower back. Itchy and burning, Carlton tore open his clothes. The base of his spine was swollen. His skin was becoming riddled with open blisters. Desperately racing for help, he pulled the garage door open just as convulsions began.

Staggering back into the warehouse, he never made it to the car. Thick blood oozing copiously from his nose, mouth and ears, Carlton Jains writhed on the cement floor, spreading a stain in the shape of a snow angel. After an agonizing three minutes, he gave a final twitch and lay still.

I was surprised to discover that Magda's phone had been disconnected. It was the only contact method that I possessed. I had left her a message giving my new number in the States, but she had not called. I assumed it had something to do with moving to Eastern Europe, and figured on giving it a few days. Surely she wanted to hear from me, as I had promised her my financial support.

Margaret Jains had gone to her club. Petersen waited at the mansion, hoping Carlton Jains would surface. When the house phone rang, it was a homicide detective with bad news. After the officer described the scene, Petersen warned that there could be radiation involved. Determined to see for himself before telling Maggie, he immediately headed for Georgetown.

Heeding the physicist's admonition, the detective had summoned the hazardous materials squad. Petersen was forced to wait behind the crime scene tape with the other cops and spectators.

After radiation levels were deemed safe, Petersen accompanied the detectives into the warehouse. The body had been removed, but the bloodstains were graphic. Petersen identified the missing machinery, but stopped short of explaining the truth about the experiment. It would suffice if Carlton were believed to have suffered from radiation poisoning. Until he could figure out what had gone wrong, Petersen did not wish to be shut out of the investigation, or conversely, arrested under suspicion of complicity.

There was no sign of foul play, but the remains had been quarantined for fear of radioactivity or some possibly infectious disease. The officers asked if Petersen would come to the hospital to identify the body. Until arriving at the morgue, Petersen was holding out hope that it would not be the corpse of Carlton Jains. After the viewing, he dutifully went to inform the deceased man's wife.

May Seventeen

Piper had left for home; apparently she and Charley had been splitting their time between her place and his. I hoped it was not my presence that was keeping them apart for the next few days. This minor misgiving was immediately forgotten when Charley showed me an article from the on-line edition of the Washington Post.

Financial Tycoon Discovered Dead
In Georgetown Warehouse

Police have confirmed the identity of a body found last night in a K Street warehouse as that of Washington financier Carlton Jains, III. No other details have been released.

Witnesses reported that the area has been placed under quarantine by the Metropolitan Police Department, and that hazardous materials experts are on the scene. Officials have declined to comment, citing the security of the ongoing investigation.

The article continued, briefly outlining Jains' family history, and listing a few of his accomplishments. I gave Charley a questioning look.

"Dude, I don't know what to think. Petersen's been calling every day, wondering if Piper's all right. Now his buddy checks out, no details."

"You think there might be a connection?"

"The site has been quarantined. What if he did a similar radioactive procedure on this guy, and something went wrong? Maybe that's why he keeps checking on Piper, wondering if she has the same problem?"

"Does Piper know about this?" I scrolled back to the top of the page, and scanned the article again.

"Nah. I doubt if she reads the Washington papers. Usually, I don't either. I noticed the name Jains on the wire service website, so I clicked on the link."

"You don't feel comfortable calling Petersen?"

"Left a message, but he hasn't called back."

The Police Department's forensic specialists had finished collecting what material they needed as evidence. The investigators realized that analyzing the nature of the equipment at the warehouse was beyond their expertise, and asked for assistance from the FBI. The Bureau delivered the teleportation machinery to the physics laboratory at Johns Hopkins University for examination. Petersen was forced to invoke his high-level credentials before being granted access.

The cadaver had registered high but not dangerous levels of radioactivity, and was now scheduled for a routine autopsy. It would take several days for the results to be returned. Without knowing the actual cause of death, Petersen was left to worry; what was the status of the Senator and the other people whose initials were on the vials? How could he find out without arousing suspicion?

In the high-security lab, Petersen checked the recent activity of the computer Jains had used, pulling up files containing mathematical models of the most recent broadcasts. Carlton had transmitted gamma rays tuned to a specific target. First, Petersen examined the intended recipient's genetic code. The data appeared to be normal, although without something for comparison, there was no way to know to whom it belonged. Next he took a look at the material that had been modeled as the prototype for the entanglement transmission. There was something drastically wrong with these sequences. Considering the peculiar request for the file containing the monkey genome, Petersen immediately suspected both what Jains had been attempting, and why it had gone wrong.

Since the Johns Hopkins physicists were already scrutinizing the entanglement apparatuses and the intended purpose of the electromagnetic devices would not remain a secret much longer, Petersen requested that DNA specimens be sent to the Institute of Genetic Medicine for analysis. Along with forensic profiling for purposes of identification, full genome sequencing was performed to look for abnormalities.

After the analysts obtained the results of the tests, the nature of Petersen's experiments became obvious, and word of the achievement circulated the close community of scientists. The professional researchers at the secure facility were not eager to publicly release such sensitive information. To prevent speculation, the mutations in Carlton Jain's cells were officially attributed to radiation exposure.

Close inspection of the arrays confirmed Petersen's suspicions; Jains had inadvertently contaminated all the genetic samples with molecules of his own DNA. When transmitting the gamma rays, he had become both prototype and target for the entangled particles. His intention had been to splice in monkey genes in an attempt at making his enemies grow tails. It had been an ill-informed endeavor; what he had actually transmitted directly to himself was muddled code. Incomplete sequences were reproduced in the developing cell nuclei. All subsequent growth was deformed. Carlton Jains had in effect eradicated the genetic blueprint for his own body.

Agent Jim Sanderson called and apologized for not having taken my warning more seriously. Donald Petersen's work was still considered classified, and his involvement in the death of Carlton Jains had drawn the attention of the Department of Homeland Security. Sanderson assured that the technology had now been taken under the auspices of the federal government, and that the physicist's activities would be closely monitored in the future. In a secure laboratory, Dr. Petersen was now reconstructing what had taken place.

The Federal investigator insisted there was no need for me to concern myself further. I hoped that this time it was true, although I was intensely curious to learn the details.

There was still no word from Magda, and I began to worry. I hated to call on Ingrid; she had made it abundantly clear that my contacting her caused nothing but grief.

During our confrontation with biological terrorists the previous year, Ingrid, Charley, and I had worked with a stern-faced private investigator named Gerhardt Brun. Herr Brun had developed a sort of fatherly fondness for Ingrid Luft, as well as a brotherly camaraderie with Charley Pulaski. I knew he regarded me with suspicion, or perhaps jealousy, but I thought I could count on his benevolent nature, and decided to ask him to find out what had happened to Magda and the child, without involving or hurting my ex-girlfriend.

Gruff as ever, Brun acted as though aware of the situation, grunting at the salient points during my explanation. Upon discovering that the intrigue would involve Ingrid, and that I trusted him to protect her personal welfare, the old detective brightened and promised to help.

May Eighteen

Hector Ramirez continued to prove his mettle. He had publicized the results of my expedition to the Peten Basin in a Spanish Language article appearing in el Periódico, a Guatemalan national newspaper. I had been accorded proper recognition for the discovery, and credit for the photographs and video I had taken of the Uchben Itza.

Largely based on my work, Ramirez had put in motion a plan to create a foundation dedicated to the preservation of the lost tribe and its habitat. The human rights of indigenous Mayans had made the headlines. It was a good place to start.

I pulled into Charley's driveway to find him pacing in the front yard with the phone to his ear. He mouthed the word "Petersen," and stopped walking so I could overhear his end of the conversation. I didn't understand half of what he said. After the call ended, Charley explained. Carlton Jains had run wild using the gamma ray machinery, with calamitous results. Repeated exposure to radiation had triggered cellular responses that destroyed the man's body. The physicist had reassured again that Piper was safe.

Now that Jains was out of the picture, Petersen intended to focus his attention on implementing the quantum computers. The work was to take place at a secure government laboratory. He promised that no more human experimentation would take place.

Charley remained skeptical. I could tell he was preoccupied and wished to concentrate on the problem. I left him poring over the complicated device on the kitchen table.

Tim Radcliff carefully checked for graying roots. Three days had passed, and there was no sign of aging. He tried to recall how much time had elapsed between the initial warning and the subsequent discoloration of his hair. He had disobeyed "La Mambo," but pride and defiance would only last for a few days before apprehension began to nag at the politician.

The case had been designated SCI, sensitive compartmentalized information. The FBI did not have access to reports filed by other agencies in the intelligence community, and made no connection between the voodoo threats and the death of Carlton Jains. Despite his righteous arrogance, Senator Radcliff would be doomed to spending the next few years wondering when the voodoo priestess was going to strike again.

May Nineteen

Piper was back at Charley's place when I returned in the evening. At happy hour, we discussed the situation over a few chilled beverages. I wondered what the two of them planned to do with the quantum experiments.

"Dude, I still gotta build the proportional chamber. Somebody's got to be wise to Petersen's jive."

I glanced at Piper. Apparently she had become used to Charley's speech mannerisms.

"It's just like you've been saying for years, Steve," Charley went on more seriously, "science must provide a system for dealing with the ethical issues created by its new abilities. Our old belief systems are inadequate when facing advanced developments. Besides, do you trust the government to provide the moral fortitude, much less the scientific oversight, for policing Petersen's experiments? Until an appropriate authority is established, it would be unconscionable for us to allow him free reign."

"He hasn't exactly exercised appropriate prudence," Piper agreed.

"Regardless of who is first to develop it, the new technology is inevitable," Charley concluded.

"What about your experiments for locating people?" I was concerned about the ethics governing that eventuality.

"Piper has agreed that technology of that nature could easily get out of hand."

Piper nodded her assent. "We'll continue to refine the process in case someone else develops the idea, but our results will remain secret."

"Although, if it works, we could surreptitiously use the method if the need arose," Charley concluded.

My brilliant friend had invented a cure for the common cold, and despite the potential for immense profit, destroyed the entire project because he felt it was unethical to foist unknown effects on the biosphere's distant future. The entanglement technology would be safe in his hands. Whatever drove his system of belief, I was glad that Charley Pulaski would be monitoring the activities of Donald Petersen.

Epilogue

May Twenty

I had not found a paying gig, but an old friend had told me about a beach placer mine refining rare elements near Jacksonville. In the process of sluicing sand to recover monazite crystals, ancient native relics had been uncovered. The mining company did not want the operation held up by archeologists, and intended to keep the discovery quiet. One of the surveyors had an attack of conscientiousness, and called a colleague to leak the story. To avoid unflattering publicity, the owners of the firm had agreed to allow access before continuing to dig.

Unlike most of the academic community, busy in the first weeks of their summer projects, I was in a state of readiness, waiting for opportunity. I hoped to get the drop on the other scientists, and document the find before it was too late.

May Twenty-one

I checked out of the motel and stopped by Charley's before leaving for north Florida. For the time being, Charley was unable to monitor Petersen's activities. Now that the physicist was working in a secure location, it seemed the radioactive transmissions were being shielded.

The interior of Charley's house still resembled the inner works of a giant electronic device, wires leading all around the house connecting mysterious boxes. I wondered why the machinery was still set up. Apparently Piper had become fascinated with the subject, and they were continuing to experiment. Their current project involving the molecular composition of minerals sounded like an attempt at alchemy.

Using Charley's address, I had tentatively begun to reenter mainstream American life, opening a new bank account, buying a used car, re-creating a paper identity. I would not be able to float around indefinitely, but by not committing resources to maintaining a permanent domicile or typical lifestyle, it was at least possible to do some exploring before becoming pinned down.

May Twenty-two

Gerhardt Brun's phone call came early in the morning. I was still a little groggy, drinking my first cup of hotel-room coffee.

"I must tell you, Herr Shaw. I do not approve of your activities. I hope I can count on your assurance that you will not disclose any information to Fraulein Dr. Luft that might cause her pain."

"To what activities are you referring, Herr Brun?"

"The womanizing and drug use, Herr Shaw."

"What on earth are you talking about?"

"Allow me to explain from the beginning, Herr Shaw. The baby has been sold."

"*What?*"

"Yes, this is correct. The Croatian woman, Magda, found a wealthy American couple that wished to adopt."

I was so stunned that I could not respond. The detective continued, "I do not know who else was involved. Arrangements were made for the couple to inspect the infant. The Americans wished to verify the child's hereditary…pedigree. They hired a private investigator. This investigator allowed me to see the dossier that was compiled on condition that I would agree to warn you not to pursue the matter."

I could not imagine what this implied, but Brun's tone alerted me that the dossier was important. "What was in the file?"

"First, genetic samples were required to verify you as the father. This matter was complicated by your travel in Latin America. However, the couple wished to complete the exchange as quickly as possible, and paid the detective agency to follow you despite the cost."

I thought back to the incidents when I had sensed someone trailing me, the times my rooms were searched. Apparently they had acquired some of my DNA.

Brun took my silence as a cue, and continued, "Once paternity had been confirmed, photographs were also desired, at first merely to demonstrate that your appearance was acceptable. In an attempt to point out your fine qualities, Magda explained to the buyers that the purpose of your trip was to raise money for the care of the infant. This made the couple quite nervous, afraid you would later make a claim for custody of the child. The investigators were instructed to 'get some dirt on you,' I think that's how you say it. Some information that could be used to discredit you in that case."

I tried to think, had I committed an errant act, a faux pas, anything borderline during my trip?

"The first photographs are murky, but in them, you are clearly shown taking drugs with a group of men at a seedy bar in Honduras. Evidently, this was not by itself considered proof of moral depravity, but as you repeatedly crossed international borders, the investigators thought you might be involved with smuggling, and continued to follow. Sometime after that, you apparently disappeared in Mexico City. The detectives were forced to wait until you returned to Florida before they could pick up the trail."

They had missed out on the Arizona trip, including my arrest at the hands of the Department of Homeland Security. I had a fairly good inkling what the next transgression was going to be. "They photographed me at a hotel with a young lady."

Herr Brun's German accent suddenly seemed sinister. "The pictures are very...graphic, Herr Shaw. I believe some of the... activities shown in the photographs may even be illegal."

Jillian. I tried to imagine where the camera could have been hidden. A wonderful day of nurture and love distorted by voyeurs and peddled as smut. Blackmail. I can't even begin to express my outrage.

"So you understand why I say this would be hurtful to Fraulein Dr. Luft?" Brun's voice had become background noise.

I robotically gave my word. Ingrid would not hear any of this from me.

June Twenty

Donald Petersen swiped his new ID card through the slot, and entered a six-digit pass code. After he entered the laboratory suite, the airlock closed behind him with a satisfying hiss. He was finally right where he should have been all along, working for the government in a high-security institution.

No one had ever discovered the attack on Senator Radcliff, but the politician was back to normal. Petersen still had no idea whose initials were on the other vials, but it didn't matter. The unused materials had been destroyed. Carlton's scheme would remain a secret.

When all the equipment had been reassembled for the investigation, Petersen had performed a demonstration that stunned the physicists at Johns-Hopkins. Immediately grasping the impact, the scientists notified high-level officials. Observers from the CIA committed the Agency's support to the project. Petersen now had seemingly unlimited funding. A car and driver chauffeured him to and from an upscale apartment and the advanced experimental facility. Donald knew the royal treatment was being provided primarily to keep him under surveillance, but it mattered little. This was the big time, playing for enormous stakes, and he was finally in the upper echelons.

With the resources of a major physics laboratory and a corps of scientists at his disposal, Petersen had easily proved the feasibility of quantum teleportation-based targeting systems. This initial success would provide job security while he completed a macroscopic entanglement technique that could identify and alter the chemical makeup of a specific individual while passing without effect through all other organisms.

Petersen focused on the idea that the method could be used to eradicate hereditary ailments in a population *en masse*. That the radical design could easily be adapted for the slaughter of millions was none of his concern.

At last, the physicist felt free to explore the parameters of subatomic reality.

June Twenty-one

I'm staring out to sea as I write this final entry. It's time to start a new journal; this notebook is full, and will be consigned to the trunk of the car until I land somewhere. For now, I am watching ships on the horizon. The wind carries the ocean's salty tang and the promise of adventure.

Photo: Kate Peachey

CARL PEACHEY is a guitarist from Washington D.C. He resides in Key West, Florida, with his wife, artist Kate Peachey. *Quantum Voodoo* is his third novel. For more information, visit carlpeachey.com.

CPSIA information can be obtained at www.ICGtesting.com
Printed in the USA
LVOW051209220912

299873LV00002B/4/P